Foreword by the Editor

Welcome to the second installment of the Demonic Visions series. This new collection of macabre tales includes short fiction by each member of the Demonic Visions team. Every new book that we publish will take you deeper into the minds of these talented writers, and acquaint you with their various styles of prose. So enjoy, and I hope that you will join us for the entire Demonic Visions saga which is intended to last many, many years and span many, many volumes…

~Chris Robertson, author of *Death Dreams Deluxe*

Cover art by Steve Wenta, artwork on Facebook: *Visions of Dislocation - the art of Steve Wenta*

Lettering and visual effects by Grant Cross, artwork on Facebook: *Grant Cross Artwork*

Table of Contents

Other Books by the Writers:

Peter Adam Salomon - *Henry Franks*

Marc Sorondo - *Aurora*

Marc Shapiro - *High Strangeness*

Robert Friedrich - *The Darkness Within: A Novella, Enlightened by Darkness - Vol.1 First Encounter, Enlightened by Darkness - Vol.2 The Invasion, Enlightened by Darkness - Vol.3 As Darkness Spreads, Enlightened by Darkness: Complete Trilogy, The Book of Metal Lyrics*

Christopher Conlon - *He Is Legend: An Anthology Celebrating Richard Matheson, A Matrix of Angels, Midnight on Mourn Street, The Oblivion Room*

Ken MacGregor - *An Aberrant Mind*

Joe McKinney - *Dead City, Apocalypse of the Dead, Flesh Eaters, Mutated, The Savage Dead, The Red Empire and Other Stories, Inheritance, Dating in Dead World: The Collected Zombie Short Fiction of Joe McKinney, Dead in the Water, Lost Girl of the Lake* (with Michael McCarty), *Night Work and Grimoires, Deadman Wade* (with Sheldon Higdon), *Dog Days, Dodging Bullets, The Crossing, Crooked House, St Rage, Plague of the Undead*

Patrick Freivald - *Twice Shy, Special Dead, Blood List* (with Phil Freivald)

Mark Slade - *A Six Gun and the Queen of Light, Hellspeak: A Pete Chambers Book*

Naching T. Kassa - *The Venihi, Master of the Shade*

Julianne Snow - *Days with the Undead: Book One, Glimpses of the Undead, The Carnival 13* (collaborative novella for charity)

William Holden - *Words to Die By*

<u>J. T. (Troy) Seate</u> - Novels: *Valley of Tears, Tears for the Departed, And the Heavens Wept,* Novellas: *Something About Sara, Connor House, A Resting Place*

<u>K. Trap Jones</u> - *The Sinner, The Drunken Exorcist, The Crossroads*

<u>Shenoa Carroll-Bradd</u> - *The Minstrel Angel*

<u>Rick McQuiston</u> - *Twelve Days of Christmas Horror, Giant Book of Nightmares, To See as a God Sees, Where Things Might Walk*

<u>S.C. Hayden</u> - *American Idol, Rusty Nails, Broken Glass*

<u>Matt Drabble</u> – *Gated, Asylum - 13 Tales of Terror, Abra-Cadaver, After Darkness Falls - 10 Tales of Terror - Volume 1, Gated II: Ravenhill Academy*

1. SWALLOWED
Joe McKinney

The snake, a 20 foot long female Burmese python, slowly uncoiled as the man walked past. The snake's tongue flicked against the air and tasted a miasma of death swirling around the man, though her reptilian brain made no connection between the man and the familiar, rotting taste. The snake saw only a man, stumbling slowly, picking his way uncertainly through the tangled weeds. She saw an easy kill, nothing more.

The man tripped over an exposed root, and in that moment, the snake struck.

She lunged forward, biting the man high up on the back of his thigh, her momentum knocking him to the ground, twisting him over onto his side.

The kill was not a difficult one. Beyond a few weak attempts to bite back, the man fought little. His legs twitched. His hands groped at her flanks ineffectually. She ignored his hands and quickly coiled around him, around his waist, his neck, and began to squeeze.

Her jaws unhinged, and the man and the snake became intimate as the slow ballet of predator and prey played out to its inevitable conclusion.

***

The snake was born here in the Everglades. Her ancestors were pets released into the wild by owners who found they could no longer care for the giant reptiles. Those first generations quickly squeezed out the wetland's top predators, creating an ecological nightmare. For a time, the authorities hunted the giant snake and her many cousins, but all that ceased when humanity's dead rose from their graves and overwhelmed the living.

The snake knew none of that, of course. She knew only that she had eaten alligators and grown huge in this new world without game wardens. And at two hundred pounds, the man who tasted like death was a long meal, but went down soon enough, one gulp at a time.

***

A night passed, and when the sun came up it found the snake warming herself on a narrow strip of bald earth next to a scum covered pond. The snake had spent the night in great pain. Her flanks were swollen, distended; the muscles down her length twitching. Spasms of pain caused her head to bob. She opened her mouth and tried to vomit out the pain inside her.

But she couldn't.

And for a blinding moment the pain became so intense her primitive reptilian mind couldn't recognize it as pain. All she knew was relief as her side burst open and the man who smelled like death spilled out in a streaming gooey mass, like a mockery of birth.

She was still reeling with the pain that was infinitely more than pain when she realized that the meal had, in its turn, begun to feed upon her body.

***

Time is gone, but the man doesn't know it.

He knows only that life is gone. The heat that drove him here is gone. He must find more heat. He must find life.

He must feed.

He stands, strands of snake offal stretching like melted cheese from his body, and he begins to walk, without a memory, without a rudder.

2. BIRD IN A WROUGHT IRON CAGE
John Alfred Taylor

I remember I laughed when Father told me about the hand. Though when he shouted, his face mottled red and white, I realized he wasn't joking.

It was another side to Dad. I had always thought him the essence of normality; brutally practical, a sworn enemy of fantasy, and now he was raving. Still waters run deep, I told myself, the cuckoo nests in any head.

How would Moorcock Sheet and Tube survive it?

But then he showed me the family heirloom, as Grandfather had shown him, and I knew Dad was his usual unimaginative self; the sight of it was better than any argument or description.

He opened up the musty buffalo-hide trunk with its green-stained brass fittings and pulled out the cage inside. For a second, I thought it held a huge brown spider, until I saw the fingernails like broken roots. Then it crawled to the corner of the cage and picked up a pen.

It liked the new ballpoints. WELCOME FREDERICK IV. WE ARE GLAD TO SEE YOU. WILL YOU GIVE US WHAT WE WANT?

I didn't know what that meant, and when I did, I wasn't eager. But after Dad explained, I got out my penknife and sterilized it with my lighter. The cut didn't hurt as much as I expected, and only a few drops were necessary— "for the form," Dad said, but I don't think he understood any better than I did. I held my forearm carefully over the notebook, and afterward the hand wrote under it, smearing the page, FREDERICK IV HIS BLOOD.

So I too gained the knowledge of the hand; of the advice that had pyramided the family fortune for three generations, that had guided Great-Grandfather through his speculations in railways and iron, that had warned Grandfather six weeks before Black Tuesday, and that in 1937 gave Father a detailed month-by-month chronology of World War II and its investment opportunities.

***

It was about time, since I had been Executive Vice President for almost a year, and Dad was already thinking of retiring himself to Chairman of the Board. Now that the hand and I had a very cozy relationship. At first I would take it a new notebook every morning, tie a string through the spiral binding, and let it down through the cage bars as per instruction.

I had once tried to do it my way, without the string, and the hand had thrown itself up to turn over in midair and claw open the ball of my third finger. I had a tetanus booster immediately and never took the risk again.

But I asked it all sorts of questions, not just business questions, though I asked more of those than Dad did—after all it was the hand and I who planned the company's diversification. All sorts of questions—I wanted to know where the hand came from, what it wanted.

"What are you?" I would ask. "Where did my Great-Grandfather find you?" The hand would pick up the pen, shuffle and slide across the page, and all it would leave would be HAHAHA or WOULDN'T YOU LIKE TO KNOW.

I asked Father if he knew anything about the hand, but all he knew was that we'd always had the hand, and what Great-Grandfather said was all there was. So I went back and read the bleached-brown script of Great-Grandfather's diary, and learned what I already knew: Great-Grandfather had paid somebody else to substitute for him in the Civil War, and made his first fortune out of quartermaster contracts, and gone west afterward. But he says next to nothing about the hand or where he got it, though he seemed to have more to do with the Indians than your average businessman.

I never did learn much more than WOULDN'T YOU LIKE TO KNOW and HAHAHA.

Dad involved himself less and less with the company, and finally, one day in June 1966, he called me on the intercom and asked me to join him. I gave our special knock and he let me in. We've always kept Grandfather's office as he left it; the gaudily painted safe no burglar would look at twice, was open. The buffalo-hide trunk was on top of it while the cage that held the hand was on the desk.

"What's up?" I asked.

"It's time," he said in a gray voice, and I noticed he looked gray too; his face was damp and pale and his lips bluish.

"Time for what?" I said, and he gestured toward the cage.

The hand was capering back and forth beside the notebook, where it had scrawled JUNE 19 8:11 PM YOU WILL DIE OF A CORONARY. PLAN ACCORDINGLY.

"It can't know," I said, then noticed Father was trying to keep himself from trembling.

"It knows," he said. "It told my father—your grandfather—when he was going to die to the minute. I said the same thing you did, and he told me I was wrong. Then he proved it. Pour me a drink. Bourbon." So I went over and poured him a drink from Grandfather's decanter.

And Father died of a coronary at 8:11 on June 19.

He had planned accordingly despite my skepticism, and Moorcock Industries went on without a tremor.

By that time I was asking the hand "Will I have a son?" For years Jessica and I had tried. YOU WILL HAVE NEITHER SON NOR DAUGHTER wrote the hand. The doctors said it was Jessica, so I made other arrangements. Every mistress knew exactly how much it was worth to bear my child—at the end I was willing to divorce Jessica—but none ever conceived.

And last week it said I would die today. But I'm proving it doesn't know everything. I've built a fire in Grandfather's fireplace, a good hot fire. Now I'm opening the safe, opening the buffalo-hide trunk.

The hand knows what I have in mind. It's hanging upside down on the cage top and trying to claw me, but the handle was designed long on purpose.

Now the cage is in the fire. The hand is hopping angrily against the top and sides, slapping the bars so hard the cage rocks, its withered tissue scorched and singed already.

We'll see who lasts longest.

3. LOOSE ENDS
Chris Leek

I sat in my old armchair not feeling the springs that poked me through the duct tape repair on the seat cushion. I no longer felt much of anything. I stared out the open window at fields I had worked all my life and took a long pull on my bottle. I hadn't showered in more than a week and I could smell my own stink, or maybe it was Miriam I could smell; her bloated corpse was still swinging from the roof beam in the back bedroom. The head-doctor I took her to told me not to leave her alone. I was only gone for ten minutes. I blamed myself. I expect she did too. Her bugged-out eyes seemed to be full of glassy accusation.

Miriam was such a gentle soul. She wouldn't even turn the tap on a spider if one showed up in the sink, which was why I found it so hard to understand how she could take a claw hammer to our German Shepard. She had smeared old Butch across the kitchen floor like he was some sort of modern art masterpiece. Miriam couldn't understand it either and she never came back from it, not really. Oh, she pretended like she was alright and after a month or so she even had me fooled, maybe not all the way fooled, but enough for me to go out for cigarettes. When I came back puffing on a Marlboro and saw that thing grinning at me on the kitchen table, my heart almost gave out. Then I caught sight of Miriam's legs dangling in the evening sunlight and I wished it had.

My dad had brought it home from World War Two. He said it was a souvenir from Africa. I guess it was, although a monkey skull ain't exactly a picture postcard or a snow globe. You would almost think it human, only it was smaller and when you looked close, the shape of it was all wrong, kind of squashed up like it had been sat on. In truth it ain't like no ape I ever seen. My mom hated it, said just looking at it made her feel funny. Back then it had a hold of dad pretty good and he would just shrug his shoulders and tell her to quit looking then.

I didn't care for it either. It was almost as if I could hear it talking. Not words as such, more like pictures, ideas really, bad ones that would get me the back of my dad's hand if I took to them. My baby sister, Joan I think she heard it too and that's why she started cutting on herself. They took Joanie away to a hospital in Pine Hills, one with bars on the windows that didn't allow visitors. She never came back either.

A warm breeze blew in through the window, making the rope around my dead wife's neck creak. Our bedroom was the same room where my mom had swallowed a whole bottle of sleeping pills before opening a vein, just to make sure. History likes to repeat itself, leastways around here it does. I drained the last of the whiskey and set the empty bottle with the others on the floor. It was time I finished something other than fifths of bourbon.

I got up and I staggered into the bedroom to cut down Miriam. I'd been wallowing in my own grief for too long and the summer heat hadn't been kind to her. The drone of insects filled the air as I gently lowered her onto the quilt and tried hard not to gag. I wrapped her up and half-dragged, half-carried her out back. I had buried old Butch at the edge of the big field, so as if he was able to look he could see all the way down the valley to the river. Miriam had always loved that view.

The soil was loose, but it was hot work and I wasn't young like I used to be. "I love you, girl," I said, the words sticking in my throat as I eased her into her grave. It was a long time before I got done crying, but then again, 37 years is a long time to love the same woman.

Dad could only see it clearly after mom passed. He tried hard to get rid of the skull then, but it was too late for that. It stuck to him like shit to a wool blanket. Whatever he did, the thing came back. In the end he drove 50 miles up state and dropped it in Deer Lake. Nearly a whole year went by and dad got to thinking he had it beat. I guess I did too. That is, until we came home from the feed store and found it waiting for us on the front porch, with green lake weed hanging from its empty eye socket.

That was the finish of my old man. He told me to run the truck to town and gas it up. After I left he went inside the house and put on his dress blues and ate a bullet. I found him face down on the floor with blood splattered over his medals and the top part of his head all but gone. The monkey skull was lying next to him, a single, neat bullet hole punched through its ancient bone.

Balled up in his hand was a note. It said: Lester, I think I know how to kill it. If this works, at least you'll be free of it. Forgive me, Dad.

Miriam and I never had any kids. I thanked God for that and picked up the shovel again. I was stone-cold sober for the first time in days. I expect the prospect of digging my own grave had a lot to do with that.

I had buried the skull much deeper before, a good hundred feet deeper, at the bottom of the old well. Then I laid charges and bought the stone-lined shaft down on it. It had taken the little fucker forty years to get out of that one. Another year or two would have probably been enough for both me and Miriam to go out on our own accord, although that didn't matter much now. I finished the hole, dusted myself down and went to the barn to fetch it.

The static in my head got louder when I opened the barn door. It could have been the mother of all hangovers kicking in, but I knew different. The air inside the barn was dusty and stale and July hot, so as breathing it hurt my lungs. On the work bench, in amongst a jumble of rusty tractor parts was an old feed sack, tied up with bailing twine. The sack felt a lot heavier than it had a right to. I took a hammer from my tool box—the same one that Miriam had used on Butch—and a stick of the dynamite I kept to clear beaver damns on the river and went back out to the field.

I dropped the sack into the grave, feeling the dull thud of eternity in my own mind when it hit the bottom. I climbed down and knelt beside it. My hands were shaking as I cut the twine and peered inside. The skull looked back at me; a sickly yellow thing that seemed to pulse in the gathering dusk. There was a circle of fresher white bone that marked the passage of my dad's bullet. He hadn't killed it, maybe he slowed it down some, but a thing like this isn't in a hurry.

"Let's get this done," I said to nobody and reached in the sack.

The feel of it made my flesh crawl and the hornets' nest inside my head buzzed angrily as I set the skull on the dirt.

"Complain all you want you son-of-a-bitch. You and me's gonna dance," I said and raised the hammer.

I brought it down on the skull, putting everything I had left behind the blow. Someone screamed, I guess it was me. Pain exploded in my head and the vision in my right eye sputtered out like a damp cigarette. The hammer fell from my grip and I collapsed against the side of the grave. Blood gushed down my face, running in my mouth and pouring off my chin to soak my shirt front. The agony was almost divine, except it didn't come with any harps and angels. I blinked my one good eye and through the red haze I saw the jagged hole I'd smashed in the skull. My hand went to my own head and found a matching depression there. I leaned over and threw up a pint of good whiskey.

Pictures flashed through my mind, they told me how easy it would be to just lay down and die; how it would all go away if I did. I didn't pay them no mind and took the dynamite from my pocket, sliding the slim finger of explosive into the hole in the monkey skull until I felt the pressure of it pushing on my own brain.

"Let's see you can dig yourself out of this one, you bastard," I said and thumbed a match.

***

"I don't think I'll ever get tired of this view," Maggie said and hugged her husband.

"Me either," Brian replied, hugging her back.

The couple stood on the back porch watching their two boys playing in the dirt over by the big field; making mud pies and getting filthy in the process. Maggie didn't mind; boys will be boys after all and besides, it was Brian's turn to get them bathed tonight.

The farm house had been a derelict when they bought it; overgrown and roofless with an oak tree sprouting through the rotten floorboards in the front room. It had taken two years of hard work to make it into a home.

"Hey sport, what you got there?" Brian called out to their eldest, Ryan.

A faint sense of unease washed through Maggie when she saw Ryan holding something that looked like a jaw bone; she guessed it was probably from a fox or a raccoon.

"Put that down, honey, it's dirty," she said letting go of her husband and starting over to the boys.

Ryan ignored her and pocketed the bone. His little brother, Tommy was kneeling in front of him intently studying something in the dirt. Ryan smiled and swung up his shovel. Maggie started to run.

***

Maggie couldn't stop hearing the dull wet sound of the shovel cleaving open Tommy's head. She heard it when the first clump of cold earth landed on her baby boy's coffin; heard it again in the scratch of the ink pen when Brian signed the forms to commit her other son to Pine Hills. She could still hear it now, even as the rope bit deep into her neck and she kicked out at the perfumed air.

15

Wren Jackson called 911 again, each ring a stab at his heart. He hung up at fifty, turned back to his mother, and burst into tears. The phone came apart when it hit the floor, and the battery pack scattered behind him.

His mom said nothing, did nothing. She sat at the dining room table, as she had for several minutes, spoon of cereal halfway to her open mouth, eyes trained on her iPad and this week's edition of Insider Secrets magazine.

Wren's hand quivered as he grabbed her unyielding, unmoving shoulder and shook. She rocked in her seat, but didn't jiggle or shift or do any of those things a person's supposed to do. Milk slopped on the table, and with it a soggy mass of once-crispy corn flakes. He grabbed her face with both hands—still warm to the touch—and kissed her forehead, as he'd done a thousand times in fifteen years.

She did not pat his cheek and say, "Love you, Pickle."

The walls opened up, and he stumbled back. Through tear-blurred vision he scrambled into the bathroom, jerked open the cupboard, and grabbed the orange-brown plastic bottle with the child-proof cap. Through panicked breaths he swallowed two Ativan, turned off the light, and huddled on the floor next to the toilet, rocking. Doctor Ward had said that the safety of the dark, tiny room, coupled with the benzodiazepine, should stave off a panic attack, or at least cut it short.

A half-hour and a vomit-spattered toilet bowl later, Wren came back into the kitchen on shaky legs. The sun shone through the dark curtains that his mother had hung to help him with his disorder, a blazing reminder of the wide open world just beyond the door. He shuffled on unwilling feet to the window, steeled himself, and looked outside.

The world swallowed him, and he drowned in the sky. Gasping, he forced his eyes down, down, to the trees, the houses, the street. Mr. Gonagle stood frozen in his bathrobe, spraying his car with a hose, cup of coffee in his left hand. Water chugged and drizzled down the asphalt driveway to the storm drain. A forgotten bucket of soapy water sat next to him, as unmoving as the beagle that sat beside it, calcified in mid-bark. Up and down the street revealed similar scenes: little Jeannie Graff lying in the grass on her pink bicycle, feet still on the pedals, face bright with an exhilarated smile; Mr. Daniels crouching in front of his open mailbox, plumber's crack poking out of his jeans; Mr. and Mrs. Walker on their stoop frozen in mid-smooch, she in PJs, he in a camo windbreaker and a fishing hat, off for some Saturday entertainment with the guys.

He closed his eyes and stepped back, squeezing out the world. The darkness enveloped him, cradled him, kept him safe. Cracks of light crawled through his brain, worming their way through the weak parts, but the Ativan did its job, and with a few deep breaths he kept his wits. Dad would know what to do.

Colonel Jackson didn't work on Saturdays. He should be home, even though he didn't answer his phone. Or maybe he'd gone to work to respond to the whatever-this-is. Either way, Wren could go there and wait. He packed up a few supplies—bottled water, the last of the granola bars, his medication, his cell phone charger—grabbed the doorknob, and stopped.

Twenty-four blocks under an open sky. Wren couldn't drive, didn't even know how to ride a bike. Through the door, the outside mocked him. He dropped the backpack by the door and sat on the couch, safe in the dark. *I can go tonight. I can do it in the dark.*

He turned on the TV and booted up Call of Duty: Ghosts. He gasped in relief when he saw his regular crew logged in. He put on his headset and sighed as the music washed over him. As close to friends as he'd ever had, they hailed from Washington, New York, even Japan, and though they'd never met in person, they promised exactly the comfort he needed. And maybe they knew something he didn't. "Hey, guys! Anything weird going on in your neck of the woods?"

The music played on. He wandered through the maze, and his hands shook on the controller. Players stood there, weapons ready. Nobody moved, nobody spoke. Wren tore off the headphones and screamed, and screamed and screamed, stopping only when his lungs couldn't produce enough breath.

The roof opened to a blazing sky, the sun's fire laying him naked before the universe. Blind and gasping, Wren shuddered and writhed. His throat burned, his stomach twisted into a cruel knot, his dry mouth clamored for water he'd never taste.

He came to later, soaked in sweat and the stink of his own piss. The power had failed, and his phone had died. The red cast of light through the windows told him it was dusk, but he wasn't ready to know for sure. Instead he pulled out a chair and sat next to his mom, still mid-bite.

He brushed his knuckles down her cheek—still warm, though her chest didn't rise or fall—and exhaled.

"I'm sorry, mom. I don't know what to do. You've always kept me safe, kept dad from shoving me outside, even when he thought it was the right thing. You knew it would kill me, but you've loved me anyway. I don't know what to do, where else to go. But we don't have any food in the house, and if I'm still moving there has to be others, right? Someone else?"

She stared at the iPad.

"I don't know if you can hear me, but I want you to know that I love you and I'm going to get help. I'm going...out there. And I'll be back. I'll bring doctors, scientists, whatever there is. If you get better before I'm back, wait for me here or leave me a note. I love you."

He kissed her cheek, stood, and approached the door.

This time, I win.

He grabbed the knob, steeled himself, and turned. It didn't budge.

He let go, only he didn't. He meant to, he wanted to, but his hand stayed on the knob. He stepped back, only he didn't. Inches from the door, he shrieked, but only in his mind.

5. SKINWALKER
B.A. Holland

Distant sirens wailed in the desert lands nearby, just as they had been all day. The rocky cliffs threw dark shadows across the landscape as the late afternoon sun began its plummet toward the horizon. Despite the multiple white jeeps with blue lights passing by, the San Diablos County Sheriff's car did not follow. The young twenty year old redheaded deputy couldn't help but wonder what had happened at the Top Secret government facility but she knew that it was all she could do; wonder.

She pulled onto a dirt road to answer the call of a possible domestic dispute. The road wound up the hill till it crested the peak with a view of the vast dry lake bed that spanned for miles beyond the horizon. The short, slender redhead stepped out of the 4x4 Sheriff's jeep and took a moment to look over the edge of the bluff. She could see lights all over the distant runway miles beyond. The military certainly had some sort of incident but the civilians of San Diablos would never know what it was.

The cool desert air grabbed hold of her pony tail as she turned and headed away from the edge and walked toward the house. As she approached the old home, she couldn't help but feel as if something was watching her in the distance. The front porch protested her steps with groans and snaps as she stepped across the weathered wooden planks. Before she could knock, the door swung inward. Its surface roared as it scraped across a groove carved into the floor by time and repetition. The officer's dark eyes widened at the sight of a nude young man before her. The officer turned away for a moment and looked at him sideways.

"We had a phone call that was made from out here about thirty minutes ago. It was a hang up. We – ah..." Her soft voice trailed away as she looked back at the man. He didn't seem phased in the least to have answered the door in the nude.

"My clothes... they are in the wash. I'm sorry. I was worried about what was happening at the airbase. Is everything – alright?" he asked. Kelly felt a hand on her shoulder and with it, an unusual, overwhelming feeling that came as a tingle and caused her hair to stand on end. At the same time, there was temptation. She didn't know which feeling to fight and which to accept as she looked back at the man.

"The military's handling it. This home is listed as owned by a *Nancy Taylor*?"

"My mother. Out of town."

There was something about his eyes... she couldn't quite place it. Something behind them that didn't seem quite right. It was as if they weren't moving and didn't focus upon her. The more he put his hands on her, the more she felt other overwhelming urges which she couldn't control. Battling the attraction with underlying fear, attraction gave in. Soon the bedroom floor of the house was strewn with the deputy's uniform as two nude figures mingled under the sheets. His body was unusually warm; his skin, softer than a usual man's. His eyes – still something wrong with his eyes... She couldn't look into them. She could feel him growing closer to climax as she leaned herself against the headboard. She found herself looking out the window at the airbase a moment. She gasped as the pleasure threatened to take over her common sense. She knew it was stopping time.

"Shouldn't you... stop now?" she moaned and hoped that he knew what he was doing. Warmth came and the young man twitched inside her. She knew that he had done the unthinkable. She breathed in deeply as she too felt the brief rush of ecstasy that came with her. She held onto his arms and looked into his eyes. Kelly cursed him for not pulling out; cursed herself for letting it happen.

"Get off!" She pushed him away. He pulled out of her without protest as she grabbed her clothes. The attraction faded away immediately, and she navigated away from the strange man… he was nothing but a strange man now. What happened to those feelings she felt before, she wondered.

Now there was only terror.

Kelly stumbled out of the back door. All she wanted to do was get away from the house. In her car, the radio blared with the county sheriff's voice. *Kelly... Kelly respond!*

"Kelly here. Sorry. I checked out the house. It's fine. Only the son is home."

"By himself?" The sheriff sounded surprised.

"Yeah."

"Where's his mother?!"

"I don't know..." Kelly felt a rumble under her belly. She had left in such a hurry, she didn't even bother to put her clothes on.

"Her son is ten, Kelly."

Kelly clicked the microphone and looked back to the house.

"I'll be right back."

She pulled her gun from the holster and dropped the pants and shirt to the ground. On the way back in, she nearly stumbled across something. She knelt down to make out shapes in the sand – bodies... a middle-aged woman, and a young boy – the boy's eyes were missing.

She stood back up but the pain in her belly intensified to the point that she fell over and gasped. She screamed as a slender figure emerged from between her legs, expanding into adult human form as it pulled itself out of her. She gasped as the fully-adult human form expanded into a near carbon copy of herself with no eyes in its sockets. The umbilical cord was still attached to her as the new entity leaned over the fear stricken young woman. The imposter pulled the gun out of Kelly's shaking hands. The other Kelly slammed its thumbs into her eyes and pulled them out of her face with ease.

"Need your eyes..."

Kelly's lifeless corpse lay still. The other naked figure gathered her clothes off the ground.

6. THE KITTEN
Megan N. Watson

When does the mind truly reach the apex of insanity? I have often thought myself to be insane, but then I had always heard that the insane are blind to their illness. What else can explain the rabid fits of rage? The blackouts of nights past, the ripped clothing? Am I insane?

I've heard insanity starts at birth. As one grows and experiences the cruelty of childhood, the madness increases, slowly consuming the sane portions of the mind. The older the child, the more perilous and unpredictable the personality becomes.

Perhaps that's why my, icy at heart but big on appearances, mother shipped me off to the prestigious Holmeswood Academy for Girls when I was seven. Despite my temper, the interactions with my peers were pleasant. I learned early on that keeping my anger in check made life a lot easier, especially after a rather nasty incident in third grade English class. No one will ever touch me without permission again, accidental or not. But as the years passed, my surliness reared its head with increasing frequency. I couldn't control it.

One day I was relaxing beside a brook in the woods behind the school. It was senior year and I was enjoying an afternoon off after midterms. The day was beautiful and the slight breeze felt glorious as it gently swept through my hair. I was staring into the waters of the brook when I heard a faint cry. Upon investigation, I discovered an adorable black and white kitten. I sat with that kitten, by the babbling brook, for what seemed like hours. Everything felt so calm and peaceful, then suddenly my heart started to pound and everything went dark.

When I awoke, the sun had started its descent, casting an orange glow on the world. For a second, all seemed okay, just a weird fainting spell. Then the realization hit. My hands felt sticky and I didn't hear the purring of my new friend anymore. A muffled scream emanated from my mouth as I discovered blood all over my dress, my hands and arms, my blonde hair. Tufts of bloody black and white fur littered the area around me. Frantically, I ran around looking for the kitten, praying that the scene was not what it appeared to be. I headed towards the bush where I had first found her and lifted the bottom branches. There, in a neat little pile, were the mutilated remains of the kitten. Panicked, I searched my brain for something to console my growing fears, but all I found was lost time. Looking at the sky wrenched me back to reality, curfew was fast approaching.

The scene of the crime had to be dealt with, no one could know of this. I buried the remains as fast as I could, then jumped in the brook, strategically smearing mud to hide the blood. Darkness covered the sky as I raced back to school, long past curfew. Thankfully I was received with sympathy, and some laughs, at my dirty, soaked uniform and scraped elbows and knees. No one was the wiser.

Slowly the nightmare of that terrible day faded into the back of my mind and everything seemed fine for a while. Months passed with no problems. One day I noticed that several girls from my dorm hadn't been in class for some time. Most assumed that they had transferred, until our Head Mistress called an assembly. The girls hadn't left the school, they'd been savagely murdered. Their mutilated bodies had been found, that morning, near the babbling brook. My brook. I left the assembly, feigning a stomach ache, and the school nurse excused me from class for the rest of the day. The illness may have been fake, but my stomach was nonetheless churning with anxiety.

Relieved to be back in my room and away from the world, a nagging suspicion was whirling. I knew there had to be a connection between the murders and the kitten. Was it me? Was someone with a horrid sense of humor messing with my head? Nothing made sense. I had no memory of anything. I hadn't even had a blackout since the kitten.

Unable to decide how to handle my emotions, I turned to cleaning my room. It began to pour outside and the room became damp and chilly. A pile of clothes separated me from the comfort of my bed. As I tore through them, looking for a sweater to warm me, my hands felt a strange garment, stiff and crunchy like snow covered blue jeans. My hands trembled as I picked up the bloody clothing. Every student at Holmeswood had their names sewn into their uniforms so that there would be no mix ups. Hoping against hope, I pulled the fabric apart at the waist band. The tag popped up and there was the name of the owner, Lisa Stark. One of the dead girls. Further inspection produced another uniform in similar condition, except this one was mine. I told myself this was a sick joke, that someone planted the clothes. It had to be a joke.

I collapsed in a heap, sobbing. How could I've committed these disgusting, violent acts and not remember them? My heart started to palpitate, faster and faster, until it felt like it would explode. My hands grew clammy, a tugging in my belly swelled, traveling down to my feet and up to my head. I started to feel separated from my body, like I was looking at myself from above. I realized my cries were now drowned out by a quiet laughter that was growing louder and louder, sounding more evil with each decibel. Was that coming from me? My mind flooded with visions of the dead girls swirling around me, screaming, "FREAK! FREAK!", pulling my hair, laughing at my tears. Laughing with a cadence created only by young girls.

***

Ten years, I've been locked in this tiny cell. I still don't remember anything. But this place, this miniscule one window room, is where I will spend the rest of my life asking my questions to an invisible audience, questions that have no answers.

7. SOUR
Bruce L. Priddy

Axe and a gas can in my hands, I walk across my field to the barn. Ten yards away, the barn is just a black stain in a fog that has smothered the town. From inside I hear Beth howl and howl. That thing in there is no longer my bride. It wears a face stolen from her.

This damnable fog, clinging and relentless, stinks of rot. I had stood on the hill with the other townsmen on the day that university man confronted the horror. I heard the frenzied, thundering croaks as the thing was sent away, the same sounds that now bellow from my barn. Then the fog seeped in from the sky and never left.

Inside of the mist, the sun is weak. The trees have lost their leaves, birds fallen from the branches. Our crops spoiled in the fields. Our livestock stunted. And we waste away... except for my Beth.

We thought the university man sent the horror back to whatever hell the Old Wizard had conjured it up from. I should've known better when my Beth told me she was pregnant. We hadn't married but three months back in September, and we were being careful. But dear God, we all know better now. "Dear God"? That's nothing but a horrendous lie.

Maybe Doc Davis could've done something for Beth, given her some sort of comfort. Maybe, that is, if he hadn't put a bullet through his temple after attending Miss Sally's miscarriage.

Damn me to Hell, but Beth had to be put in the barn so I could get a bit sleep. I should have done right by her - when she was still my Beth. But what loving husband could face that hard truth, even as his spouse grew and bloated? After what I saw this morning, I can't ignore it any longer.

Earl Sawyer called me up and said, "Joe, get your gun. Meet us in Hutchins' field. Something got one of his heifers."

I was the last to get there. Sawyer had rounded up Fred Farr, Henry Wheeler, Wesley Corey, and Curtis Whateley. The men stood with Sawyer and Hutchins round the cow. She was blossomed open, her insides spilled, staining the withered grass black. Tongues of fog lapped at the ragged edges of the rent heifer. Destroyed as she was, I could tell she'd been deformed, distended. Like my Beth. My stomach wanted to heave.

"Is it back?" Curtis asked, panic rattling his voice.

"Herd's all still here. What's left of them," said Hutchins. We all let loose an audible exhale of relief. Wheeler thanked the Lord. How can any man with sense still believe?

Hutchins wasn't finished. "Got her calf, though." He pointed to a trail of gore disappearing into the fog.

We followed. The path of bloody purulence took us to the creek at the back of Hutchins land. As we approached, we heard something splashing and gasping in the shallow water. Weapons ready, we stepped to the bank.

We beheld the aborted fruit of the heifer's womb. It seemed to be a combination of cow, lizard, and some spawn from the ocean's nightmare depths. A wizened, bearded human faced gaped at us, like a land-stuck fish gulping. Those goatish eyes seemed to smirk when it saw us.

Hutchins' shotgun blasted away that mocking countenance. Still it moved. We all fired our weapons, and rent that corruption to bits. Each part sprouted appendages, hooves. We didn't let up until the creek's weak waters ran a greenish-yellow and carried every piece of that blasphemy away. I'm not sure we killed them all.

Curtis screamed. "That face! I spied that face through the telescope on the hill! It ain't gone! It ain't gone!"

Wheeler took my shoulders in his hands and looked me in the eye. "That was inside her, Joe."

I ran. I don't know why, nothing was going to change.

Curtis kept screaming as I fled. There was a gunshot. Then he was quiet.

He was right. The university man thought he sent the horror away. It was only scattered, into the sky, the soil, the water. It settled in our balls, our wombs.

We've gone sour.

As I walk into the barn, Beth's howling ceases. From her bed of hay, she lifts her head, unable to move any other part of her body. She is nothing but a bulbous pile of flesh with shriveled limbs.

"It won't let me die," she says, the words falling from the chasm in her throat. Over and over she says this, all coherence lost since she took a knife to herself when she could still move. "It won't let me die."

I set down the axe and gasoline. Parts of her swell and bulge, following me as I walk around her bloated form to place a kiss upon her forehead. "I know," I whisper against translucent skin thick with purple veins. "But I'm going to help you."

8. PRESENCE
Mark Slade

I am here.

Perched upon a simple wooden chair, my knees drawn up to my chin, my arms wrapped tightly around my legs. My bare feet are barely dangling off the edge of the seat. My eyes are steadied upon the linoleum kitchen floor. Each of the decorative squares slowly being overcome by a drifting shadow.

I can't stop trembling.

Although I am naked, I have just risen from bed, I am not cold. No. that is not the reason I am shaking so violently. It is....this....thing....a shadow....a lurking shadow that persists in consuming everything in its path.

As I have said, I was awakened from a deep slumber. I had heard sighs....or maybe...and I know it sounds a little.....crazy. I heard a woman in ecstasy.

And yes. I recognize those sighs of ecstasy.

It is Gail.

I met Gail while shopping in the drugstore. I needed medicine for my wife. My wife, Leah....is a good woman, a good wife. But....she has days when she will not get out of bed. It is, I know, a terrible thing I am about to say. I am glad we do not have children. I am always at the office, selling airtime for a dying breed: FM radio. And Leah, well, she hardly gets out of bed because the walls of the bedroom are too gloomy.

I tried painting them different colors. After a month of bright reds, yellows, country greens, orange, even. I grew tired of a job that I never got paid for: being a decorator.

We went to a well-known and all too expensive analyst. Psychiatry is a con game. I still went along with it. Leah seemed to get slightly better. Only three days out of the week she stayed in bed. So this analyst prescribed medicine for Leah.

Maybe that psychiatrist is to blame for all of this. Through her I met Gail.

Yes. Gail is very different from Leah. Leah is slim, very slim, and mousy. I used to say I had a thing for mousy, quiet girls. Leah almost always had short blond hair, and small piercing blue eyes. But she also has very luscious pouty lips. Gail, has long dark curly hair. She is tall, voluptuous....child bearing hips. Those large brown eyes are hypnotizing, like a tall refreshing glass of water. And those cherry red lips always quenched my thirst. She was tall, very long legs. And it was like she knew they were her best feature. She always wore short skirts.

Gail was the pharmacist. She got to know me from ordering that medicine for Leah. It was a medication, as Gail would tell me, doctors in asylums prescribe. She said she was concerned about its use. That was how our affair began. Short chats in the drugstore turned into long sob stories told over coffee. Which led to dinner, which led to emails, cell phone numbers being exchanged, phone sex, sex in the car, sex in a seedy hotel, sex at her house — when her boyfriend, Don, was away on school functions. He's a football coach at the high school.

Eventually, it led to us renting this cottage twenty miles from our homes. My lie to Leah was a business trip to the Tri-cities. Gail told Don she was visiting a sister in New York. Perfect. We ate her cooking, I tended to cutting firewood. We went for long walks, made love every day for the last week, pretended to be a happily married couple.

Those long walks have become our end. Our comeuppance, as people say.

We took our usual walk in the woods, past tall glorious trees with their leaves turning from bland green to glorious oranges and yellows. We went too far, and I told her so. Gail wanted to find a stream that was listed on the property management's website. We found the stream deep in the woods. We stayed there all day until dusk began to settle.

I made her hurry out of those woods. I never fancied getting lost within a dark forest at night. We went left instead of right, right instead of left....we were lost. We argued terribly. She walked off and, in the distance on top of a steep hill, there was a large black mound. Strange. The mound seemed to move on its own.

No. I am not crazy. I am not Leah....I didn't mean to say that. Not at all. It just...flashed through my mind.

Gail....oh....please...Gail stepped right on the mound. That black...moving mound. It consumed. Crawled right up her pant legs, and her legs quickly disappeared! Soon, within micro-seconds her bottom half was gone. Her lower extremities had become black muck writhing across the ground. It moved upwards, devouring her chest, her neck....then all that was left was a head floating within a dark, black shadow.

I can still hear her screams. I can see her widened eyes glaring at me. That oval shaped mouth, screaming for me to help her.

One last plea. Gail was no more.

That shadow danced across weeds that were swallowed up in a frenzy. It came toward me, eating up the scenery, as people say, trees disappearing that black muck.....

It was gone.
That quick.

I stood there, cold, clammy from sweat, shaking. I made my way back to the cottage. I don't remember how. It was a memory that never happened. Regardless, all I could think of was that horrible incident with Gail and the shadow.

I went to bed, cried myself to sleep. Hours later, I was awakened by a wonderful sound of heightened female experience. I wandered sleepily into the kitchen, as the sound grew louder.

The shadow was there, devouring the refrigerator, the stove, the table, chairs, linoleum floor.....

Here I am.

I sit perched on a simple kitchen chair, hugging my naked legs close, trying to keep my bare feet from touching the black, murky shadow rising up towards me.

I heard a voice.
A calm, serene voice, in between long sighs of female pleasure.

"Tom......" the voice said.

It was Gail.

"Tom...." she says to me.

I am enchanted.

I lower my bare foot, dipping into that black, murky shadow.....

9. THEY REQUIRE KILLING
Naching T. Kassa

Her blood was still warm.

Robert Evans rose from beside the mutilated corpse, nervously licking his lips. He forced himself to breathe deeply. When he had reached a sufficient level of calm, he lifted the body and carried it to the back of the building. Then, he left 29 Hanbury Street and made his way to the dingy hotel in which he was lodging. The clothes under his cloak were bloody and needed a change.

Outside, a woman stood near the hotel. She was dressed cheaply and smelled of corn whiskey. A coy smile spread over her lips as he approached. Assuming a seductive stance, she called out to him.

"Fancy a tumble, Ducky?" she asked.

Robert stared at her, his eyes coldly calculating. She was wholly unattractive in both face and figure. In the past, he would have assessed her as nothing but a potential victim. He would have slit her throat from ear to ear without hesitation and watched her life ebb from her eyes. That was the past, however. He killed only those who required killing now.

The prostitute was waiting for an answer, shivering a little in the cold. He pulled a gold sovereign from his pocket and tossed it to her. Then, he hurried into the hotel and upstairs to his room.

Robert did not turn up the gas, as he entered. There was no need to attract unwanted attention. He bent down near the fireplace and stirred the embers with a poker. Once the fire was revived, he shed his bloodstained clothes and threw them into the flames. A soft tone sounded from across the room. He turned to the table and retrieved the device which had emitted the sound. Outwardly, it appeared to be a cell phone, but was much more than that. He flipped it open to answer the summons.

"Report, Sergeant Evans," the female voice said. The tone was professional, even brusque.

"Encountered Victim Number Four, Dispatcher Anderson," Robert replied. "Subject is now deceased. Was delayed in my arrival on scene. Victim was not killed in correct location. Had to relocate."

"Understood," Anderson said. "The final victim will be murdered in two months. Are you prepared to wait?"

"Yes," Robert affirmed.

"Control is vital here," she reminded. "No unauthorized murder will be tolerated."

"I know," Robert said glumly.

"Unauthorized murder can lead to disruption of the Time Line," she continued. "Unauthorized disruption means your instant termination."

"Understood, Dispatcher Anderson," Robert said through gritted teeth. Didn't she realize that he had changed?

"Contact will be reestablished on the Ninth day of the Eleventh month. Anderson, out." The link between past and present was suddenly extinguished. Robert tossed the Quantumphone aside.

He stared out the smoke stained window, his mind in the past. It was not the past of 1888 in which he now resided, but his own past. It was the past of 2032.

He had been in prison then, on Death Row for the murders of seven women. His execution had been scheduled for the following week. He sat in his cell, dreading the day.

Then, Aaron Munson had come to him with a life-saving proposition.

Munson, an unassuming and bespectacled little man, was in charge of the newly formed Time Police. As time travel had become possible and popular, certain abuses had been incurred. As a result, the natural Time Line had been disrupted. Munson was going to set it straight.

He had a rather strange method of achieving this end. Prisoners, enlisted by him, were to travel back in time and correct the disruptions. The cons were chosen not only for their skills, but for the fact that they were expendable.

Robert accepted the offer.

He had looked forward to the killing. It was a dream-come-true. At least, he thought it was, until he underwent the required reconditioning.

The process took three years to complete. It was the worst and the best thing that had ever happened to him. Robert was broken and rebuilt. By the end of the conditioning, he was a different man.

A commotion arose outside. Robert ignored the cacophony of alarm and slid into the sagging bed. Sleep overcame him. It was a deep sleep, though not as deep as that imposed upon the dead woman in the street outside.

***

An almost supernatural mist rose off of the Thames, the night of November 9th. It chilled the bone and warped the perception. Sounds seemed to echo opposite from their true direction. Human forms were twisted shadows, not unlike demon spawn cavorting in a smoky Hell. One such demon approached the house at 13 Miller's Court in Dorsett Street, with a singular purpose in mind.

Mary Kelly, unlike most women of her profession, possessed a fair amount of beauty. She changed her hair color when the fancy took her, but could not change the angelic blue of her eyes. They were her best feature.

Mary saw the man pass her in the fog and smiled confidently. He was surprisingly handsome, with piercing grey eyes and dark hair. He was also a gentleman, for he tipped his silk hat to her as she passed. Mary continued on toward her room, without propositioning the man. Her looks were all that she needed to attract potential customers.

What Mary did not know, was that beauty was ephemeral. Those who were lucky, lost it with age. Those who were not, had it wrung from them by a hard life.

Mary's was about to be cut away from her…an inch at a time.

Robert's grey eyes followed Mary as she entered the hovel at 13 Miller's Court. He waited a few minutes before following her. Regret turned his stomach. She had to die. It was required.

***

The smell of blood filled the room. It was the metallic smell of slaughter, of Charnel Hell. Robert licked his lips as he crept up behind his unsuspecting victim. His body was a coiled spring. He smiled.

It was a floor board which betrayed him to his prey. The protesting creak caused the man to look up from the bloody ruin of Mary Kelly and into Robert's face.

For an instant, Robert regarded the man before him. He was all together unremarkable, easily overlooked in a crowd. His dark eyes were the only clue to the monster that lurked within. The man gazed at Robert dumbly, too surprised to speak.

Robert ceased to hesitate. He rammed the six-inch blade into the Ripper's throat. Blood spurted as he severed the carotid artery. The murderer fell; face first, upon the floor.

Robert closed his eyes as the tremor of ecstasy swept over him. He breathed deeply, trying to calm himself. There was much to do and little time.

Fifteen minutes later, he stood on a secluded bank of the Thames, shrouded in fog. There, he dismembered what had been the most notorious of murderers and tossed the pieces into the murky water. The sun began to rise, burning through the fog like a bloody eye. Robert stretched and retreated from the river.

***

"Report, Sergeant Evans," Dispatcher Anderson commanded when Robert answered the summons.

"Victim Number Five is dead and the Target has been eliminated."

"Has the body been…disposed of?" Anderson asked.

"It has." His eyes shifted over to the hat box on the table.

"We are quite impressed with your work, Evans," Anderson said, adopting a warmer tone. "Frankly, we didn't believe that you could…could…"

"Control myself?" Robert said, his lips twisting into an ironic smile.

"Yes," the Dispatcher admitted. "However, because of your fine service, a promotion is in order. You shall receive it upon your return. Once you have been debriefed, you will receive your next assignment."

"Who is my next assignment?"

Anderson hesitated. Robert waited. At last she answered.

"The Zodiac. You're going to Stateline, Nevada, circa 1970.

"Very well," Robert said. He smiled at the hat box.

"Are you ready for return?" She asked.

Robert quickly crossed the room and snatched up the box.

"I am," he responded.

"See you on the other side," she said and signed off.

Robert smiled as the Mini-Wormhole began to extend from the Quantumphone. He had accomplished his first mission and finally proven himself. His new life had finally begun.

As the Wormhole began to envelope him, his entire being was suddenly overcome with guilt. He nearly dropped the box on the floor. What he had done was strictly forbidden and, worse, it declared to him that he had not really changed at all.

Then, he considered the other side of the coin. He had killed one of the greatest serial killers in history and that deserved more than a simple promotion. It deserved a trophy. He clutched the box tightly. *He* deserved a trophy.

The Wormhole pulled him away in one brilliant flash of light.

34

10. LIKE 'EM BIG
Johannes Pinter

Like 'em big.

It was the first thought that popped into Ralf's mind as he arrived at the Södertälje Syd train station and saw her standing there with her impressive cleavage.

The evening sky was cloudy and unusually dark for September. No people, except this piquant woman, could be seen outside the rural woodland station located a kilometer outside of the small town of Södertälje. But he parked the car at the far end of the long-term parking lot anyway, to get an unhurried overview of the location and situation. He had double checked the timetable. Now, around half past ten, it would be an hour until the next long-distance trains stopped. The car he was driving, a dark blue Volvo 740, was so common that no one would observe it. But if they saw him, Ralf, of thirty five years and four hundred pounds, with his round baby face and light blond hair, they would definitely remember him. So he always chose places a little off, at times, a lot off.

This was his first detour in nearly three months and the first in a long time this far south of Stockholm. The papers had written about his last girl, the one he thought he'd hidden so well in that abandoned house by the Råcksta swamp. So he'd been lying low for a while, staying home, keeping the Need at bay. He had the freezer full of *trophies* (as the police like to call them in TV series and movies); the breasts from his girls.

At first he had thawed out a new pair every two weeks or so. But as time went, it had become more often. The Need demanded it. And when he had, just a few days ago, thrown the last rotting pair in a garbage container down at the switchyard, wrapped in plastic, a newspaper and a plastic bag, he had known that it was time again.

The articles he read online claimed that his fascination came out of an unnatural relationship with his mother. But the shitheads didn't have a clue what they were talking about - he hadn't even had a mom. Almost hadn't, anyway. If you didn't count a coldhearted, dissociating, uncommunicative, sour, constantly accusing crone - then he *possibly* have had a mother. No. Why does one like hamburgers? Why does one like formula one racing? Why does one like women with big breasts? Because one does! That's why, simple as that, and there's your psychology right in your faces, stupid shrinks.

Now he sat here, watching a woman with the most exciting breasts he'd seen in years. She was wearing green rubber boots and a knee-length skirt and a jacket that looked a little chilly for this time of the year, and under the jacket she wore a thin light gray blouse with that plunging neckline. No suitcase, just some sort of canvas bag hanging over her shoulder, so she didn't seem to be out on a long journey.

After twenty minutes as she still stood there, after having turned down a cab that dropped an arriving couple, he decided that it was time. First, he double-checked the plastic bag containing the cloth soaked with the anesthetic *Sevoflurane* that he hid in the compartment next to the seat, and the meat knife beside it. The roadmap lay open on the passenger seat. He started the Volvo, glided up and stopped next to her. With difficulty he leaned over and opened the passenger door.

"Excuse me," he said, trying not to let that throbbing arousal affect his tone. "Are you familiar with the roads around here?"

The woman leaned forward, and Ralf got a glimpse straight down the front of her blouse, which confirmed that he had chosen the right girl (only naturally large breasts are affected by gravity like that), as her face appeared in the open door. She had long, strawberry blond hair with braids interwoven, one from each temple. Her light Scandinavian appearance was seasoned by distinctive features and dark eyebrows. But when she met his gaze, he was nonplussed. At first he thought she was doped, but then he realized that she appeared so much older than he had anticipated. Not that she was old-aged, because she wasn't, maybe twenty-five tops. But her eyes were ... ancient. Grayish brown, with fine wrinkles around the edges and the whites slightly yellowed. For a moment he sensed that she'd seen the whole world; not like she had traveled a lot, but that she'd seen the world *change*. Not seen the world in length and width, but in *depth*. It was an uncomfortable feeling that caught him off balance. He let his eyes sweep over her breasts (sweet Jesus, so big and round and...) and then he was back on track.

"This map confuses me, and -"

"Lift?" the woman asked.

Ralf could not believe his ears. This was almost too easy; she literally threw herself on him. Too bad, in a way; he liked it when he had to bargain and persuade. It was part of the game, made the juices flow. But maybe he could make this a game too; become the one to convince.

"It depends", he said. "Where you going?"

"Nearby."

He pretended to ponder for a moment.

"Okay, jump in."

As she slipped into the passenger seat, Ralf glanced as she strapped on her seatbelt, how it settled between the mighty hills (hadn't her nipples stiffened under the fabric?). Then he got the car in gear and they left the station behind.

"You live around here?" he asked.

The woman nodded hesitantly.

"In town?" he continued.

"Around."

"Good. You just let me know when to turn, okay?"

"Okay."

She had some kind of accent, but he couldn't tell whether it was foreign or dialectal. He steered the car out on the bigger Nyköping Road.

"I just have to make a short errand, then I'll drive you home."

The woman leered at him and nodded.

Sparsely deployed streetlights generated moments of yellow illumination along the nighttime road. As they passed through the light, he noticed that she quickly looked away, as if she secretly watched him in the darkness. She was most certainly disgusted with his plump body, that's why she'd looked. Just like the others.

After five hundred meters he turned left into the smaller Glade Road that stretched into the woods. He'd done some scouting earlier, so he knew he could work here undisturbed. The asphalt turned to gravel, and after another minute they were in the middle of no mans' land. Ralf glanced at the woman, who looked at him with a stiff posture. She surely now wondered what he was doing out here in the woods - he knew that he would've.

"There. Now I just have to…" he said and discreetly unfolded the bag beside his seat.

But when he turned around and raised the soaked cloth, he was surprised as the woman concurrently reached toward him.

***

It didn't take much; a grab and a quick twist of the head, and his obese body became limp in the seat. She nearly ripped his head from the body from excitement, but then realized that the whole interior would become covered in blood. So she walked around the car and pulled out the big man onto the ground. God, she wanted to eat so badly, the hunger tore at her bowels so ravenously that she thought she'd go crazy. But it was not time just yet, not here and now. Later. In the forest. At home.

She took off her jacket, the blouse and skirt and put them in the bag. She didn't like the clothes, they made her feel snared. But contacting humans demanded it. She stood there pale and naked, only rubber boots on, breasts hanging over her furry stomach, her hollowed back open like an empty box. It wasn't easy to be a Huldra these days, with all the vehicles and technical and digital connections between mankind, and fewer and fewer men straying into her hunting grounds by foot. Her last feeding was over a month ago and it had been a thin man.

She looked down at the fat man in the light of the car's headlamps. If more men of this size came her way – she could last a month or longer. Salivation began to run freely from the corners of her mouth. How she longed to tear him to pieces, drink the blood, eat the flesh and intestines and marrow of the bones.

With some effort, she lifted the massive body in her arms and began her trek away from civilization, into the dark heart of the woodlands. It would be a tough walk, but it was definitely worth the effort.

Like 'em big, she thought.

11. OPERATION WENDIGO
Aaron J. French

How long have I been here?

That was the question. Memories he retained were like dreams, a swirling mass of images and experiences, thoughts and emotions. Not one distinctly true. But neither were they egregious fantasies.

They just *were*.

Was it like this? Was it like he went to sleep every night and passed through The Gate of Death, only to find himself here, unutterably alone in this frozen wasteland, with nothing but the arctic winds, snow bluffs, and ice peaks to keep his company?

Perhaps he did wake up some mornings. Perhaps that was what all those swirling images (memories) were about. If he had another existence, apart from this unthawed hell, maybe it was going to be all right. Maybe this *was* just a dream.

God, he hoped so.

He was thin almost to the point of emaciation, and his skin pulled tight against his bones, making them stand out. The fur that covered his body was ash-gray, and long locks of gray hair hung over his head. He had elongated arms like an ape which ended in fixed black claws. The fur was sometimes itchy, but at least it protected him from the cold. *Something* was protecting him from the cold because he sure as hell wasn't freezing to death.

That's because you're already dead.

No, it's because you're dreaming.

No, it's actually because you're a beast.

He combed the chaos in his brain and located one of those memories he had such a hard time understanding. This one showed him landing in a small jet airplane on a strip of black tarmac enclosed inside a fenced-in military compound. Jagged ice peaks reared up behind it. This he could believe, for if he looked even deeper he found more memories of a military nature, boot camp, working at the base, even seeing some combat.

But was it true? Had he been a soldier?

He climbed up the mountainside like he always did, anchoring his towering physique with wide flat feet. Every so often a little shower of loose ice piddled down the slant. He knew that if enough of that got going it would spell disaster. But his body, animal though it was, possessed a great sense of balance. He was able to move with the grace of a ballerina.

When he reached the top of one of the peaks, he settled into the cave-like shelves there within the ice. He sat at the ledge, gazing out into the distance. Nothing but miles and miles of snow and ice under a gray sky, with more mountains in the distance. Not a trace of human civilization.

It's okay because any time I'll be waking up, he told himself. This is one of those dreams that repeats itself, and when I do wake up I'll be a United States soldier.

He felt good just saying it. He had taken a position. Somehow that seemed to waylay a bit of the confusion.

He laid on his back staring up at the frozen ceiling of the cave, the icy grooves and ridges. Then his doubts returned, like they always did, and his mental feelers dove back into the pits of his unconscious, searching for clues.

He had nightmares, but who didn't? One was this horrible scenario in which, as a soldier, he had been living on the base with the fenced-in tarmac, him and a few others who'd gotten off the plane as a group. Women and men. He couldn't seem to recall what in the Sam hell they'd all been doing in the middle of this arctic nowhere land, but there you had it. Eventually they started running low on food and were quarreling a bit. The heating units began to malfunction, and in the end they had resorted to cannibalism.

But that can't be true. I don't believe it.

He was the only one to have made it out alive. And it was he who had eaten up the last of them—

Flashes of blood-covered hands, mutilated corpses, sinews and entrails dangling from his teeth.

Christ.

He sat up and looked toward the horizon. He thought he was imagining it. This was just a dream, he wasn't seeing this. No. Soon he would rouse to the familiar buzzing of his alarm clock.

But it wasn't going away.

He squinted—yes, sure enough. He knew what it was. A Sikorsky UH-60, Black Hawk Family. Army rescue helicopter. Coming straight toward him.

His heart thudded with excitement. Maybe this whole thing wasn't a dream, maybe he really was stranded here. Better safe than sorry.

He must get to higher ground.

Are you crazy? Look at you. You're like a demonic Sasquatch or something.

He'd forgotten about that. But what choice did he have? He had to risk it. And hopefully this impression he had of himself was only a hallucination caused by the cold.

He left the ice-cave and started climbing higher. Again and again, those unsettling trails of snow piddled down at his feet. He usually didn't go this high, even though his mountaineering skills were superb. When the mountain wanted to go, it went. And you went with it.

As he ascended, his memories brought up a final horror. This one was certainly a dream. He had wandered away from the compound on a death wish, out of food and water, freezing to death, when some god-awful creature had emerged from the snow. A spirit, he wanted to call it, a demonic spirit. He recalled its obscene eyes and salivating jowls, eyes black as death, loping over the snow fields like a gorilla, and howling like a lion.

He had no chance: it was on him instantly, tearing his flesh apart, like a sheet of paper. It slit his throat with a taloned claw and drank his blood. It slashed a wound in his gut and drank his entrails, leaving him a bloody mess in the snow.

But that was it. There the memories ended. It must be a dream, because it was obvious he wasn't dead. If he were dead how could he be climbing up this—

But you are dead, at least your body is, and now you're this grotesque lumbering thing, a creature, and you have tasted human flesh, and you want to taste it again...

He grinned. He couldn't argue with that. If he knew one thing for certain it was that he had this hunger unquenchable by normal means. It wasn't the kind of hunger you died from. It was the kind that gnawed at you and drove you insane.

A hunger for human meat.

Because after all, now that he was the spirit he didn't have to eat, not for survival anyway.

He didn't like it. He had enough on his mind already without dragging delusions like that into the equation. His strange appearance—and most likely lots of his memories—were a product of the extreme cold. If he could just make it back to civilization and thaw himself out there'd be a normal, psychosis-free individual underneath. He was sure of it.

He had advanced further up the mountain. Several times he craned around to make sure the UH-60 was still coming, and it always was, was so close now he could hear the faint *thwump thwump* of its propeller blades.

He grew so excited when he heard this sound that he picked up the pace. Crunch, crunch, crunch, he footed through the snow, leaning at the waist a little to account for the upward slant. It was not easy work and he soon became winded, but he refused to relent. If this was his chance at freedom, he sure as hell wasn't going to miss it.

However the snow beneath his feet was quickly dislodging, and each time he pounded another step into the ground, more shook free. He knew this was dangerous but he didn't care, he had to reach the top.

Soon so much of it had fallen that he could hear it sliding down the mountainside—a low swishing sound. The mountain itself began to tremble, then it was all going, a whole gigantic slab of it.

With luck, he reached the flat summit just as the shelf beneath his feet broke away. He stood on the hard icy surface, hands on knees and panting, as the roar of the avalanche filled his ears. He peered over the edge, to where the vast white cloud was roiling up like mist.

Catching his breath, he straightened and scanned the sky, and sure enough the UH-60 was heading right for the avalanche site. He backed up several feet, positioning himself in the most open area, and began waving his arms.

The chopper rumbled into view, its blades competing for sound with the falling snow. He noticed that this UH-60 was equipped with M60 machine guns. This seemed odd, for usually the rescue choppers weren't fitted with such firepower. He supposed it didn't make much difference.

He started jumping now, flailing his clawed hands. The long gray locks bounced against the back of his neck. His big body left depressions in the slabs of frosted rock. The chopper flew in close, circling him, and he could see several soldiers through the glass windshield. They were looking down at him and seemed to be shouting.

They see me! No more of this nightmare, I'm going home!

The UH-60 did a few more circles, then started coasting away. His heart sank down into his stomach, but then they were looping around and heading straight for him. Suddenly he heard the electronic wheeze of the M60s as they came online, followed by the gasping whine of the Gatling barrels.

He turned and started to run as bullets shredded through his flesh.

12. THE CLUB
Michael Schomaker

The air is frigid and dark. I can't see more than 3 feet in front of me as I push forward; the dense cold fog hides my path. The rocks of the substrate I'm running on are bruising and cutting the bottoms of my feet, as I run at full speed. Terror consumes my soul and I am running for my life, but why? Who am I running from? I don't know and there's no time to figure that out now, I must reach safety. The uneven ground makes it nearly impossible to move without losing balance.

In the distance I see a soft red and blue glow illuminate the fog ahead of me. What it is? I don't know but what choice do I have but approach? As I near the illumination I can hear the faint sound of music getting louder. I emerge from the fog, and my surroundings come into focus; the blue light revealing an old rundown clapboard-sided pub. It appears open. There is music playing from inside, but no vehicles within the lot. As I run the only words I can read upon the building are the red and blue neon sign. It blinks on and off in the window, reading simply "the Club".

Still at full speed, I hit the old saloon style doors and they fly open, banging on the walls and shaking the building. My entire body is trembling from the adrenaline coursing through my veins. I can finally stop for a moment, my lungs burning with every breath. Just as I do, I look up to notice that the club is full of people and they have all turned to look at me. I contemplate explaining that I don't know why I'm running or who I'm running from, but it is a task that I'm certainly not up for at the moment. I glance behind me, out the door, and wonder if who or whoever pursued me still gives chase. This brings the terror over me again, and I immediately turn and hastily sit in an empty seat against the wall. When I look up the other patrons look away and pretend not to stare.

As I sit catching my breath, I try and remember the night's events, trying desperately to recall how this madness had begun. Why was I running, from who or what, and from where?

"What will you have hunny?" I look up to find the waitress standing over me. She has long, brown curly hair, and wears a tiny black leather outfit. Her voluptuous breasts are barely covered by the blackened hide. Her long legs are accentuated by her outfit, rising to her equally ample backside. "Well?" she asks.

"Oh I'm sorry, little tired, I'll have water."

"Water? Water it is." She laughs and walks away.

I can't help but watch her, and as she walks away I finally notice the décor of the room. Strobe lights flash within each corner, making everyone look as though they move in slow motion. Poles adorn each corner, with half naked women swinging from each in a hedonistic trance. It suddenly occurs to me that, *"This is a strip club."* Instead of thinking this I realize that I've said it aloud.

"Why, yes it is baby, like what you see?" the waitress questions, seemingly back to my table instantaneously.

"Um, yeah, definitely, I just had a rough night," I answer. My mind is aflutter with feelings of foolishness and fear.

"I know you did Hun, now here's your water. My name's Jinn if you need anything else."

I thank the woman and again watch her walk away. But as she leaves something she said rings in my head. *"I know you did."* It rang strangely in my mind. Was she just trying to be nice? It doesn't make any sense. And what of my phone and my wallet? Reaching frantically into my empty pockets, I see I'm wearing a black suit. I don't remember putting this on, or why I'm dressed so formally.

With my head down starring at my clothes, a woman comes up behind me and reaches around my neck. She puts her lips to my ear and whispers. "Hey you, how about a dance?"

As I turn toward her the smell of sweet perfume fills my nose. "My name's Seraphim, Sera for short." Her breasts press up against my back and she lingers awhile with her mouth close to my skin. I don't feel like a dance but there's definitely something about her.

"Actually, I don't have any money," I tell her.

"Oh it's ok, everything is free here dear." A song I have never heard starts playing, yet for some reason the newness of it is strangely comforting. She stands in front of me, her hands caressing her almost naked body, moving side to side with the sultry rhythm of a siren. She reaches behind her back, unclasping her delicate, white lace brazier, slowly releasing her pale breasts. By this time I had almost forgotten about the night's events, until she whispered something else into my ear. "You just have to choose Hun." Softly, she turns my head toward each corner of the room.

In the left corner I notice all of the girls dancing for other patrons. One of the girls swings sensuously around the shiny brass pole, grazing her black dress upon the ground. On the other side of the bar I see a woman crawling with feline-movement sexiness toward the edge of a raised stage. Her perfect skin is the very picture of beauty, covered in white lace. As my dance finishes I want to talk to her about her comment but she was too quick and has moved on to the next man seated in front of me. With a shy wave and smile she was gone.

All of my attention is now on the two corners of the oblong bar. I notice a man stand up on the left side of the bar and follow a woman through an old wooden door. The Champaign Room I assume. The sweet perfume smell was all but gone and a pungent odor of burning food slowly overtook the room after the wooden door had opened. I turned to the opposite side of the room and was interrupted by the sound of gunfire as five shots rang out suddenly. I hit the floor and slid under the table, yet no one else in the room seemed to move.

I scan around the interior of the bar trying to see if I can determine what happened. A dark haired woman leans under the table and smiles.

"You all right?" she asks.

"Didn't you hear the gunshots?" I ask timidly. Slowly she helps me up and back into my chair.

"Oh, you don't know yet. My name's Vine. Why don't you let me dance for you." A dark, heavy rock and roll song begins to play over the speakers. Vine lifts her leg and straddles mine, all the while thrusting her pelvis against mine. The music is loud and all of my earthly worries dissipate, so I close my eyes and lose myself in the moment.

With my eyes closed and mind wandering, things start to come to me in flashes. I see Vine dancing in front of me down a long alley. She slowly starts to disappear. Two men approach me wearing dirty tattered clothes, faces unkempt with scraggly beards. "Give me all your money." One of the men calls out. Just as he does, the other pulls a revolver from his pocket and five shots deafen my ears, and I fall to the ground clutching my chest.

I open my eyes and call out, "I'm dead?"

Vine slowly caresses my face and says, "Don't worry baby, I'll take care of you." Looking deeply into her eyes I somehow feel at peace. Sinking back into the chair I glance over to the right side of the room and a fellow is following Seraphim through a steel door beside the stage. "Come with me baby, your soul can be purified. I'll make all of your dreams come true." She stands up and takes my hand. We start walking toward the wooden door. Vine whispers to the barkeep, "Yama, I got one more," with a smile on her face.

As we walk toward the door an image floats into my mind; me lying in a pool of blood within a dark alley. Vine opens the heavy wooden door and my mind is fuzzy with the feelings and images of my own death. I feel uncertain, and I turn to look around the bar one last time. Jinn is in the corner with another customer, and she is smiling as she watches. All of the dancers in white watch also but they are somber. As Vine leads me through the door the heat is nearly unbearable. I stop a moment in the threshold.

"What's in that door over there"? I inquire as I motion toward the steel portal.

"Oh don't worry about that door; you've made your choice."

"I've made my what?"

13. LILY'S GRAVE
Chris Reed

Liz said she wanted to make my fortieth birthday a special one. And since we didn't have much money to spare, she offered to grant me a wish. "Go ahead, Nick," she said as we sipped coffee at the diner down the street from our apartment. "Anything you want."

"Anything?"

"Anything. Don't hold back."

I thought for a moment, but it seemed like everything I wanted could only be achieved with a check book. Finally, I said, "I don't know. Really, I can't think of anything."

Liz leaned forward so the people seated near us wouldn't hear. "What about your deepest, darkest fantasy? Something you've never told me before."

After four years of marriage, there wasn't much I hadn't shared with Liz. Well, maybe there was one thing...

I leaned forward until I was close enough to smell the coffee on her breath. "If I tell you, you're going to think I'm crazy."

"Go on," she said. "Whatever it is, I'll do it for you. I'll strap on a dildo and bend you over this table if that's what you want."

"No thanks," I said.

"Then how about a three-way? My friend Melissa's into that stuff. You know, the one that works at the gas station? You think she's attractive, right?"

"Sure, she's good-looking," I said. "But you know how I feel about monogamy."

She rolled her eyes. "Well, then, what's your idea?"

I fiddled with my cup, trying to figure out how to say it. "I don't think it's legal."

"Just tell me!"

I leaned all the way over the table and whispered in her ear: "I want to fuck a dead person."

Her eyes widened a little, but she didn't freak. "A female, right?"

"Of course a female," I said, easing back into my seat.

She looked relieved, then concerned. "That could be risky."

"Not to mention impossible," I said, "considering we don't know any dead people."

"That's what the obituaries are for," Liz said. She turned around to the table behind her and grabbed a newspaper that the last patron had abandoned. She placed it in front of her and dug through the pages until she found the death notices.

I sipped my coffee and watched her scan the paper. "Here's one," she said, pointing to a spot halfway down the page. "Lily Anne Campbell. Eighteen. Died Tuesday at Hurley Medical Center."

"Is there a picture?"

Liz turned the paper around and held it up so I could see. It was the girl's graduation photo. Blonde hair. Nice smile. Probably still a virgin.

"Cute, huh?" Liz said.

"Yeah, but eighteen's really young. What if it was a car accident or something? Her face could be all messed up."

"What about that old expression you men like to use?"

"Which one's that?"

"I believe it goes something like, 'Pussy ain't got no face.'"

"Or in this case, no pulse," I said.

Liz snatched the paper out of my hands and spread it out on the table in front of her. "It says here that funeral services will be held this afternoon, followed by the burial at Glenwood Cemetery. That's not very far from here."

As I drained my cup, I studied the look on my wife's face, trying to decide if she was serious. "So when do we dig her up?" I asked.

"You officially turn forty at midnight."

***

We parked down the street at a gas station and walked to the cemetery. My old army duffle bag hung from my shoulder with our supplies inside: two flashlights, two shovels, and an ax to crack open the coffin.

We climbed the rusty iron gates at the front of the cemetery and started up the narrow dirt road that snaked through the property. When we were far enough from the main road, we turned on our flashlights and began looking for Lily's grave.

Liz was crouched down, sweeping the beam of light across the weathered stone facades. "These people all died in the eighteen hundreds," she whispered.

"Let's work our way towards the back," I suggested.

As we lurked among the tombstones, heading deeper into the cemetery, the markers became more modern and the dates more recent, until we came upon a cluster of graves just a few years old.

49

"She has to be around here somewhere," Liz said as we maneuvered around the marble markers, throwing light on their inscriptions.

Liz stopped so suddenly that I almost ran into her. "Here it is!" she said. She dropped to one knee and aimed her light at the tombstone. There were lilies carved into the marble, and below her name were the words OUR LITTLE FLOWER.

"Pretty," I said.

"Let's hope the girl still is," Liz said. She laid her flashlight in the grass and took a shovel out of the duffle bag.

As I watched Liz dig, I was overwhelmed by my love for her. The way her lean muscles flexed. The sweet sweat that gleamed on her skin. The determination in her eyes.

"Are you going to help me, or what?" she asked. When I didn't answer, she turned around. "Come on, Nick, grab a sho—"

I brought the ax down hard, splitting her face like a cord of wood. She fell over with her eyes open, her mouth frozen around a word it would never finish. I held her head down with the heel of my boot and yanked the ax out of her skull. The cleft in her face oozed blood as dark as used motor oil. I pulled her shirt up over her head to cover the mess, thinking about that old saying we men like to use.

"You know how I feel about monogamy," I said as I took off her shoes. Then I unbuttoned her pants and slid them down her still-twitching legs. "I could never cheat on you, Liz. Not even with a dead girl."

Then I turned off the flashlights and celebrated my birthday with my own little flower.

14. EXPERT OPINION
Shenoa Carroll-Bradd

The officer at my door looks almost apologetic. His presence gives me a little goose of panic at first, but I keep my face still and my voice steady. "Officer Howell, good morning. How can I help you?"

He meets my eye before glancing over my shoulder at the fishing poles and shark jaws on the living room wall. "We had someone wash up on the beach this morning." He glances behind him, then to either side, as if someone might be eavesdropping. "We'd like you to come take a look, just to confirm our suspicions."

I keep my face very still, though my heart rate climbs. "And what are your suspicions?"

Howell looks around again, even though there's no one else up this early, then leans in to whisper, "Shark attack."

I fight to keep the smile off my face as he escorts me to the scene.

***

Around our tiny beachfront town, I am generally known as the go-to "Shark Guy". I run a mini-mart and gas station where every inch of wall space is covered with shark jaws, shark paintings, shark souvenirs and t-shirts.

Shark attacks are rare around here, but I've got a feeling that's about to change.

I've read all the books, and I've seen Jaws at least once a week since its release. The opening's my favorite part, where the skinny-dipping slut gets dragged around like a cat toy. Ever since that movie came out, everyone's been real skittish around the water.

***

Officer Howell leads me to a cordoned-off spot on the beach where two officers flank a lump under a tarp, both looking everywhere but down. They glance up and give me grim smiles when we approach, then back away. I recognize them both as frequent customers, and one as the father of a honey-blonde darling named Tanya.

I gesture toward the tarp. "Any idea who it is?"

Howell's lips pull tight. "We're not releasing the victim's name yet. Just please, look at the wound patterns and tell me if they're consistent with a shark attack." He puts on gloves and peels back a corner of the tarp, careful not to expose the corpse's face. Her skin is pale blue-grey, like the dawn light creeping over damp sand.

I lean in to inspect the ragged tears along her toned midriff, and the long, bloodless gouges in her thighs. He keeps her face hidden, but one pale hand lies curled on the sand, nails polished bright pink.

I used to watch those nails trail over bags of potato chips and tap against sweating coke bottles as Jennifer Reyn perused my store. As the mercury rose she had visited my mini-mart more and more, wearing less and less. I'd watched her, circled, tested the waters with jokes and small talk.

I bend closer to study the wounds. They'd spread like laughing mouths in the violence of the surf. "Yep, these definitely look like shark bites. You can see where the flesh was torn…" I point, careful not to touch her skin, remembering how warm it had been, how supple. Like peaches. Like dreams come true.

The ragged teeth marks hid the knife marks so well. I bit my lip at the memory of tearing that sweet flesh with a set of mako jaws held between my hands like scissors.

I stand up again. "Better be careful how you break the news. Wouldn't want to start a panic."

Howell looks even paler as he covers Jennifer once more. "Don't mention this to anyone until we make an official announcement."

I assure him I won't and wave to the other officers before heading home.

Before, I had been much too afraid to act on my desires, certain that I'd be caught. But now, with a monstrous shark circling in the public's psyche, I'm no longer caged. I'm free at last to hunt the summer waters, where the sky above is full of tanned, toned, kicking legs, and I'm the only predator.

15. WRITING FOR EXPOSURE
Joe McKinney

I found it at a garage sale. An IBM Selectric III - the exact same machine I'd learned to type on in the 7th Grade.

The tired old widow running the cashbox saw me eyeing it.

"That was my husband's. Twenty bucks it's yours."

Next to the typewriter I saw a huge box of old Arkham House hardcovers – Henry S. Whitehead, Robert E. Howard, Fritz Leiber, a dozen others – each one in a protective plastic sleeve. Very nice. Her husband and I would have got on like a house on fire.

"Make it thirty if I can have the old books there," I said.

She glanced at the box, then at me, and shrugged.

***

At my desk, I ran my fingers across the keys. Pushed a few. The golf ball print wheel struck the platen with a series of solid, satisfying whacks.

I ran a piece of paper into the machine, then opened my copy of *Ancient Sorceries and Other Weird Stories* to Algernon Blackwood's novella "The Willows" and started copying out the intro, just to get a feel for how well the machine typed. I got through the first few sentences before I realized the type was coming out blue.

I stared at the words.

I read once that James Tiptree Jr. always used blue ink to type her manuscripts, and that the only mystery bigger than her true identity was where she got typewriter ribbon that color. *Guess I'll need to find out*, I thought.

But then I looked back at Blackwood's story.

The first few words were disappearing. As I watched, the letters actually rose from the paper, broke apart like smoke off a smoldering cigarette, and evaporated into nothing. Before I knew it, the first few sentences were gone - right up to the point where I had stopped typing.

Stunned, I typed another word.

It disappeared from the page.

I typed out the rest of the story in a frenzy of excitement; and when I was done, Blackwood's story had vanished. The page numbers had resorted themselves to fill the gap left by the missing story. The table of contents didn't show it.

I had no idea what to think. I went to my laptop and did a Google search on Algernon Blackwood. History has not given Blackwood the full recognition he deserves, but you can still find a bunch on him. And I did. Only there wasn't a single reference to "The Willows."

Not a word on his masterpiece.

I went to the fridge, got a beer, sat on the couch, and stared at my new typewriter. I had all the predictable thoughts - demonic possession, magic, LSD on the keys, a very clever prank.

Finally, I decided to try a little experiment.

T.E.D. Klein.

His story, "Black Man With a Horn," is mentioned just about everywhere. It's one of the landmarks of modern horror fiction. I got a piece of paper and started typing.

Same thing happened.

It was gone from his collection, *Dark Gods*. It was gone from my copy of *Cthulhu 2000*. All references to it in Joshi's *Icons of Horror and the Supernatural* were gone. The Internet had never heard of it.

The story seemed to exist only in blue ink.

Realizing I was probably committing career suicide, I submitted "Black Man With a Horn" as my own the next day.

The Magazine of Fantasy & Science Fiction bought it for five cents a word.

And the sale came with a phone call from Gordon Van Gelder himself. "This is going to sound weird," he said, "but as I was reading your story, I had the strangest feeling. It was like it had been missing from my world. Like I had suddenly caught up with an old friend, but one I never knew was gone. Does that make sense?"

My heart was pounding. "You bet it does," I said.

***

Five years later, on my thirtieth birthday, I was horror's hottest short fiction writer.

And the better I did, the thinner the resumes of horror's big names became. Stephen King became strictly a novelist. The same happened to Peter Straub, Laird Barron, Joe R. Lansdale, Gene Wolfe, Reggie Oliver, Dan Simmons, John Langan, Ray Bradbury, Lucius Shepard, a host of others.

By the time I was forty - with three Hugos, a World Fantasy Award, the Shirley Jackson Award, and six Stokers - I owned modern horror.

***

Ellen Datlow wrote an article on me. She said I was a master stylist, one of the greats, but that I couldn't write a sympathetic female character to save my life.

I thought: *Who in the hell does this woman think she is? I'll show her who can write women.*

I got to work on Octavia Butler's "Speech Sounds." Then Nina Kiriki Hoffman's "The Pulse of the Machine" and Connie Willis' "Even the Queen." After that, I went through M. Rickert and Nancy Springer and Poppy Z. Brite and Lisa Morton.

At NECON, two years later, Ellen tried to apologize. She was very professional about the whole thing, but I was drunk. She was wearing red heels. I told her, "Hey, I saw those shoes on TV last night - except when I saw 'em they were sticking out from beneath Dorothy's farmhouse."

How many other writers you know can say Ellen Datlow broke their nose in public?

***

I always wanted to save the girl in Tom Godwin's story "The Cold Equations." Poor thing, I felt sorry for her, getting blown out the hatch like that. So I copied out the story, but worked in my own solution.

It was a no go.

The story started to disappear from the David Hartwell and Kathryn Cramer anthology I was copying it out of; but as soon as I got to the point where I was making changes, the words coalesced back out of the air and settled onto the pages of *The Ascent of Wonder*. I was stuck on what to do until I remembered that Don Sakers had already answered the problem of saving the girl in his story "The Cold Solution." I copied out both stories and sent them off to *Analog*, requesting they run in back to back issues.

Huge hit. *Analog* Reader's Choice Award. My first Nebula. And a valuable lesson learned.

***

I turned to novels.

Forty-one of them in twelve years, to be exact.

Ghost Story; The Shining; IT; The Conjure Wife; The Other; Fahrenheit 451 - all mine.

But something was missing. I had nearly universal respect in the horror community, but I was still just another genre writer as far as the *New York Review of Books* was concerned.

55

I felt bitter about that, and the bitterness ate at me until I couldn't live with it anymore.

And so, in a hotel room in New Jersey, after a night of hard drinking at a convention, I got out my copy of *Love in the Time of Cholera* and set to work typing out Edith Grossman's translation.

Sure as always, the letters turned to smoke and drifted off the page.

I didn't even bother to check the Internet. I sent it off to my people at Simon & Schuster and they loved it. They said I had arrived on the literary scene.

They organized a huge publicity campaign.

But, as it turns out, Robert Silvers, the editor over at the *New York Review of Books*, is an amateur Gabriel Garcia Marquez scholar and when he got hold of the ARC for my book, he raised the red flag.

Translating, I discovered, is an art too. Grossman's translation had become my own, but not the original. That was still out there – unknown, in the United States at least, to all but a few diehard Latin American Literature fans - but still out there.

Now Simon & Schuster has called a meeting.

They say I have some explaining to do.

16. ABALAM
S.C. Hayden

Maggie sat, ass cheeks clenched, on the wooden plank that served as a bench. She was hyperventilating. The guy on her left, a fat Mexican in a wife-beater with his arms covered in gang tattoos, had been stealing glances at her throughout the last round. She didn't care. The guy on her right was sweating like a whore in church and his eyeballs were about to pop out of his head. Skinny, pockmarked, and gap toothed, he was an obvious meth head and was tweaking pretty hard. Again, she didn't care.

She was focused on the dogs. The one she thought would win, the big brindle with the wedge shaped head, had developed a serious limp. The white one had darted in and taken a chunk out of his rear haunch and it was slowing him down something awful. That little white mutt turned out to be a lot faster and meaner than he'd looked.

She didn't really care who won. She was probably the only person in the filthy smoke filled garage where the fights took place who didn't have any money riding. She was certainly the only woman. The fact that she was a woman and didn't bet, made her suspect to a few of the guys who ran the place. One of them had grilled her pretty hard, thinking she might be a cop or a reporter. But Maggie wasn't a reporter and she certainly wasn't a cop. Maggie was there for one thing and one thing only, she was there for the blood.

The brindle circled to the left, trying to guard his injured side. The white went in low and fast and got a lock on the brindle's neck. He shook his head and blood splatted round the pit. People were screaming and pounding on the plank benches. The big Mexican stood up. He had a hard-on pressing through his jeans. Maggie slipped the knife out of her pocket, held her breath and thought about him.

She remembered when he first came to her in the big house just outside of New Orleans when she was six years old… She was walking down an endless hallway. There was a faint light somewhere in the distance. Something, more felt than heard, was padding along behind her. She started running. She wanted, *needed*, to reach the light, but the faster she ran, the farther it receded. She stumbled and fell through endless darkness, and when she woke, ice cold and panting, she knew she wasn't alone.

Somehow, she'd carried something, *someone*, out of the dream with her. She felt him moving inside of her, a stowaway clinging to her very soul. It wasn't an unpleasant sensation, quite the opposite in fact. She felt whole.

From time to time, he left her, and when he did, she felt a near intolerable emptiness, but he always returned at night and made her whole again. Sometimes, he whispered his name in her ear, but she could never hear it clearly, so she called him Mr. Ableman. That wasn't quite it, but it was close enough.

When she was sixteen years old, he taught her about fire. Later that summer, the big house burned down with her mother and father inside. The fire inspector said it might have been faulty wiring. It was nothing short of a miracle that Maggie had been sleepwalking. When the fire crew arrived, she was standing on the front lawn, still as stone, watching the fire roll and churn.

After the fire, she went to live with her aunt in Baton Rouge. It was a life of doilies, cat hair, and endless gospel radio. And on the weekends, it was a life of bible waving, tongue talking, and snake handling.

It was a boring life, but there was an escape. At night, alone in bed, she would clear her mind and open herself. And when she was *open*, Mr. Ableman would come and lie with her, lie *inside* of her, and tell her secrets.

It was her aunt who recognized the signs. It was her aunt who called the preacher. He came the next morning. Some cracker bumpkin with a pudgy corn fed face and a syrupy grin. He opened his bible, held his hand in the air and read a few passages in his county fried drawl.

Maggie didn't think for a second that it would work. She certainly hadn't felt anything, but later that night, when she opened herself and waited for him, he didn't come. He didn't come the next night either. He never came again.

Shortly afterwards, her aunt too, was killed in a fire. Once again, they found Maggie standing outside with a strange faraway look on her face, watching the house burn down to the ground.

An errant thought sailed through her mind. What if she went back to Baton Rouge and sued that preacher for damages? She imagined the tabloid headline and giggled. "Woman sues exorcist, wants demon back! Read all about it."

There was a high-pitched yelping. The yelping morphed into a frantic terrified squeal. The brindle bucked, kicked, and shook, but the white held tight. Maggie drove the tip of the knife into her palm. *Ahhhhh.* She squeezed her hand into a fist, held the pain as though holding a living thing. Blood dripped. Her palm throbbed.

She let the noise of the crowd wash over her. She inhaled the blood, sweat, and animal stink. The excitement, the fear, the lust, the pain, it all washed over her and for a second, for a fleeting moment, she was almost there, almost in that special place where everything was right, almost with *him.* So close, so close she could taste it, but not quite.

A few last spasms and the brindle was still. Maggie unclenched her ass cheeks and exhaled. She slipped the knife back into her pocket. Between fights, she wandered into the dirt parking lot to take in a little moonlight and think.

There was a 20-foot length of rope in the trunk of her rattletrap Pontiac Firefly. It was enough rope to throw over a tree branch, tie a noose, and put an end to the madness. She could do that. She could. Or, she could shake her ass a little and lore one of these hard cases back to her doublewide, knock him over the head with the lead pipe she kept behind the door and tie him up. When he came to, she could open up her straight razor and see if she couldn't recreate that special feeling. See if she couldn't fill the space that special someone left behind.

What to do? She'd have to do one or the other. That much was certain. The night was young and there was plenty of time to decide.

"What's your hurry, sweet cheeks?" The voice came from behind. She turned back, already grinning. It was the big Mexican with the tattoos and the wife-beater. He was covered in sweat and had a crazed look in his eyes. Her grin widened.

Sometimes the answer just falls into your lap.

17. LYTHALIA CALLING
Adam Millard

Jack sat staring through the window towards the woods at the rear of the garden, the way he had for twelve consecutive nights. Darkness had fallen; the sound of the wind rustling through the trees was the only thing he could hear. Courtenay House's garden was barely visible through the fog, and for a moment he panicked at the thought of not seeing *her* tonight.

The girl; the single-most terrifying – and yet resplendent – woman he had ever seen had visited him at the stroke of twelve for the last dozen nights. The first time she'd appeared – dancing amongst the cinquefoil – he'd been paralyzed with both fear and fascination. Who was she, and what the hell was she doing in his garden? Part of his mind had screamed at him, urging him to go out and send her packing, or call the Bluebottles, who would no doubt cart her off to the cells for the night, or at least until she'd slept off whatever powerful elixir she'd imbibed to send her jigging through the undergrowth in the middle of the night. Another part of him – the more curious and adolescent half which cared nothing for consequences and even less for decorum – instructed him to quietly observe. She wasn't hurting anybody, was she? The plants would need replacing, but that was a small price to pay for the splendorous exhibition the girl was putting on.

Just for *him*?

That first night she'd danced for an hour, kicking through the garden like some mythical sprite. Jack couldn't recall blinking once during the whole performance. When she'd left – disappearing as clandestinely as she had appeared into the woods – he'd realized how sore his eyes were, and after applying drops he'd gone to bed and thought about her, about the way in which she sprang lithely from one foot to the next. He'd slept none that first night, not that he'd actively tried to switch off.

The second night he'd been tending to the dog – allowing it to shit, scratch, sniff around a little – when the girl appeared from the trees. He couldn't believe that she would return, and as he dragged the dog towards the house, so as not to startle the girl, he'd wondered whether she was really there, or if his wishful thinking from that day had manifested itself in a vision.

Charlie, his Red Fell Terrier, had run whimpering into the house, its business for the evening prematurely concluded, but Jack had watched from the shadows, mesmerized once again by her movements. She'd practically floated across the Amaryllis, her feet constantly shrouded with an emerald miasma.

Had that been there the previous night? Jack couldn't be sure.

The third, fourth and fifth nights she'd appeared and performed, and it was upon the sixth night that Jack had realized she wasn't human.

The word *Goddess* came to mind, though it wasn't the kind of word Jack liked to chuck around, willy-nilly. It conjured images of robed beauties playing chess with pieces carved from diamond and platinum. This girl *was* a Goddess, but not of that ilk. She was something else wholly, and Jack knew that somewhere along the line, their paths would inextricably cross and things would change forever.

But he'd kept his distance, watching from the sanctuary of the house or deep within the shadows provided by it. There was, he knew, a possibility that she might disapprove of his audience should she become aware of it, and that was something he wasn't willing to risk just yet.

He *had* to watch her; he had to see her dance, for if *he* didn't then it would all be for nothing. She might as well not exist.

Rain began to pepper the window. Jack watched as thin streaks dragged down to the sill, partially obscuring his view. It didn't worry him too much. The clock hanging upon the wall assured him that it was ten-fifteen; plenty of time for the rain to dissipate.

Once again he pondered the unimaginable, that she would not appear tonight. "Don't be a *fool*, Jack," he whispered, clouding the window with his exhalation. "She'll show."

The strangest thing was, he couldn't recall his life before two weeks ago. Everything that had come before had drifted into obscurity, as if nothing else mattered. His mother would have a coronary if she heard about it; that he was allowing a girl to frolic in the garden to which she so painstakingly tended. Edith Drummond was the epitome of old-fashioned, rendering her unapproachable as far as girls were concerned. Jack had never been able to discuss his romances with his mother, and this one – not that it was a romance, not even in the remotest sense of the word – would certainly be filed under S for *Secret*, and also N for *Never Tell Mother…*

With the rain gently pattering the glass, and the clock ticking behind him, Jack relaxed. Within three minutes he was drifting, weightless, his mind working overtime to placate him. She would be there when he woke up; he knew that her performances were all for him.

She must know, must feel my gaze upon her…

Panic washed over him as he bolted upright in his chair. He spun, allowed his eyes to adjust to the darkness of the room.

He sighed. The clock read one minute to midnight.

"I haven't missed her."

He turned his attention back to the garden, where a thick fog had descended while he slept, carpeting everything from the graveled courtyard to the woods. The wind pushed it gently along the ground. Jack was just happy for the abeyance of the rain.

And there she was, right on time, hovering along on her viridian mist. Her long, brown hair flapped loosely around her face. Jack wanted nothing more than to bunch it up into his fists and inhale her scent.

She danced and gracefully cavorted; Jack watched and nervously hoped…hoped that she might look to the window and see him, beckon him down to her so that they might dance together, lose themselves in each other.

She looked stunning tonight. Ethereal yet tangible, and just beyond reach, though hadn't she always been?

"Not tonight," Jack whispered. He stood from the chair, unable to look away from the dancing girl. He knew he had to, though. Ten seconds was all it would take. Ten seconds and he would be outside with her, and they would dance together, becoming one.

He blinked, sighed, turned and rushed for the stairs. Taking them three at a time – and almost crippling himself in the process – it took less than three seconds to reach the ground-floor. He hurtled through the kitchen, grabbing for the keys which dangled from the locked door. As he fumbled erratically to unlock the door, Charlie whimpered from his basket. Did the dog know she was out there once again? Could it sense her, or hear her reveling in the copse? "It's okay, Charlie," Jack mumbled. "Daddy's just popping outside for a moment." Charlie settled, lowering his head. If Jack had turned in that moment and noticed the countenance of his pet, he might have considered calling the whole thing off, returning instead to the safety of his bedroom.

Finally the key turned. Jack spilled out into the inclemency of the night. He scanned the garden, fearing he'd made a mistake and that she had finished her routine and withdrawn, as was her wont, to the woods.

Then he saw her, cavorting by the pond. Was it possible that he could *love* her? It certainly felt like it, not that he had a basis of comparison. His mother would indubitably tell him it was nonsense; that it was impossible to fall for a girl who had done nothing more than trespass and drunkenly dance – and on her Clematis, nonetheless…

"Excuse me." The words leapt from his mouth. Had he been in control he might have continued to hide amongst the shadows, silently, but it was too late now.

She stopped, landing with a less-than-nimble thump upon the grass. Her neck arched as she glanced in his direction. Her expression was not of shock, but inevitability, as if she had expected to be caught.

Jack suddenly wished he'd remained upstairs; she would never return, not now, not after this. Her joyous midnight dancing was over, and Jack felt something tug at his heart – an emptiness – which he wished he could eliminate.

Then she did something he could never have anticipated. A smile, beautiful and impish, crept across her face. She wasn't disgusted, as Jack had first thought. She was happy. Perhaps this wasn't the end, after all.

Perhaps this was the beginning of something else.

Yeah, mother. Who's laughing now?…

Jack took a tentative step into the garden. Just because she was smiling didn't mean she wasn't frightened.

"I've watched you dance since the beginning," Jack said, hoping his honesty would somehow put her at ease. Although, now that he'd said it he couldn't help feeling that this admission portrayed him as creepy.

She smiled, took a step towards him, and said, "I know."

He'd expected a lot of ripostes, but not that one. That one was a game-changer.

"You know?"

She nodded, still smiling. As Jack cautiously approached, he noticed something he hadn't from the window. The emerald mist was dissipating, seeping away from her as if she no longer had a need for it.

And as the mist dissolved, he saw something that wasn't possible. It couldn't be possible.

Her legs didn't finish at her feet. In fact, her feet were nothing like human. They were covered with bark; an orange sap oozed out over her ankles and between her toes. Vegetation of some sort twisted up around her shins, stopping just shy of the hem of her dress. At first sight, one would imagine it as nothing more than a trick of the moonlight, but Jack was close enough to realize that the vines trailing off into the woods were as much a part of her as the hair on her head; hair that was a combination of slender twigs and rotting ivy.

"I don't—"was all he could manage, for something emerged from her mouth. Parting her lips and snapping her jaw in the process, a branch leapt out of her throat and coiled around his neck. Her wide eyes were now a luminous green, a hue similar to the fog which had shielded Jack from the truth. She gargled, though not in pain at the wooden protrusion, but in ecstasy. She flicked her head to the side and Jack stumbled to the ground, clawing at the tightening branch around his throat. He could breathe, but only just.

She headed for the woods at the back of the garden. Jack dragged along behind her, through the flowers that his mother – *Oh, mother, what have I done?* – would find dead at first light. And Jack hoped that this thing, this beautiful thing that had danced and frolicked with the innocence of a child, carried him far from Courtenay House so that his mother would only stumble upon the dead flowers in the garden, and not a dead son, as well.

The trees soon blocked out the moonlight, but Jack could see stars through the overhead branches; stars that were long deceased, ancient worlds that had been destroyed by impossible creatures and cosmic beings. And Lythalia – he knew her name, now, for he could feel it, hear it, resonating through the branch coiled around his neck – was a Goddess, after all. He just hadn't expected her to be Lythalia, *The Forest Goddess*.

Later that night, they danced together for the one and only time. If Jack had lived to tell the tale, he would have been lying if he said he hadn't enjoyed it.

18. DAY DREAMS
Christopher Conlon

It was when she began laughing that I killed her.

I don't deny it. The evidence is there for all to see. Yes, I killed her. But *murder*?

Can a monster be murdered?

We met, as people meet. In our case it was at our work. She insisted on calling me "Charles," which is my name—Charles Day— but no one calls me it. I'm Charlie. I'm Chuck. Friendly, well-liked around the plant. But to her I was Charles. I liked it even as it embarrassed me, even as the other men on the line would smirk as she walked by, black hair bouncing on her shoulders, hips swaying, and greeting me in her low, sultry voice: "Good morning, Charles."

It was after we'd been sleeping together for some weeks that I noticed something. At first it seemed meaningless, but as night passed night, it became undeniable.

I no longer dreamed.

Now I've always been a man with an extremely active dream life. I don't suppose my dreams are much different from any man's. Figures from my childhood, dramatic scenes of conflict…and, of course, sex. I've always been a prolific sexual dreamer. But those dreams stopped. And then all my dreams stopped. The overnight hours were nothing but a dark fog and I woke up depressed, disoriented. We really have little understanding of how vital dream sleep truly is.

Of course I was waking, as often as not, with her beside me, and her gorgeous face and hair and body would quickly disabuse me of the notion that anything was wrong. We made love a great deal—before work, after work, and, yes, a few times during work. She was one of the boss's assistants and knew where we could do this without risk of discovery.

And yet I didn't dream, and so my sleep was at best thin, soupy, unsatisfying. I found myself tired all the time.

Finally I told her about my problem.

"Oh yes," she said silkily, "of course. I had to stop those dreams of yours. Especially the dirty ones involving other women. I can't have you dreaming about *that*."

I laughed, of course. But I noticed that she didn't.

That night I had a dream, my first in months. It was very brief. I stood on an endless dark plain, like the surface of the moon. Suddenly she was there before me, smiling with teeth that looked strangely sharp, like little razors. "You thought I was joking, didn't you?" she said.

I opened my eyes. We were facing each other in the bed, our bodies entwined, our faces inches apart.

"I had a dream," I whispered in the dark.

"I know you did. It was about me. I said, 'You thought I was joking, didn't you?'"

I gasped and pulled away from her. "How did you know?"

"Charles," she purred, "I have them all. All your dreams. And now you'll only dream when I want you to. And you'll dream *what* I want you to."

I jumped out of bed, stood before her. She rolled onto her back and put her arms lazily behind her head, hair disarrayed and beautiful on the white pillow.

"Why?" I asked.

She smiled. "It's what I do. It's what I am."

I moved around to her side of the bed and sat next to her. "You've done it before?"

"Only a million times. Prisons and mental institutions are filled with my old boyfriends, Charles."

"No. It can't be."

"You'll never dream again except, once in a while, if you're *very* good, I'll let you dream a little bit…about me."

"Give me my dreams back! They're mine!"

"Not anymore they're not."

"But they…they're what I am. Everybody is—what they dream."

"What does that make you now, Charles?"

"Give them back to me!"

"I can't."

"Why not?"

"Because," she said, and smiled again, "I ate them."

That's when she began to laugh. Her mouth opened wide, wider, like a shark's, like a whale's, like some prehistoric beast's, a cavernous impossible mouth and down there, straight down her throat, I could see the shimmering remnants of my dreams, visions of my long-dead mother and father, my brother who died in infancy, my first girlfriend, the golden retriever I had when I was eleven, all dream-distorted but somehow all the more real for that, the only way I could ever reconnect with any of their lost souls, in dreams. And now they were gone from me forever, taken from me, trapped within her.

You see, I don't deny that I killed her. I don't deny that I shoved my hand into her awful mouth, jammed it down her throat, I don't deny that I felt cartilage ripping and smelled blood and heard her terrible smothered choking. I don't deny that I grabbed, grabbed, grabbed for my dreams.

And then she was dead. But can anyone truly call it murder? When she stole away the core part of me? Wasn't it really self-defense?

They took me to a place—someone did. I can't remember clearly. It was many years ago. When I look at the sighing, twitching, murmuring men around me I know I'm seeing some of her old boyfriends.

But she's dead. She is. In that way, maybe I did something, performed some service to the world, even though I myself am lost, lost forever, lost for all time.

I've never dreamed again.

19. DOUBLE DOWN
Devlin Giroux

It's not that I liked seeing the corpse, don't get to thinking that shit. The whole thing was the raccoon next to the railroad tracks. Dead, but still drew your eye and mind, little bastard just begging to get poked with a stick to see if the thing popped.

Same thing here.

I stared at the once man. He…it…whatever the hell we are once we shit ourselves…swayed from the end of a noose. I didn't tie the damn thing, and I sure as hell didn't wrap it around his neck…and under his four chins. Be sure of this, though, I'm the reason for his drop and stop exit.

"Know what they're calling you, Mr. Montrosse?"

Lice across the soul, that voice.

"No," I said, giving my latest take a push. I'd rather watch a fat sack of dead-thing swing than look at the creature jawing me at that moment. "Still haven't let me in on who they are."

"Because, Mr. Montrosse, it would be like slitting Santa's throat, I imagine," said Mr. Gone. I just knew he was shining that smile at me. Could feel it burning my neck. "The Suicide King."

"What about it?" I said. The card fell into my hand. Been with me since that first take. A friend in fading royal colors.

A laugh as cruel as 3 a.m. spilled from Mr. Gone. "Your moniker, Mr. Montrosse. The Suicide King. All your takes have ended themselves, have they not?"

"Something wrong with that?"

He stood next to me. Didn't need to see him, and there was no hearing him. Just knew he was there. It was the side I wanted to douse with kerosene and set a match to in hopes of burning off the whisper of his presence that I could swear was crawling on me.

"None of us would pass judgment on your choice of expression," Mr. Gone said, as he too, gave the dead fat man a push. "But it does seem…distant. Cowardly."

The card disappeared to…wherever it went when I no longer wanted it. That moment was the first time since we met, back when I was among the right and righteous, that I looked at the man. Never thought it was possible for someone who looked so plain to be so damn ugly. It wasn't a physical deformity, mind you. Mr. Gone looked like a mailman, or the guy picking through junk mail.

No, it was the smile, and the eyes. You hear about people who walk the world all smiling death and dead eyes, but this man, this thing that had reached into my life and changed it into something completely divergent, he devoured death. It sustained him. Take after take, he lapped it up. One look and there was no doubt, this was a being ready to smother the world, smiling the whole while.

"Because killing the kids requires a hero, right?" I said.

"That's just fun." He gave the corpse another push, a demented father at a playground.

Maybe it was his touching my take, or the little girl titter he vomited up, or I just felt like seeing if I could take him, but I stared. Stared deep. I searched out that part of him that longed to rest, to just stop and set aside all things; sought out the voice that whispered soft death—an end to pain and responsibility.

All I got was shined by another damn smile.

And for my trouble I got the finest ass kicking a man could ask for. Mr. Gone set to me faster than a preacher to a penny. In those agonizing seconds I learned why his takes were never seen again. I know if it wasn't for what his "they" had done to me, there'd be nothing left of me to tell this.

"Just don't get the same spray," Mr. Gone said. "No catharsis whatsoever. No art. You've left me voiceless, Mr. Montrosse. I can't have that."

Just the corpse and me again.

"You didn't see that," I said to the swinging meat.

All my wounds closed with the pins and needles of frostbite. I held my hand up in front of my eyes. Well, one eye was still making its way home, but that's just a detail. I flexed the fingers and thought about what this new life was going to be like.

One take after another?

Forever working with things like Mr. Gone?

I never would've called myself yellow while I was still wasting air, but the thought of spending eternity with that ugly bastard made me do something all new. I trembled. Those fucking fingers of mine wouldn't stop shaking.

Black.

A beep. A hundred years away.

Another.

The image came together at the edges, snapping into place. This was not my way. I faded in and out. He did this. I stood, looking for that soul-staining smile. Doctors and nurses ran all around, chasing what machines were screaming out warnings. And it sounded like every damn one of them in the hospital was hooked up to someone about to kick.

The sign read Pediatric Ward. That ended all doubt. He'd brought me here. Was he playing at something?

"This way, Sue," said Mr. Gone, his voice slithering through the ridges across my mind.

I followed the sights he sent, the thoughts clearer than my own. Sharp, clean, no ambiguity to their form or reason. This was the mind of the once-man I was tracking.

He was standing over a young girl as she stared at the wall. Wasted and green, no hair and all despair. That was this girl.

No cards.

No balloons.

No teddy bear to chase away the nightmares.

Life had taken a shit on this kid. Really the best way to put it when a poor kid like her had only Mr. Gone for company. Not that she saw him. At least she had one blessing come her way.

"She ready for you, Sue," said Mr. Gone. He ran a hand over her head. An agonizing spasm seized her. The once-man thing moaned as she writhed, arms to her stomach. "No, I didn't do it to her, but why let it go to waste?"

"You knew where this would go even as you zapped my ass here, didn't you?" I asked.

Mr. Gone's smile disappeared. "She wants to die. Look around Montrosse. No one here. No one coming."

"And not her fault." I took in the chaos around me. "What did you do, Gone? You set this up."

"Fault? Not her fault? Of course it is." He stepped away from the girl. She rolled onto her side and whispered prayers to something, anything, to help her. To give her something. Just one fucking thing. "They're all at fault. For thinking life is theirs to begin with. Take her, Montrosse. Show me The Suicide King."

The girl whimpered, in too much pain for more words wasted on empty air. I wanted to tell her someone was indeed listening, even if it was some bitter asshole who was chucking cards only a few days ago.

I was listening.

No more pain, I told her.

Use the blanket.

I watched her, even through agony, twist the blanket into a tight coil.

Tie one end around the bed frame.

It was hard, but she managed it.

The other around your neck.

She rushed now, as much as the pain let her. She was seeing the end of the tunnel now.

I read her name off the patient room information board. Some careless nurse had wiped away the first couple letters: omi.

Let it be over, Naomi.

She nodded, the slightest shadow of a smile spreading across her sickly face.

Throw yourself over the side…and let go.

I didn't hear what happened next over the sound of clapping.

"See?" said Mr. Gone, his hands slapping together with even more gusto. "That is something I can take back to the others and tell them I do not recruit cowards. That was catharsis. That, Mr. Montrosse, was the work of a virtuoso."

I glared. It was all I could muster.

20. SPRINGHEELED JACK
Maggie Carroll

Fog drifted over the city, quiet and muffling. Sally hurried along Merrymeeting Road, sniffling and cursing the weather. Even for the less savory types such as herself, it was a God-forsaken hour of the night. But her last client of the evening, a well-to-do gent from uptown had kept her longer than usual. When he and the missus were on the outs, shaking him off was trouble.

Sally paused at Cook Street, looking down at the tightly-packed row-houses and wiped her nose thoughtfully. Mary lived that way, in a house bought and paid for by her rich, married lover. Mary was a good woman, even if she prattled on about how *good* life was since becoming someone's mistress. She would shelter Sally until the sun came up.

Sally rubbed her hands together, blowing briskly across the tips of her fingers. The heat made them ache and she grimaced, flexing. This night was fit for neither man nor beast. She blew across her fingers again, pulling her ratty sleeves over them as best she could, and started down Cook.

Halfway to Mary's house, the hair on Sally's neck rose. Unease rippled down her spine like ice. Mouth suddenly dry, she glanced around. "I ain't takin' no more custom!" she hollered, but her voice was muffled and fell flat. She squinted into the mist, moving forward step by cautious step, but only gauzy grey gloom met her searching gaze.

Moments passed, and the overpowering feeling of being watched grew. Sally shifted restlessly, nerves strung nearly to breaking, and wondered if she shouldn't just hurry back to shelter in the church. She glanced over her shoulder in the direction she'd come...

...and shrieked to wake the dead when she came face to face with Springheeled Jack.

He had misshapen features, scarred cheeks and jagged yellowy teeth, and odd eyes that peered in different directions. He was dressed in black, cloak and tails, with a black helmet on his head; close enough to breathe on her neck. "Stay away!" he hissed.

Sally jumped back, fumbling in the folds of her skirt for her protection; an old sock stuffed with pennies. Before she could swing it, Jack uttered a weird, high-pitched noise and leaped back into the fog.

Sally whirled, clutching her sap, breath hissing through her teeth as she searched for Jack. The street was quiet again.

"Jesus, Mary and Joseph," she swore breathlessly, crossing herself. They said Jack was an escapee from the Mental, taken to scaring the bejesus out of the residents of Merrymeeting. She'd not put much stock in the stories, figured them for drunken tales told round the pub.

Having come face to face with him, Sally knew him as a minion of Hell, come to claim her. She had to get walls around her. To hell with the church. Mary was only a moment away. She hiked her skirts up past her ankles and ran.

Jack jumped at her out of the fog again, as she came around the corner of Mary's street. She screamed, hands flying up to protect her face. "Stay away," he hissed, hands raised and fingers clawed. "Stay away."

Sally braced herself for death but, incredibly, Jack leaped away instead of attacking her. It was a jump of inhuman strength, carrying him across the street and up three stories. He vanished as the fog closed around the rooftop. Sally was alone again.

She picked herself up, eyes raised to the rooftops. She wasn't sure, but she thought she could see a hunched figure up there, where Jack had scrambled. *Stay away*, she heard, hissed through the fog. It echoed oddly, and that brought the hair straight back up on the nape of her neck.

Best she was on her way.

She hurried down Cook Street, all but stumbling over Mary's front stoop. There was a thump above her, an ominous, crouching presence. She didn't look up, not even when the sibilant voice came again: *stay away!*

"*You* stay away!" she yelled back, pounding on the door with the heel of her hand. "Mary? Mary, let me in!" She rattled the knob, startled when it turned in her hand. Mary never left her door unlocked.

Stay away! she heard again. With a shudder of fear, she pushed into the porch and slammed the door behind her. There was a scrape from above the door, an angry screech, and then silence again. Sally leaned against the door for a moment, just a moment, to catch her breath.

As she leaned there, it occurred to her that Mary hadn't answered her. She opened her eyes. "Mary?" she called as she peered into the house. Faint firelight shone from the living room, and Sally thought she saw movement. "It's Sally!"

There was no answer. Sally moved towards the living room, and paused in horror as her eyes adjusted and she saw the mess. Mary was meticulous, had been even when she was just a common tramp. She was especially proud of her knick-knacks, lined up neatly on the mantel. Trinkets that now littered the floor; porcelain and clay pieces crunching under Sally's feet.

Mary's books were torn and scattered about. The drapes hung drunkenly from the window. Embers glowed in the hearth, catching on the edges of pages from the books and flaring them into brief fires. A shadowy lump lay hunched on the settee.

"Mary?" Sally's voice cracked on the name and she swallowed hard as she crept forward, reaching out a hand. At the brush of her fingers, it shifted. Mary fell out of the shadows, dead-eyed and pale.

Sally bit back a scream, falling on her backside and scrambling backward. Her hands and feet scraped through debris. She registered sound behind her at the same moment her hand closed around the top of a boot.

The scream tore out of her then as she was seized by the hair and dragged upright. She spun, hands scrabbling at the grip on her hair, and came face to face with Mary's lover, cruel-eyed. Silver flashed in his other hand, a knife still stained with Mary's blood.

"He tried to save you. Warned you to stay away." His face was grim and cold, and so was the blade that bit into Sally's throat. "You should have listened, whore."

21. THE PATIENT IN THE ATTIC
Arran McDermott

Dr. Jennings didn't normally do house calls. Mrs. Peabody was a friend of one of his regular patient's Aunts and she said she desperately needed his help. Her son had shut himself up in the attic for months and wouldn't come down. She wanted a psychological evaluation before she decided whether he needed to be committed. Jennings explained he wasn't a psychologist, but the matronly lady offered him £1000 just to give his opinion and refer her son to a specialist, if needed. Jennings couldn't turn that down.

He arrived at the house at dusk. It was a two-story Victorian that had obviously been remodeled a great deal over the years. There was a small window in the peak where the loft was, but it had been papered over.

Mrs. Peabody invited him in and offered him a cup of tea and a digestive biscuit. Jennings politely refused. The house was as quiet as a tomb and he just wanted to get out of there as soon as possible. She filled him in with a hushed tone as they walked up the stairs.

"He used to be a normal boy. Then he lost his job and his girlfriend broke up with him. He moved his mattress up to the attic one night and just stayed up there. He won't even come down to eat or use the bathroom anymore. It's breaking my heart."

"Does he talk to anyone?"

"Not anymore."

They reached the top step and it creaked loudly. The sound put Jennings even more on edge. Mrs. Peabody reached up to the ceiling and pulled on a cord. The steps to the attic tumbled down with a crash. She handed the doctor a torch.

"You'll need this. He keeps smashing the bulbs."

Jennings reluctantly took it from her. "I'm not so sure this is a good idea. He may react aggressively to outside interference."

"Nonsense, Nigel's not a violent boy. Please see if you can help him. We had such plans for him."

He nodded and climbed the steps. As he neared the hatch, an aroma of dust, sweat and stale urine invaded his nostrils. He turned the torch on as he poked his head up.

The attic was huge. It seemed to stretch beyond the actual boundaries of the house. It was filled with all kinds of junk: boxes, moth-eaten clothes, discarded toys, rolls of insulating material and even a grandfather clock. He saw the mattress tucked away in one corner, but there was no sign of any living person.

He climbed all the way up and stood there, reluctant to go any further. He waved the light back and forth, looking for any area where someone could be hiding.

"Nigel," he called out in the loudest tone of voice he dared use. "I'm Dr. Jennings. Your mother asked if I could speak with you."

There was no replay. He turned back to the hatch.

"Mrs. Peabody?" he called back down. "Are you sure your son is up here?"

There was no answer and his swinging light found no one standing in the hall below.

"Mrs. Peabody!"

Again no answer from below, but he did hear some kind of acknowledgment from the attic. A muffled cough.

Run, his rational mind instructed. *Get out of here, now.*

Yet he couldn't. His legs were fixed in place. His heart was pounding and his breath came out in rapid bursts.

"Nigel, is that you?"

He heard a shuffling noise that seemed to be coming from the corner where the mattress was. He shone the light over but there was still no one visible. He found the strength to move one foot, then another. He walked with a slow calmness that he didn't feel.

"Nigel, you don't have to be afraid of me. I'm not here to hurt you."

He reached the mattress. It was covered in food crumbs and other stains. Bugs crawled over it. Jennings turned away in disgust, and found a pair of eyes staring at him from the shadows in an alcove.

He barely stopped himself from screaming. Crouched in the alcove was a man who appeared to be in his twenties. He was freakishly thin and the arms that poked out of his tattered shirt were covered in cuts and sores. His hair was dirty and looked like it had been pulled out by the roots in parts, leaving random bald patches. But the face was the worst.

It was a sickly yellowish color. The eyes bulged out of their sockets. Blood was dried on one ear. The nose looked like it had been repeatedly broken and his mouth hung open, revealing blackened, rotting teeth. It was the face of a nightmare.

"Stay back," Jennings warned him.

Then something unexpected happened. The man began to cry. His body was racked with sobs.

"Help me," he moaned.

"Nigel, what happened to you?"

"My name's not Nigel!" he spat, suddenly angry. "And I'm not her son."

"What do you mean? How did you get here?"

"She-," he started to say but then stopped, frozen with fear.

Jennings heard a creak behind him and turned to see what the sickened man was looking at. Something struck his head with tremendous force. Before he passed out into blackness, he heard the other man screaming.

He awoke some time later to find himself on the mattress. His hands and feet were tied with thick rope that was attached to the rafters overhead. He tugged on them but they would not budge.

"I'm sorry I had to deceive you," a voice said.

He looked up and saw Mrs. Peabody sitting a few feet away. She studied him with concern.

"I hoped this time Nigel could be the perfect son I always dreamed of. But he disappointed me again. He's gone now, but you'll stay with me, won't you?"

"I don't know what you think you're doing," he said as calmly as he could manage, "but you have to let me go."

"I can't do that. My own son was taken from me before his time. I have no one else to look after me. You won't have to stay tied up forever. Just until I know I can trust you to be a good boy."

She lifted up a cloth bag and reached inside. "I'll even leave you a playmate."

She took out something round and wet and placed it beside the bed. Her previous "son's" glazed eyes stared at Jennings.

"Sweet dreams," she said, blowing him a kiss.

She walked away and descended the steps as Jennings screamed and hurled abuse at her. None of his protests met with any reaction. Moments later the hatch closed loudly. Then he was alone in the dark. Well, almost alone.

22. SMOKE
Kerry G.S. Lipp

"You smell like smoke," Mike said, face in my neck as I straddled him while removing my shirt. I didn't answer. His clumsy hands struggled with my black bra as I stared, hating him but loving the sex, even when it wasn't that good. With Mike, it never was.

We'd been together for about two weeks and it was always the same. Me initiating and Mike feebly fumbling with my bra like he was cracking a safe. *Guys, it's not that hard.* Bras aren't that difficult to operate and all mine were simple. It should've been an easy one-handed job for every male on the planet, but for some reason it was impossible for Mike. If you can unlock a door, you can unhook a bra. It isn't brain surgery.

With two stuttering hands, he finally got it undone and my full round breasts fell less than an inch from his mouth.

I wanted to come, needed to, but that wasn't going to happen with Mike. Neither his tongue, fingers, or dick could get the job done. If I wanted to come with him, I had to finger myself while I rode him. And on top of all his performance flaws, he just had to make a "you smell like smoke" comment. It was at least the tenth time he'd made that comment. Bad news for Mike.

I still wanted to fuck, but I could barely look at him. I adjusted myself on top of him, since he could never quite find it himself, and he slid in. I was half-tempted to spin around so we could still do it and I wouldn't have to look at him. He moaned and I threw my head back. An act, but he bought it — they all did. They all thought they were the best ever. Sadly, they had no idea. My hand was the best. The second best had been a girl. The third had been a married guy with plenty of experience. Mike, like most of them, didn't know shit. Still, I needed something.

I tossed my head so my hair tickled his chest and, right then and there, the son-of-a-bitch said it again.

"Your hair smells like smoke."

Strike two already and he'd only been inside me for all of thirty seconds. That, coupled with him not being good at sex, really pissed me off. It takes a lot for me to give up on sex. Whiskey dick, a two-pump chump, or a fatherly figure is about it. After failing rule number 2, I'd just about had it. So I let him have it, snapping at him.

"Look," I said. "I smoke. You know I smoke. Get over it or I'll get off of it. Got it?"

His eyes widened at my outburst.

"Fine," he groaned. "Forget it."

I continued to ride him. He pawed at my tanned breasts. For once, it actually didn't feel that bad. Then he moved his hands to my shoulders and thrust up. From my shoulders, his hands crept up to my hair and he started to pull me down, a fistful right at the root. The sensation drove me crazy.

Had he been reading books on pleasing women? It sure seemed like it. A very pleasant surprise. He tugged hard and my neck jerked. It felt great with him inside of me. I balanced myself atop him and fingered myself with the other.

I came. Mostly from my own finger, but the hair pulling definitely didn't slow down the orgasmic wave. My body shuddered and the arm keeping my balance twitched and strained as I felt that sweet tug on my hair.

Mike smiled dumbly up at me while the orgasm rocked my body. In either the heat of passion or pure stupidity, I leaned my head forward and kissed him hard on the mouth, darting my tongue in. He returned the kiss for a second then released me.

"Your mouth tastes like an ashtray," he said.

This pretty much led to me being the most pissed off I've ever been. The look I gave him shattered his newfound sexual confidence. I was amazed at how fast Mike could drive me from pleasure to rage. I'm beautiful and I'm letting this little slimeball fuck me, and he's not even my fucking boyfriend. He has no right to talk to me that way. I made up my mind right then.

Mike was going to die.

I was still on top, so I began to grind away against him. He'd gone soft inside me, but I could feel it growing again. I rode him with porn star grace. Each time his timid hands touched me, I brushed them off.

When he tried to change positions, I slapped his hands away. He relented each time. He was a weak pussy. A *real* man would've flipped me, maybe hit me back, and I would've let him. But not Mike. He squeezed my tits again and started to moan aloud. When I saw him coming, saw him defenseless, I started slapping him in the face with my fists, opened palms and even nails. I wondered what that felt like, ejaculating when your nose was splattered against the side of your face. All pleasure? All pain? A twisted concoction of both? I wasn't sure.

My fists didn't stop until the purple satin sheets were black with red blood. He barely fought back. My fists didn't kill him, but my hands did. I hit him until he passed out and once he was out, my hands circled his throat. After all the comments about smoking, I laughed as his lungs failed him. Killing him felt good, even better than the last couple. I could clean this up and make it all go away and then disappear like I had in the past. No problem. I was getting good at this.

But first, my craving was kicking and I needed a fix. Before I put my shirt back on, I took a towel to the sink and mirror and wiped off the blood. It was mostly on my hands and my face. I licked a few splats off my lips and my body almost rocked with yet another orgasm. Wearing only the skirt with nothing underneath, tasting the dead man's blood on my lips, I let my fingers head south. I came hard standing up.

After crashing down I got back up on shaky legs. I had all day to clean this up, and it wouldn't be hard, but first I needed a cigarette. Some people say that the best cigarette is after a meal. That's bullshit. Some people say the best cigarette is after sex. That's bullshit. The best cigarette is after the kill. In Helter Skelter, Vincent Bugliosi said that members of the Manson family slept, satisfied, for days after Cielo Drive and the LaBiancas. Susan Adkins and Leslie Van Houten were a couple of my favorites, and God I sure hope they enjoyed a cigarette before they passed out.

My lighter flared up on the porch and I lit my Camel. What a day.

As I pulled on the heater and scrolled through my phone, I heard a tired voice.

"Would you mind putting that out, miss?"

My initial reaction was to tell the voice to fuck off and die. But it was just the old man who lived next door to me.

When I looked away from him, he gestured at my cigarette. "That smoking. It'll kill you."

"Maybe. A meteor could fly out of the sky and kill me at any second too. So could an undiagnosed illness. I'm well aware of the risks."

"So why don't you put it out?"

"Because I don't *have* to. And I don't *want* to. It's my right as an American to smoke if I want to."

"But it's going to kill you," he said.

I lost it. Again. "And just how do you know that it's going to kill me? You got a crystal ball? If anyone's gonna die, you old fuck, it's you."

"You young people are so rude," he said, shaking his head turning around to leave.

"How so? You come over here and tell me to quit doing something perfectly legal in my own home and yet I'm the rude one?"

I was pissed. No doubt I'd kill him in broad daylight if I could get away with it, but a cop lived adjacent from me. Front yard murder is always a bad idea.

"Well Miss, a lot of people don't appreciate the second-hand smoke, and are sensitive to it."

This motherfucker just pushed my hot button.

"Okay, Mr. Weatherby," I said.

"I'm Mr. *Sampson*."

"Fuck, fine, whatever, Mr. *Sampson*. Look. This state has banned smoking in all restaurants and bars, hell, even inside most casinos. You can't smoke within 50 feet of any public building. If you drive a car to work you can get arrested for smoking in the vehicle because it's considered 'smoking in the workplace.' And health insurance is completely fucked. I'm smoking on my front porch and if you have a problem with that, Mr. Sampson, go fuck yourself.

"Now just a minute, young lady-"

"Or better yet," I interrupted, "why don't you tell me where I can smoke without being accosted because it's apparently not inside my own home."

The old man staggered and his whiskered face twitched. Red flushed his cheeks under his white beard. They puffed out. He obviously wasn't anticipating an argument. Stupid old fuck. What did he expect? That I'd just hand it over and be like, "you're right and thank you so much for saving my life, my kind savior." Bastard didn't know me at all.

"Have I ever come to your house and told you what to do? What food to eat? What pills to take? Or what books to read? No. Fuck no. And I never would. That, Mr. Sampson, is the essence of rudeness. So yeah, please, leave me the fuck alone and I'll leave you alone."

Sampson's mouth dropped open like an elevator with the cables cut.

"Now you listen here…" he started.

"It's cold out here. Tell you what - I'll put this out if we can finish this talk inside," I said.

I took one last hit of that post-sex, post-murder cigarette and savored it. Mr. Sampson, somehow thinking he could still convince me about the evils of smoking, climbed the concrete steps. I admired his passion and conviction, but I was still going to kill him.

I held the door open as he stepped inside.

"My wife died of lung cancer, missy, and I saw what she went through, and forgive me for trying to keep you from the same fate."

I'd figured something like this was coming. When you live to be 80, people you know have probably died in just about every possible way, from shotgun suicides to car crashes. People become passionate when they lose a loved one. And I even saw the sadness in his eyes. I considered hearing him out and letting him go, but then he said it.

"It smells like smoke in here."

I snapped.

I grabbed a brass candle holder from the end table by the door and clobbered him across the skull, knocking him unconscious. Now, I usually don't do this sort of thing with this sort of person, but Mr. Sampson had burrowed deep under my skin.

I dragged his elderly body onto a chair. I duct taped his hands to the arms and his legs to the chair's legs. It was a high-backed chair. I put tape around his chin and forehead to hold his cranium in place.

I was going to teach him a lesson about smelling like smoke.

I drank a beer and sat directly across from Mr. Sampson, waiting for him to open his eyes. I was on my second beer when they fluttered open. As soon as I saw the first twitch, I lit a cigarette and blew smoke into his face. His eyes snapped open and he stared at me, trying to figure out where he was and what was going on.

"I don't know how long it will take you to figure it out, you old fuck, but I was minding my own business, smoking a cig on my front porch, and you would have lived the rest of your life in your garden or watching the History Channel or doing whatever shit old fucks like you do. But you had the nerve to tell me to put out my cig. And *that* pissed me off. That's bad for you."

"Help!" he screamed, though his voice was weak. "Somebody help me. She's going to torture me!"

I pulled the smoke from my lips and put it out on the index fingernail of his right hand. He screamed.

"Every time you scream for help," I said, lighting another cigarette, "I'll put one of these out on you. Understand?"

"You're crazy," he muttered, but he didn't scream. His sad old eyes sat deep in his doughy skin. He coughed as I blew smoke into his face.

"Is this how you thought you would die, Mr. Sampson?" I asked. He shook his head no.

"I didn't think so," I said. "It's never what we anticipate, is it?" He shook his head again.

"Maybe this will teach you a lesson then. I'll show you why I'm not scared one bit of lung cancer," I said.

"But… But…" he started and trailed off.

"I'm done talking to you, Mr. Sampson," I said.

"What? You're *crazy*."

"Yeah, yeah, shut up."

"All I'm trying to do is help you!"

"Have you ever seen somebody do this?" I asked, lighting a second cigarette and blowing the smoke into his face. "Smoke two at once? It's my specialty."

I put both cigarettes in the ashtray, letting them smolder. Smoke dragons billowed up toward the ceiling.

He began to moan, but I slapped him silent. "I told you. I'm done talking to you."

Then I got up and grabbed the roll of duct tape. His body strained, atrophied muscles struggling to free themselves. I laughed. I ran the duct tape several times around his mouth, leaving only his nose free. His eyes bulged out. Pure terror.

"I'll bet when I'm done with you, Mr. Sampson, you'll wish you'd died of lung cancer years ago." With the pointed cherries of both cigarettes flaring volcano orange, I jammed them, burning ends first, up the old man's nostrils.

"Can you smell that? Does it smell like smoke?" I asked, laughing. I could hear the ends sizzling on the tender flesh of his nose, could smell burning nose hair. He fought for a desperate breath and sucked the hot cherries even deeper into his nasal passages. Then I pinched his nose shut while the cherries burned and he suffocated.

I'll bet that felt a lot like lung cancer, I thought as I watched. I was proud of my creativity.

It took him a long time to die.

Earlier that day, I thought that a post-murder cigarette was the best ever. Now I know for sure, that the best cigarette is the one you smoke while you're watching someone die.

I made a mental note to try this again.

I went to the store to buy more suds and smokes. I usually didn't smoke two packs a day, but hell, I usually didn't kill two people a day, either. I need more of both.

The clean, crisp air outside felt great. I turned. A car was pulling into the driveway.

The cop.

I waved to him with a cigarette in my hand, figuring that was more innocent than waving with a beer in my hand.

He waved back; made his way over to me. He sat down next to me and I offered him one of the three beers left in the six pack I'd brought out.

He grabbed one, twisted the top and downed almost half of it.

"Rough day?" I asked.

"You wouldn't believe me if I told you."

"Yeah, me too."

"You smoking?" he asked.

"Yeah."

He grunted. "I used to smoke, years ago, but I quit."

I nodded.

"You know – you probably shouldn't smoke."

I got up. "Want to come inside for a bit?"

The man looked surprised. He looked at me. Looked at my breasts then the beer. Looked back over to his house.

He finally nodded and pursed his lips.

"Sure," he said, draining the last of his beer. "Why the hell not?"

I opened the door and he followed me inside.

"Jesus," he said with a grin, "smells like a forest fire in here."

Squinting my eyes, I closed the door behind him.

It was going to be a long night cleaning the house…

23. THE FIRST CUT IS THE DEEPEST
Matt Drabble

"What kind of a man are you anyway?" Wendy Baird sneered as her glass of merlot sloshed over the rim and splattered on the once pristine antique lace tablecloth.

Dr. Lawrence Baird cowered beneath his wife's cruel glare as the eyes of the other table incumbents looked away embarrassed.

The dinner party was supposed to have been a pleasant way to pass an evening. Lawrence was Chief Surgeon at St. Martin's Hospital. His job was one of importance and skill, and behind the glinting glare of a scalpel he was a God. But as soon as he stepped outside of his operating theatre he was lost within the constructs of the real world. He had been married to Wendy for almost 10 years now, and despite her seemingly endless bag of personal barbs, he had thought that this was marriage, and that this was life. She was a bitter woman obsessed with his career far more than he had ever been. He made an excellent living but her eyes were always firmly fixed on the next rung of the ladder. He loved her deeply and considered her constant blunt batterings a small price to pay for her hand.

He began to dab at the staining wine until she batted his hand away angrily.

"Just leave it you bloody fool, you'll only make it worse, like everything else you touch!" Wendy sniggered drunkenly.

She was everything that he was not. While he was a small and quiet man, narrow of stature and build, she was a whirlwind of beauty and life. He was 10 years older than her at 45 with a slight paunch that was impregnated by indignity. His hair had receded past the point of surrender and his round black glasses only added to his anonymity. Wendy however had maintained her beauty queen figure through a strict diet of alcohol and cigarettes over food. Her hair was sculpted by a salon on the other side of town as she barely lifted a finger in self maintenance, preferring to use his credit cards to employ the services of the experts that she believed she so richly deserved.

He smiled at her with the sort of regular compliance that ran through their marriage like a poisoned candy center.

"God you make me sick," she said coldly. "I should have married a man with balls, not a limp dick like you. You know he can barely get it up anymore," she laughed turning towardir guests, not caring who was listening.

"The new administrator seems to be working out well," Dr. Rhys Hixson said breaking into the awkward silence. He was the head of Radiology and one of Lawrence's few friends. He was an older man of 55 but distinguished with it. He sported a wave of silver groomed hair and exuded the healthy glow of a golf enthusiast, or maybe yachting if the weather was fine.

"Yes I have heard good things about her," Lawrence agreed.

"Yeah I bet you'd love to go sticking your little prick in some new piece of ass at the hospital," Wendy slurred. "Not that your little member would ever get you anything except laughs."

"Would you like a little salmon?" Rhys' wife Alice asked Wendy in an effort to perhaps soak up a little of the wine that she had been packing away all night.

"I bet you've got no complaints in that department, eh Alice?" Wendy sniggered as she nudged the doctor's wife.

Alice merely smiled uncomfortably while trying to maintain a sense of decorum. She was an attractive woman, younger than her husband but with an air of sophistication and quiet dignity.

"Really Wendy you should try and eat something," Lawrence offered meekly.

She answered him with the blackest of looks that sent his gaze ever downwards in spiraling shame.

***

"I really don't know why he puts up with her," Alice Hixson said in the car as they drove home.

"I'm sure that she's not all bad," Rhys replied as he drove.

"Oh really Rhys, she's absolutely horrid to him and he just sits there and takes it all like a browbeaten puppy."

"What can I say, he loves her," Rhys shrugged.

"You work closely with him, can't you get him to see sense?"

"I really don't think it's my place to," he bristled uncomfortably.

"Oh you men, you can send a rocket to the moon but woe betide you to actually have a real conversation," Alice sighed heavily as she looked out of the car window into the dark night beyond.

***

Rhys looked over at his friend as they toweled off from a strenuous round of golf. He knew that his wife was right and he should try and intervene, but it just didn't seem his place to do so. "So how are things old man?" He asked a little too casually.

"Fine, fine," Lawrence answered with a forced smile.

86

Rhys could see that the surgeon's face looked pale and drawn. Throughout their round he had been constantly fretting over the time and he knew that Wendy would undoubtedly be the cause as always. "And how's Wendy?" He added.

"Oh you know," Lawrence shrugged. "Same as always. She's looking at some houses over in Bainford; apparently the hospital over there is looking for a new Chief of Surgery."

"Bainford?" Rhys said surprised.

"Wendy thinks that it will be a good move for us, more money, more prestige," Lawrence said quietly.

"And where exactly do your plans fit into all this?" Rhys asked a little more sharply than he'd intended.

"Oh I think that it's a good idea," Lawrence replied with a face that said he thought it was anything but.

"Really Lawrence, isn't it high time that the word *no* entered your vocabulary? I mean you've always told me how happy you are at St. Martin's and that your house is your dream home, why on earth would you even think about moving?"

"A marriage is a partnership Rhys, it's all about compromise," Lawrence recited.

"As far as I can see your marriage is all about Wendy and what she wants out of life." Rhys felt like he was crossing an imaginary line, but also that if he was going to cross it then he might as well go the whole way. He took a deep breath. "She's no good for you old man, there I've said it. She bosses you around something terrible and it's painful to watch for your friends, or at least those that she's let you keep."

Lawrence looked at him long and hard with a sad desperation in his eyes. "I love her," he finally said. "And I couldn't live without her, I wouldn't want to."

Rhys looked at his friend and saw that it was hopeless. No matter how many times she kicked him or how hard, Lawrence was just going to keep coming back for more.

***

Two days later Alice was walking along the high street. Rhys' birthday was coming up and she was looking for the perfect present. She loved her husband deeply and wanted nothing more than to put a smile on his face.

She had spent the morning wandering between stores seeking inspiration when she spotted Wendy across the road sitting outside of a swanky looking restaurant. The weather was warm and as usual

Wendy was dressed in as little as possible. She was about to call out when she saw that Wendy was not alone.

A man walked up to her table and sat down opposite her. The man had his back to her, but he was elegantly attired and she wondered for a moment if he perhaps worked at the hospital. He had a confident stride that she had often found in doctors.

The man reached out and touched Wendy's hand. It could have been an innocent enough public gesture, but his fingers lingered a little too long, and Alice quickly turned away.

She kept her secret for three days before finally breaking down and confessing what she'd seen to her husband.

"But you can't be sure," Rhys said naively.

"Rhys I've held enough hands and had my own held enough times to know what I saw, that harlot is cheating on poor Lawrence and you're going to have to tell him."

"Me? Why exactly am I in the hot seat all of a sudden?" he exclaimed.

"Because you're his friend and he deserves to know."

They spent the rest of the evening and into the night arguing before sleeping back to back in cold silence. She hated to fight with Rhys and couldn't understand his reluctance to get involved.

"Alright I'll tell him," he spoke into the small hours of the morning as the sun was getting ready to peer over the horizon.

She hugged him and slept until the alarm went off. She rose quickly and made him his favorite breakfast as a thank you, of course now that she had gotten her own way.

They ate in stony silence as he pouted. She was about to speak words of comfort when the phone rang and they both looked at each other with furrowed brows. Whenever anyone rang at this hour, it was always bad news.

Rhys answered and stood there nodding and offering the occasional word of consolation. She just knew from his tone and expression that someone must have died. She steeled herself for the bad news when he eventually hung up.

"Who was it?" she asked preparing herself for the worst.

"It was Lawrence; it appears that I won't have to have an awkward conversation with him after all, she's left him."

***

The first two weeks were a constant surveillance job as they kept a vigil over Lawrence to make sure that he didn't do anything stupid. The man was inconsolable at losing his wife to another man. Wendy had cleared out their bank accounts and taken all of her expensive clothing and jewelry when she'd left.

It turned out that unbeknownst to them Wendy had left before on more than one occasion. She had disappeared with several men, often for days at a time, but Lawrence had always taken her back willingly and happily. Alice couldn't help but lose a little of the admittedly shallow well of respect that she had for Lawrence upon hearing this.

For two weeks Alice never saw Lawrence without a bottle of whisky in his hands and she had started to wonder about his sanity. His eyes were constantly bloodshot and his face was sallow and drawn. He reeked of despair and suicide and she made it hers and Rhys' mission to ensure that he was never alone.

The worst part of all was the fact that when he spoke, he constantly said that all he wanted was to take her back again. Alice had hoped that he would eventually see the light and realize this for the blessing in disguise that it truly was, but she now knew that he would never accept that.

Eventually time moved on and Lawrence's drinking started to recede. Once he had used up all of his owing holiday time at the hospital it became clear that Wendy wasn't coming back this time, and that he would have to get back to work at some point. Rhys was a continual voice of reason in his ear, and eventually one Monday morning Lawrence was showered and shaved and back in the saddle, at least on the surface.

The days became weeks and the weeks stretched into months and slowly Lawrence emerged from his shell of denial. He had always maintained that Wendy would come strolling through their door again any day now, but eventually even he was forced to admit that this time it was for good.

Lawrence had furnished them with practically zero details about the man that had stolen his wife away. Whether he knew or not, Alice couldn't say, but as far as she was concerned whoever had taken a woman like Wendy away from her loving husband deserved everything that they got.

"You're moving?" She exclaimed over a Sunday dinner that had become a ritual between the three of them.

"Greener pastures and new memories," Lawrence replied gently. "I don't want you, either of you, to think that I'm not eternally grateful for you taking me in and looking after me, because I am. Without your love and patience I probably wouldn't still be here," he said darkly.

"But you seem to be doing so much better now old man," Rhys said.

"Then it's exactly the right time for me to be on my way."

"But where will you go?" Alice asked concerned.

"Do you remember a few months ago me telling you about the position over in Bainford?" Lawrence asked Rhys.

"The Chief Surgeon opening?" he replied.

"Well apparently the chap that they employed hasn't worked out and the position is vacant again. So I thought to myself, why not? It's about time that I started moving on and this seemed perfect."

"You've already got the job?" Alice enquired surprised.

"I interviewed last week and they offered it to me this morning," Lawrence beamed.

"And this is really what you want?" she asked gently.

"I think it really is," he replied.

"Then here's to you my old friend," Rhys said raising his glass. "To new beginnings," he toasted.

"New beginnings," Alice and Lawrence agreed.

***

"We've got a bad one coming in Dr. Baird," the panicking voice spat down the phone. "Road traffic accident and the woman's in a right mess."

Lawrence had been at the hospital for almost three months now and his new position had brought about a change in his personality. Gone was the timid, henpecked husband to be replaced by a quiet and studious man and a doctor of confidence. He was just starting to get a grip upon his new charge and move on with his life. He worked all hours but did not mind the long days as his large but comfortable house held only the four walls for company.

He left his office and shucked on the white coat that was his armor against the blood and mess that passed through his department. The hospital was quiet due to the lateness of the hour and the patients slept soundly, many of whom upon a tide of medication.

He headed quickly downstairs towards the emergency ward where the latest poor soul would be wheeled in on a stretcher straight from the ambulance. But it was their lucky day; he was the chief surgeon, the head cutter, the man with the magic hands and steady nerve.

He bounded across to the ward with a confident gait and a whistle in his heart. This was what he was born to do and this was the gift that he had been given to share with the world.

The doors smashed open as the gurney was wheeled through into the emergency room. The staff was on a skeleton crew rotation due to the wee hours and he was the only doctor of any note on duty.

The body on the gurney was female with short blonde hair matted across her face, encrusted in blood. He cared little for any information that wasn't relevant to his course of action. He wasn't interested if the patient had been drinking or was on drugs or even a criminal, they were simply puzzle pieces to fit back together again.

"What have we got?" he asked the first paramedic.

"Female, road collision, multiple fractures to the spine, right leg broken in more places than I could count, left leg almost severed," the man recited efficiently. "Internal hemorrhaging and significant blood loss. She slipped away twice on the journey in, but we managed to bring her back both times. Pulse is weak but holding."

"Okay people on three," Lawrence ordered as they prepared to lift her onto the bed.

He began to run through the various checks and found the paramedic's work to be excellent. One of the nurses at his side absently wiped the woman's face clean of blood and brushed the hair from her forehead. Lawrence almost died on the spot when he stared down into his wife's eyes. The hair was different and her face was fuller and rounder than it had been, but it was Wendy.

He knew that she had been sent back to him by God himself, with all the hospitals in the country she had been wheeled into his. He steeled himself and steadied his hands; he was a surgeon, and he had a job to do.

***

Several months later Alice hung up the phone and stood shocked and confused.

"Who was it?" Rhys implored with concern splashed across his face. "What's wrong?"

"It was Lawrence," she replied in a strange disconnected voice.

"Is he alright?"

"She's come back to him."

"Who has?"

"Wendy, she's back."

Rhys stared at her like she was mad. "Are you sure? I mean how did she find him? I know she hasn't contacted us to find him and I don't think he had any other friends around here before he moved."

"I've no idea," Alice said shaking her head. "He wants us to go around on Sunday for lunch; he says that she's a changed woman and that she can't wait to see us."

"Then she *has* changed," Rhys joked to a passive audience.

"I can't believe that he's taken her back after everything she's done to him," Alice sighed. "He seemed to be doing so well, new job, new town."

"Well, all we can do is give him our support," Rhys shrugged. "What else can we do?"

***

Sunday rolled around soon enough and their anticipation grew with the wait. They talked about nothing else, other than hoping that the miracle had finally happened and Wendy had seen the light. They just prayed that all of the growing that Lawrence had done in the months since she had walked out on him wouldn't be forsaken.

Rhys pulled the car up to the front of Lawrence's house as per the man's finely planned directions. Alice carried flowers and Rhys carried a fine bottle of wine. They walked up the driveway with their stomachs churning a mixture of hope and trepidation.

This was both of their debuts in visiting Lawrence's new home. The house was large and spacious looking, and in a fine neighborhood. Affluence and wealth was parked in every driveway as pristine motors gleamed with metallic statements of good taste.

The door flew open before either of them had time to knock. Lawrence greeted them with a beaming smile and happiness adorning his face.

"It's so wonderful to see you both again," he enthused as he heartily hugged them both, squeezing the breath from their chests. "Come in, come in."

They followed him in through the open doorway. The hall was long with several rooms closed off by closed doors. There was a slightly odd smell in the air that made Rhys think immediately of hospital corridors.

"How are you Lawrence?" Alice asked, quietly glad to have their friend alone for a minute.

"I'm wonderful," he smiled. "Everything is wonderful now that Wendy is home."

"Speaking of which, where is she?" Rhys asked looking around.

"Wendy darling," Lawrence called up the winding staircase. "Our guests have arrived."

The three of them stood and waited in the silence.

"Perhaps she didn't hear you," Alice suggested.

"Oh she heard me," Lawrence replied. "She'll be with us presently," he said. "Come on through and I'll pour you a drink. That looks like a cheeky number," he said pointing to the bottle of wine that Rhys was holding. "But I think that the situation calls for something a little bit more celebratory, I've got some bubbly on ice."

They followed him down the long hallway where there was what looked like a small elevator inside a brass cage.

"How big is this place?" Rhys asked looking at the cage.

"Ah I'm afraid that is rather necessary," Lawrence said sadly. "I have quite the tale to fill you in on, come through and I'll tell you."

They followed him through to the spacious lounge that opened out into an open plan room with a high ceiling and dining room attached.

"Please sit," he indicated.

Alice could let her curiosity wait no longer. "What happened to Wendy? Where has she been all this time?"

"Well as you know we have had problems in our marriage for some time. I've told you that she had left me several times before, but she'd always come home in the end. Look there was blame on both sides," he said holding up a hand to quiet Alice's disapproving look at the suggestion of his own culpability. "Well this time I thought that she was gone for good I don't mind admitting. That is until God saw fit to reveal his plan and bring her back to me."

Alice heard something heavy moving upstairs and wondered if the ever so precious Wendy had perhaps put on a few pounds during her sabbatical.

"You think that God brought her back to you?" Rhys asked dubiously.

"Oh no question about it," Lawrence nodded seriously. "All the towns and cities in the country, all the hospitals, and all the shift patterns and she was brought back to me."

"Wait a minute she's been in an accident?" Alice asked concerned and feeling a little guilty over her hopes that Wendy was not the perfect figure that she had last laid eyes upon.

"Yes and a bad one at that," Lawrence answered with his head bowed low.

"You should have called us old man, when did this happen?" Rhys asked worriedly.

"A few months ago now. It was touch and go for a while there, but we pulled through, just as it was supposed to be," he smiled broadly and Alice inexplicably felt a small shudder of unease.

She heard the elevator crank into life and it begin to descend. The metal box rattled its way downwards, presumably carrying Wendy. "And they let you operate on her? Aren't there rules against that being as she's your wife?" she asked.

"Fortunately it was late at night, or early in the morning depending on which way you look at it," he smiled. "I pretty much had the run of the place and was able to work unimpeded. Once she had been stabilized and out of danger I was able to bring her here. I converted one of the rooms upstairs into an operating room and worked on getting her back to perfection."

Rhys exchanged a look with Alice at the idea of home-school surgery. It couldn't be ethical and surely the hospital wouldn't have allowed it, if they had known.

"Where had she been, you know when she ran off?" Alice couldn't help but ask as the elevator landed on the ground level.

"She hasn't said and I haven't asked," Lawrence said firmly. "What's happened in the past has no bearing on our future together. It's all ancient history now."

Alice heard the metal bars of the cage slide noisily across as the elevator doors opened. "Aren't you worried," she said quietly. "Aren't you worried that she might…, you know run away again?"

"Oh no," Lawrence smiled pleasantly. "I've seen to that."

Alice turned to the door and suddenly had a sick feeling of dread in her stomach. She heard the sound off a small engine purring along the hallway towards them. As Wendy's motorized wheelchair turned into the room she threw her hands up to her face in sheer horror and screamed at the sight.

Wendy wore a floral sleeveless lilac dress that lay upon her thigh. Both of her arms above the elbow had been amputated along with both legs below the knee. Her hair had been brushed and styled by a loving but amateur hand. Thick makeup was smeared enthusiastically across her pale face, but applied without a woman's precision or skill. Her mouth was a gaping black hole hanging open, minus a tongue, and her eyes were staring straight ahead brimming with tears and bulging with insanity.

"I don't think that she'll ever run away again," Lawrence smiled darkly as he poured the champagne.

24. THE GHOST WHO HAUNTS ME
Charles David Bennett

In or around 2015 hours last Sunday night, the ghost who haunts me rattled the circuit breakers in my kitchen. This had been going on ever since I moved into my new digs about six months prior (an event I've learned to set my watch by). This was not the only strange and unusual activity, however. My cat Shadow would regularly wake me up at Jesus-O'clock-in-the-morning with her eerie, mournful yowling. After yelling the standard obscenities at her I usually fell back asleep, though, sometimes it would creep me out enough that I would get up, make coffee, and watch the tube. There was also a large, perfectly oval, brown stain that appeared upon the ceiling which a plethora of cleaning compounds would not remove. I had scrubbed the paint off, but the stain remained. Even after several new coats of expensive stain removing primer and ceiling paint, the stain reappeared twenty four hours later, and I knew that I had one.

They say that a normal, intelligent mind doesn't believe in ghosts, and I agree, as I do not believe in them. I do, however, believe in gravitational osmosis, which is the tendency to pass through the fabric or membrane of space/time so as to equalize concentrations on both sides.

None the less, I finally broke down and dialed the landlord, and left a message complaining about the haunted breaker box. The following Monday, Juan the maintenance man showed up at my door. Juan's a short, stocky, pleasant Latino fellow who seemed to enjoy his job. He used his multi-meter as I watched, and then said, "The circuit is good." Which it was, as I had seen with my own eyes right there alongside him.

Though, when I said that it always rattled in or around a quarter past ten p.m. he just looked at me like I was bat shit crazy and repeated his assessment. Afterward we joked and chortled for a time about other things, until his cell phone rang and he had to depart immediately. No sooner than closing the door behind him, the damned thing started rattling once again.

"Robert? Is that you?" I said into the roaring silence that followed, but there was no answer, nor nothing onwards. I shrugged, then, grabbed my keys and wallet and stepped out to put some local affairs in order. Several hours later I returned home and, while packing a couple bags, I believe that I witnessed something completely insane.

You see, I thought I had seen the image of myself standing outside of my bedroom window, looking inward. Not a reflection mind you, but my own face standing on the other side of the window lattice, looking inward.

I rushed outside but nobody was there; and that damned circuit breaker was rattling like hell the entire time. It finally popped when I reentered. I left it off as I had begun to worry about the fire hazard it represented, bewitched or not.

I suppose, to be honest, that I was spooked. I finished packing and tossed my bags in the car, along with the cat, and hit the road with no particular destination in mind. The fog was thick, and I put Nigel Potter's 'Spires of Heaven' in the CD player and allowed my mind to get lost in the music. I don't know how long I'd been driving, nor do I remember shutting down the music, but when I noticed that the fuel gauge neared empty, I pulled off at the nearest exit and into the first gas station. When I finished at the pump I walked through the foggy mist and into the store.

"Where is the restroom and where am I?" I asked the clerk upon entering. He pointed to the head and informed me that I was just outside a town called Rockford.

I finished my business, grabbed a rack of beer and headed to the checkout. After forking over the appropriate amount of cash, I asked him if there were any motels in the area.

"Sure," he said. "Just head back behind the store away from the main highway, make another right and there are two of them about a quarter mile down."

I thanked him, took my items, and left.

***

I checked into a place called 'The Sleep Inn.' It had seen better days but I didn't care and it was cheap. I found my room and kicked back, turned on the TV and found a local news channel. I had thought, at this point, that I was staying one step ahead of the ghost who haunted me, until I saw my face on the television screen. As I watched in disbelief I learned that the doppelganger had materialized inside a family's home just a few blocks from my apartment. It had apparently materialized out of thin air in their living room as they had sat watching T.V. The shocked homeowners were said to have watched it for several minutes in a state of fearful paralysis, before one of them thought to record it with their cellphone. The specter had then walked from the room and out of sight, where it seemed to the eyewitnesses as though it simply disappeared. From there it had taken the local authorities almost no time to identify me from the cellphone footage with image recognition technology. The media man also reported that federal authorities were seeking me for questioning, in this "unusual, and possibly paranormal, event".

It seemed at that moment to be a very good thing that I had an old fashioned dislike of debit and credit cards, and always carried cash. There would be no paper or electronic trails for them to follow. The news channel went on to say that the authorities just wanted to question Jack Velmor—that would be me—and that they did not believe that Mr. Velmor was the actual perpetrator of the home invasion, but some imposter using my identity.

"AND MY FRIGGIN' FACE!" I yelled.

I slammed four beers in rapid succession. The resulting burp was an earthquake in E-Minor. A fly began bludgeoning itself to death inside the lampshade, stopped, and then started anew. I softly mashed it, and it fell to the floor. Another body lost forever in the ugly yellow and orange shag carpeting which, by the smell, was no doubt a relic of the nineteen seventies. I turned the TV to the weather channel, lowered the volume, finished my beers and curled-up with the cat on the bed. I awoke the following morning somewhat hung over, rather irritated and tired of the doppelganger's piratical pursuit. I check out, breakfasted and headed home.

***

On the long drive home I couldn't help but wonder how many law enforcement agencies had rummaged through my home. I took a circuitous route of country roads and back streets, slowly ninjaing my way back. I drove around the block twice. There didn't seem to be any stake-out vehicles, nor crime scene tape present, so I parked a block away, grabbed the feline and much of my gear.

I set the cat down in the kitchen. She meowed and took off for a hiding place known only to her. The phone began to ring and that damned circuit breaker began rattling immediately; someone must have reset it. I left the kitchen, passed through the living room into my study, and found myself staring at the malevolent image of myself, or rather, the image of my doppelganger.

"What do you want asshole?" I said through clinched teeth, and it did not stir a muscle.

"Why your death, brother, what else?" replied the ghost who haunts me.

"I am NOT your flippin' brother!" I yelled, becoming enraged.

My doppelganger smiled then, opening its mouth to show many rows of inhuman, sharp teeth.

***

I backed up a bit, helplessly glancing round for something to strike the ghastly being. My tormentor was too fast however and was on me with lightning speed. I felt like I was being electrocuted, and then, the lights of my consciousness went out.

Four days later the authorities entered my home to find me hanging by the neck in the attic. My swollen, blackened tongue protruded from my stiff blue lips, and my bulging and fogged-over eyes gazed at nothing. The roofing trusses made a disturbing squeak as my naked body dangled above moldy crap and corrosive urine, giving the place the rank stench of ammonia and human decay. Special agent Polyester felt the need to vomit, but lit a cigarette instead, as was his custom.

"Death by misadventure," he said, and then, "Go ahead and cut him down, I've seen enough." Agent Polyester blew-out a huge cloud of smoke with a sigh and exclaimed, "Why must these jerks always do this in the nude? Don't they have any respect for their fellow man?"

He turned to leave and then paused. "It's a pain in the ass waiting around for the world to destroy itself," he said, before descending the stairs. The other CSI agents looked at each other and shrugged, and then proceeded to bag the body.

The following Tuesday a bank robbery was reported, in which several of the employees had been decapitated. The perpetrator fit the description of Jack Velmor. It was also reported that the heads of the bound employees appeared to have been chewed off. It was going to be a long week for special agents.

25. A LICENSE TO KILL
Rob Smales

The cold night wind tossed Abigail's hair, ruffling her sleeve as she hung her thumb out in the approaching headlights. An observer might have heard her repeating a two word mantra under her breath. It was a different mantra than she'd used on the last car, but her focus had been different then. *Then* she had muttered *'no cops, no cops,'* until the approaching headlights had become dwindling taillights, leaving her eyes blinking against their swirling dust.

Two hours trudging in the breakdown lane with nothing for company but darkness and the biting cold had given her a completely different attitude.

"...please stop, please stop, *please* stop..."

Even if they're cops, she thought, *at least they'll give me a ride somewhere.*

The lights came closer, the engine's hum reaching her over the constant rustle of leaves and branches.

"...please stop, please stop, please stop, pleasestoppleasestop*pleasestop*..."

The headlights drew abreast of her, illuminating the surrounding night... and drove past.

"Shit!"

She dropped her arm to her side, burying the now freezing thumb deep in her pocket, searching for warmth.

The road in front of her suddenly flared with red light, as did the trees across the road, her own shadow a dark stain on the now crimson macadam. She spun about.

The big car sat not twenty feet away, engine rumbling, brake lights brilliant in the moonlight. As she watched, the passenger's side door swung open in invitation. With a celebratory whoop, Abby dashed to the car before the driver could change his mind. She slid onto the seat and had barely reached to close the door when, with a roar, the car shot off down the road.

As alarming as that was Abby still took a moment to revel in the hot air blasting out of the heating vents. Her hands were already thrust toward the dash, fingers extended to take full advantage of the airflow, before she smelled it.

Rancid. Foul. Hanging in the air so thick she could actually *taste* it. Musty old body odor. Cigarette smoke, both fresh and stale. Someone had apparently been unable to wait for the water to boil and had simply set the coffee beans on fire. Hovering beneath it all was the dank, moist funk of mold and rot, as if the inside of the car had spoiled like a Halloween pumpkin at Thanksgiving.

In Florida.

She fought the urge to gag as the unsuitably used air invaded her mouth and nose; the powerful heat thawing numbed taste buds and nasal passages to allow the full force of the miasma to wash through her like a sickening tide.

"Oh my God," she whispered, immediately regretful — speaking created the need to take another breath, and she wasn't certain that her stomach was ready.

"Beg pardon?"

The voice was deep, male, and lightly, indefinably accented. Abby instinctively turned toward it, only to catch a face-full of the world's worst halitosis. Eyes watering, she saw a tall, cadaverous man gripping the steering wheel with hands that appeared to be sticks with knuckles. His black suit and white shirt struck her as strangely spotless considering the overwhelming stench of the car. She took a shallow breath, sipping the grotesque atmosphere rather than gulping, and managed another whisper.

"May I open a window?"

"Beg pardon?" He leaned his gaunt face closer, turning one long ear toward her to hear. "Are you alright?"

Though the voice was concerned his face remained an expressionless mask, and though he'd just expelled a cloud of tooth-rotting breath in her direction, Abby noticed another smell getting stronger as he leaned in: the funk of rot.

Maybe that suit is nice and clean, she thought, *but there's something seriously wrong with the body inside it...*

"The window," she said, risking another lungful of filth for the chance of some cleaner air. "May I put it down?"

"I'm afraid that window does not work," he said, though by his tone he didn't seem particularly apologetic about it.

"I just —" she began.

"How old are you, child?" he said. "Fourteen?"

"I'm older than I look," she said. "Please, do you think you could put *your*—"

"So you're fifteen? Sixteen at most. You really shouldn't be hitchhiking, you know. You never know *who* might be picking you up."

"Sir," Abby said, uncomfortable with the direction the conversation had taken, "thank you for the ride and all, really, but I'm pretty hungry, so do you think we could—"

"Oh, I understand hunger, child," the gaunt man interrupted once more, reaching out a long, knobby hand to pat her denim-clad thigh in a fashion she found all too friendly. The hand carried yet another smell, something that had been there all along, unnoticed, just another ingredient in the horrible odor permeating the car's interior. Now she could make it out as it wafted up from his pallid, spongy flesh. A metallic, coppery smell, with a tang all its own.

Blood.

The tires crunched on gravel as he pulled the big car onto the shoulder. Looking about, Abby saw nothing but the trees and the dark, empty road.

"Why are we—?"

"I think this is the perfect place to discuss the nature of hunger, child," he said, twisting toward her in his seat, and for the first time his face held expression: glee.

"I hunger for *you!*"

He lunged across the car, preternaturally fast, his hands coming for her... only to be caught by her own. His hands were twisted. A thumb pressed against the back of his left fist, flexing the wrist painfully; a knife dropped to the floor. Abigail looked into his suddenly terrified eyes. She leaned forward slightly, sniffing his skin.

"I should really wash you first, but like you said, this is the perfect place."

She cocked her head.

"You know, if I *looked* one hundred and eighty-six I could get my *own* driver's license. Then this would be easier. Those things are practically a license to kill in the modern age."

Tears flowed down his cheeks as her fangs sank into his throat…

26. THE FINAL SCREAM OF YOUR LIFE
Rick McQuiston

I first noticed it when I came home from work. As usual, I pulled my little white Pontiac as close to the curb in front of my house as I could and stepped out onto the cool, dew-laden grass.

The squirrel laid there on its side, half of its limp body on the sidewalk, half on my lawn. It was obvious it was injured; its hind legs weren't moving at all.

My wife emerged from the house. She still wore her pajamas, having woken up only shortly before I came home.

"Morning, Honey," I still remember her saying. She walked up to me and gave me a kiss. Her breath smelled of Listerine. We both looked down at the squirrel. "I think it's paralyzed. Probably fell out of the tree."

I looked up into the sprawling branches of the ancient oak that adorned my front lawn. It had been there long before my house was built, and my house was very old. I looked back at the squirrel. Apparently, while my wife and I were speculating on the cause of its injuries, it had died.

"Oh dear," my wife moaned. She brushed her poker-straight blond hair from her face. "He's dead."

Tiny black flies had already begun to buzz around the carcass, looking for suitable spots to feed or lay their eggs. The squirrel did not move.

We walked back into the house, me promising that after I got something to drink I'd bury the poor animal on the side of the shed.

***

Two days passed. Two more dead squirrels in front of my house.

"Maybe you should call the police," my wife said innocently. I suppressed the urge to scream a reply.

"I can't," I said as calmly as I could. "What would I say? That someone's dumping squirrels on my front lawn? They'd think I was nuts." I almost laughed at the unintentional pun I made.

"Well, what do you think is killing them?" she asked.

I could tell she was worried. I think she knew even then that something was happening that didn't make sense.

If only I knew then what I know now.

It was then, at that moment, I made a decision that forever erased the fine line between sanity and madness: I walked out my front door and over toward the sidewalk.

There were still residual stains on the cement from the squirrels, and I cursed myself under my breath for not washing them away earlier.

And then I felt something land on top of my head. I immediately brushed it off.

It was another dead squirrel, shiny black fur matted with blood and wide open, unseeing eyes.

"Oh my God!" my wife shrieked from our front porch.

I turned to look at her and was amazed and horrified to see that she wasn't even looking at me.

She was looking *above* me.

Instinctively, I followed her terrified gaze upward.

The tree squirmed with unnatural movement. Dozens of sinewy branches tangled and untangled around each other. As a whole it vaguely resembled a swarm of snakes in some bizarre mating ritual. But the worst part wasn't the branches. It was the things that were trapped in them.

Squirrels, birds, even what appeared to be a cat, although it was mangled so badly it was difficult to tell what it was. And all were being subjected to brutal punishment by the limbs.

"Get out of there!" my wife screamed from the relative safety of our front porch.

I say *relative* because looking back now she was safe there. But not for long. As I watched in horror, a branch, a fairly thick and mottled thing, shot over my head and speared my poor wife before I could react. I heard the final scream of her life as she toppled over dead. The branch then withdrew from her lifeless body.

Suddenly all that mattered to me was reaching the body and dragging it inside the house. I reasoned it would be safe there from any more attacks.

But as I began to run across my front yard I was tripped up by some smaller branches that had snaked their way into the lawn. I wound up with my face in the grass. I immediately sat back up and started to pull the terrible things off my legs. They felt warm and slippery, but I managed to free myself without too much difficulty.

My wife's body proved heavier than I thought it would be, but I was able to pull it through the doorway and into the living room. She laid there, a blank expression on her pale face. My heart burned with anguish, but the fires were doused by the realization of what happened.

The tree? How could a tree do that?

I had no answers but knew I had to call for help. Without wasting a second I snatched the phone off its base and dialed 9-1-1.

Predictably, the line was dead. A quick look out the window told me how.

The phone lines ran through the tree. I saw both ends of the severed cable dangling from swirling branches. My wish for a cell phone dwindled into insignificance when I noticed dozens of other trees squirming with impossible life, each flailing around violently, groping for victims, pulsating like water balloons ready to pop. They lined the street on both sides. I saw one smash a passing car flat as a pancake.

And then the idea hit me.

My car! If I could make it to my car I might be able to escape.

But that notion was dashed when I heard the sound of metal buckling and glass shattering. I watched in disbelief as my car, as well as my wife's car, was reduced to wreckage.

I crouched down next to the body of my wife and held her lifeless hand in mine. My will to live drained from me like so much water down a pipe. I suddenly didn't care anymore. My world (and presumably everyone else's as well) was coming to an end. A greater species was taking over. Perhaps they had evolved to the point where they had merely been waiting for the right time to strike. God only knows how long they had been capable of something like this. Months? Years? Centuries? And all the while mankind just turned a blind eye to them.

***

Two days have passed now and I was forced to cover my wife's body with a blanket. I just couldn't bear to look at what time was doing to her. There's no power so I have no way of knowing what's happening outside. I've drawn all the curtains in the house, but I can still hear the trees outside rustling around. Yesterday, I thought I saw a huge shadow across the front bay window. It was so tall that it went straight up out of sight. I assumed it was probably the tree in my front yard. Apparently, now they could uproot themselves and move about.

I look over at the still form beneath the blanket and wonder if somehow all this could have been avoided. Maybe we should've listened to all the environmentalists sooner. Maybe then we could have lived together in peace.

I curl up into a fetal position next to my wife. The memory of her last scream still rings in my ears. I can only wonder what my final scream will sound like.

27. ON THIS DARK AND SACRED NIGHT
James Pratt

In an old graveyard on the edge of town, a spirit slept in a borrowed grave. Perhaps spirit wasn't the right word. Some had called it a god once upon a time, holding festivals in its honor and singing praises to its name. Not a lord of the heavens or ruler of the mighty seas, but a god nonetheless. And though those days were long passed and its presence had dwindled in the hearts and minds of the living, it lingered on, for like the dreams from which they sprung, gods could be discarded but they never quite went away.

The spirit stirred at the first autumnal chill, for the harvest season was its time of power and heralded the approach of its holiest day. As the sacred day drew closer, its dreams grew darker and more vivid. Over and over, it relived the coming of the Roman soldiers who had torn down the sacred stones and put its beloved children to torch and sword. Dogs whimpered and the wind howled in sympathy as the spirit muttered in its sleep.

On the first day of October, the spirit spent twelve hours opening the shriveled orbs that had once been eyes. Time weighed heavily upon it, and each movement was a titanic effort. The spirit wouldn't be fully awake till the dawn of *Samhain*, the sacred day when the druid-priests gathered to give thanks to the Lord of the Harvest. In the meantime, it would stoke the glowing coals of indignation to a fiery rage by recalling the injustices of the past. Hate alone gave it the strength to resist the call of oblivion, and even then only for one night a year.

Time crawled at a glacial pace but the sacred day finally arrived. Decrepit and entombed, the borrowed body it had used the previous year was no good to the spirit now, and so a new vessel was required. Rising up out of the earth, it sniffed the wind in search of a place which reeked of fresh death. Finding such a place, the spirit went on its way. Animals scattered at its approach but people remained oblivious save for a momentary chill as it passed, sight unseen among the living. Unhampered by material impediments or fatigue, the spirit soon reached its destination. In a brightly lit room in the back of a somber-looking building, the gangly corpse of a wizened old man with features pitted and grooved as a walnut shell lay naked on a stainless steel table. It was not the fit young body for which the spirit had hoped, but the sacred hour was drawing near. It would have to do.

As it sank into the body, the spirit heard footsteps approach. Moments later, a well-groomed man in a dark suit entered the room. Acclimating itself to the new-old body, the spirit waited for the right moment to strike. As the man in the suit turned to retrieve a thin metal wand and switch on a noisy apparatus, it retrieved a scalpel from a tray of gleaming instruments. When the man turned back and leaned over the corpse, its eyes opened and flashed a wide, yellow-toothed grin. The man in the suit stumbled backward, tripping over his own feet, and falling to the floor. He stared wide-eyed as the corpse sat up and turned to look at him. It began to gibber as it stepped onto the floor and reached for him with a trembling, liver-spotted hand. The spirit briefly considered killing the man and taking his younger body, but opted to will him to sleep and take his clothes instead. The covenant allowed for a most specific tribute, and it would not be found here.

As it waited for the sun to set, the spirit thought of the olden times when the faithful had sought to appease it. They knew it stood at the Last Threshold, and only it could guard them from those things which dwelt in the Land of the Dead. Gathering in the places where the veils were thinnest, the faithful held great festivals in the spirit's honor. They danced naked and free around bonfires whose flames reached high as the midnight clouds, and roasted cats in wicker baskets that they might gain glimpses of things yet to come. Greatest of their offerings was the Wicker Man, a towering effigy filled with human sacrifices; once lit, the Wicker Man's glow filled the night as did the screams of those trapped within it.

But those days were long past. Armed with steel weapons and armor, invaders stole the sacred relics which were its touchstone to the mortal world and carried them across the wide sea. They did so without knowing the relic's true purpose, or of that which slept within them. When the spirit awoke in the New World, it knew its time had passed. What even the Romans couldn't eradicate, ignorance had finally undone. Far from its place of power, the spirit had no more substance than a dream.

But dreams could be potent things. Each year when the sacred day had arrived, the spirit had gone among the living and rekindled ancestral memories in the hearts and minds of those whose bloodline could be traced back to the Old Country. It sent dreams reminding them of the sacred night when the veils were thrown back and the worlds of the living and the dead overlapped. In time the festival of *Samhain* was reborn as a new sort of tradition, one harmless enough for a people who no longer cared to roast cats or dance naked and free beneath the light of a gibbous moon. And so, even if indirectly, the spirit received the recognition it craved. And by its own hand, the spirit would have the red tribute which was its due.

The spirit waited patiently for the sun to set. The veil would be especially thin at twilight as light gave way to shadow. There was power in the in-between places; doorways, borderlands, and crossroads; and in the in-between times of dusk, dawn, and the stroke of midnight. That was where magic lay, in the neither-nor. And so, as the setting sun painted the horizon an angry shade of red, the spirit hid its waxy, slack-jawed face beneath sunglasses and a scarf before leaving the mortuary to walk amongst the living once more.

All around it, children in garish costumes rushed along streets which had the appearance of a single, endless slab of impossibly smooth stone. The children wore masks and makeup and carried bags filled with brightly wrapped sweets. If the children could have seen the lost souls, elemental spirits, and ravenous demons with faces like gaping wounds that walked hidden beside them, their laughter would have quickly turned to screams. For a moment the spirit was tempted to pull back the veil and show them, but decided against it. It wasn't completely heartless, after all. And on this sacred night, the children were its flock. They knew not what they were truly celebrating, but they were celebrating nonetheless.

No one paid much attention to the bloodstained suit the spirit wore, for this was a night of costumes and grotesqueries, and so it walked unmolested through the town. The spirit stopped at the first holy place it encountered but found it empty, as was the second and the third. At the fourth temple, it sensed the presence of life. High above the temple and mounted on a narrow steeple was the symbol which the faithful of the upstart religion held in reverence. That seemed strange to the spirit; crucifixion had been used by the Romans as a particularly brutal form of execution whereas the religion of the Carpenter's Son was said to be one of peace and love. Shrugging its bony shoulders, the spirit entered the temple.

The spirit did not like this place for it was consecrated to a most jealous god; not content with any one thing, this god had declared himself the Lord of All Things and because his worshippers believed it, so it came to pass. At the altar, the spirit paused to regard the plaster image of the Father-Son who had required a sacrifice so mighty only the Father-Son himself would do. Creator of the universe or not, the god of this land certainly seemed taken with himself.

The spirit found that for which it sought in an office in the back where a young priest sat writing at a desk. The priest looked up from his work, a sermon he was preparing for the funeral service of a Mr. Caleb Abernathy who had died of a stroke the previous week. It would be a particularly sad occasion. Able to trace their lineage back to the Old Country, the Abernathy's had been a fixture of the community since its founding two centuries past. With Caleb's death, the proud Abernathy line had finally come to an end.

At the sound of the spirit's approach, the priest stopped what he was doing and rose to greet his visitor. "Can I help you?"

The spirit removed the sunglasses then unwound the scarf and tossed it aside.

The priest's mouth fell open at the sight of the very man whose funeral service he would be conducting two days hence. "Mr. …Mr. Abernathy?"

When the spirit had first awoken in this new land, holy men had tried to bind it within the relics where it once had slept. But the spirit was no hell-born demon. The words sacred to the holy men had no power over it. When the spirit had threatened to use its own power over the dead against them, the holy men had no choice but to enter into a covenant. Once a year, one of their own would be sacrificed as tribute. It was little compensation, but better than nothing at all. Over the decades, the covenant had been relegated to the stuff of legend, and then forgotten entirely. But the spirit had not forgotten. Even if by its own two hands, the spirit would have its due.

The time for the yearly ritual had come. The priest backed away as the spirit revealed the scalpel it had brought from the funeral parlor. Then it spoke in a quavering voice and, though its words were in the dead language of the Old Country, its intent was quite clear:

Now I rise from wormy earth
On this dark and sacred night
To demand the red tribute
Which is mine to claim by right
I stand before thee, O priest
Yet before me there are none
For I am lord of this land
Till dawn brings the morning sun

As the corpse approached, its features underwent a hideous transformation. First its mouth stretched into an impossibly wide, gap-toothed grin. Then its eyes and nose began to sizzle and dissolve, running down its face in waxy rivulets that left tiny canals of melted flesh. A flame ignited within its skull, sending a flickering light streaming through its eye sockets, nasal cavity, and gaping mouth. The true face of *Samhain* stood revealed, and the time of the red tribute was at hand.

"Dear God!" the priest cried. Back against the wall, he raised his hands defensively.

Now I rise from wormy earth, the spirit repeated, slashing the priest across the palms.

Clasping his bloody hands together, the priest closed his eyes. "Our Father who art in heaven-"

On this dark and sacred night…

***

After the ritual was complete, the spirit re-donned the scarf and sunglasses, and returned to the mortuary. The only people still on the street were teenage lovers and mischief-makers, both of whom gave the old man wide berth without complete notion as to why. When the spirit reached the parlor, it removed its stolen clothes and restored them to the mortician. When the mortician awoke, he would undoubtedly attribute the vision of Mr. Abernathy rising from the dead to a Halloween-inspired dream. Then the spirit returned to the cold metal slab, lay down, and willed its borrowed face back to its original form. Soon Mr. Abernathy would be laid to rest. It would then return to the sleep of oblivion as it had so many times before, dreaming of tributes past and those yet to elapse, as it waited for its day to come round again.

28. ROULETTE
Peter Adam Salomon

"There's no such thing as vampires," she said, her voice shaking just enough for me to hear the air rushing over her lips. Hair dyed a shade too orange hid her eyes, but I knew they were the same brown as her older sister's, though without the intoxicating intellect. Perhaps it was only the two-year age difference. At sixteen, she was still growing, whereas her older sister had already arrived.

Not that it mattered. Her sister wasn't at the party. She was. And her whisper caressed lips colored perfectly red. The hair? I could learn to live with orange.

"Vampires?" someone else asked, joining the small group of us in the corner of the basement. Flickering Christmas lights cast shadows that were more festive than creepy, despite the Halloween theme.

"That movie," I said, waving the thought away even as I was saying it. "She doesn't believe." They laughed. Hell, I laughed. It was worth laughing at. Believe? In sparkling vampires falling in love?

She laughed as well, her lips open, exposing American Contemporary Teeth (DDS approved and bland) and a tongue just the sweetest shade of pink. Her breath reached me despite the distance, a hint of bubble gum and, if I had to guess, mint toothpaste within the last few hours. Probably right before the party began.

"If there were really vampires," she said, her voice growing stronger with each word as we all watched her, "it'd be on the news or Homeland Security would be after them or something. Right?"

"Sure," someone said, "they have nothing else to do."

And we laughed, again. Oh, how we laughed. After all, it was funny. There couldn't possibly be vampires in 2014. In suburban America. At a high school party where someone smuggled in a six-pack that wasn't remotely cold.

"But what if there were?" I asked, sliding just a little bit closer to her, invading the edges of her personal space to see what she would do. The odd color of her hair came into slightly better focus. I could see where the brown roots gradually shifted to orange despite the inconsistent lighting. More importantly, I could see the steady pulse of her heartbeat keeping time along the curve of her neck, where pale skin disappeared into the collar of her shirt. At least it was open, flashing a hint of a bra strap whenever she'd lean forward. Brown, to match her eyes, I suppose.

Even more importantly, with the closeness I could smell her. Body wash and deodorant, and enough perfume so as to catch only the slightest scent. Vanilla. A kiss of strawberries. Baby powder in the undercurrents of her skin. And stronger than everything, the invigorating scent of her blood.

There are no vampires indeed.

"What if there were?" I asked again, my voice lowered as though I were speaking only to her.

Her pupils dilated as she turned to look at me, dark and emptier than I'd like. Still, she'd do, for now.

"How did we get on this topic again?" someone else asked, taking a final swig of their lukewarm beer. "What about mummies?"

"Definitely mummies," she said, shaking her head and sending waves of distractingly colored hair my way. If I'd been a step further away it would have been fine, but I was close to her, so very close, and stray dead-ends flicked across my face. It might have tickled, might have merely been a touch of her against my skin. Instead, the dye seemed to react with my flesh like acid, burning through me with an indescribable pain that I dared not show.

I raised my hand, fingers trailing over my cheek to check for blood, for raised welts as though I'd been burned. It reminded me of the times I'd been whipped and beaten for the sin of being me. But those were other lives and other memories and my fingers found nothing but unblemished skin. I smiled through gritted teeth and slid still closer to her, more aware of her scent, her pounding heartbeat and all of that delicious blood. Her pupils widened just a little bit more as she realized how close I was, how my body was between her and everyone else we were talking to, how my hands lingered on my legs, so close to her thighs, exposed and waiting beneath the hem of her skirt.

"There are mummies in the museum," she said, catching her breath on the words.

"No vampires, though," someone else said. "If they were real there'd be at least one in a museum, right?"

"Truth or dare?" our hostess said, breaking into our conversation by plopping herself down on the other side of me, much too close for comfort. Her black hair pressed against me, her shoulder pushing me toward my prey. I scooted closer, my fingers practically resting on the bare white skin of her thigh.

When no one responded, the hostess continued. "What, you're not playing a game all bunched up in the corner?"

I shook my head as someone else answered. "Vampires."

"Vampires?" the hostess asked. "Is that a game?"

I turned my head just enough to share my smile with the girl with the orange hair. She smiled back.

"Would you play?" I asked, my voice a whisper, for her alone.

She laughed again. "Depends on the rules," she said, resting her hand on my fingers where they touched her thigh for just a moment before pushing me away.

I smiled despite the setback. It wasn't, after all, her thigh that interested me.

"Much like truth or dare," I said.

For a few moments she said nothing and just stared at me, eyelids fluttering in time with her heartbeat as she nodded.

I smiled.

Mine, I thought, all mine.

I leaned in toward my prey, letting her hair brush up against me despite the pain. I let my fingers dip back down to her thigh and whispered, the words hissed out through teeth that would never be confused with American Contemporary Dentistry. "Well, maybe more like Russian Roulette, I guess."

Her skin burned beneath my touch, the flesh as soft as velvet and her breath caught somewhere between a gasp and a sigh as my lips brushed against her ear. I smiled as she bit her soft red lips, the scent of her vivid and delicious as I inhaled.

She turned to look at me, her orange hair burning against my cheek with the motion. Her lips moved but no words came out, then she swallowed and tried again.

"Rules?" she asked.

I took a deep breath, letting the subtle fragrance of her blood fill my senses. I matched her smile and leaned closer, blocking out the game of Spin the Bottle going on around us.

"Like Russian Roulette," I said, "except there's no gun, no bullet." I raised my hand from her thigh, trailing fingertips over her skirt, up her torso, between her breasts to finally stop, resting on the flickering pulse of her heart where it beat on the side of her neck.

Her skin still burned, hotter now as I felt the flesh move beneath my fingers with every surge of blood through her body.

I let my smile slowly fade, licking my lips as I moved in even closer. "Instead, I bite you. Right here." I stroked her, petting her neck where the throbbing rhythm called to me. "If there's no such thing as vampires, it'll be nothing more than a bite, like a gun clicking on an empty chamber."

She laughed then, finally understanding the rules, if little else.

"But if vampires exist," I said, moving closer still, "if they're real? Well, the bullet has a sting when it breaks the skin, but they say you never feel the pain."

She trembled, actually trembled, against me. Her body shivered beneath my steady hold on her neck. Still, she didn't move away, didn't run and hide upstairs in the kitchen with the others. She stayed, her burning skin under my fingers, her hair caressing my cheek like chemical whips.

"Want to play?"

Again, she shivered, her body heat spiking with the motion. But she smiled, wide enough for the tip of her pink tongue to brush against those beautiful red lips.

And then she nodded. "Yes."

Nothing else existed, not the music blaring around us, not the hostess engaged in her silly game next to me. Nothing but her submission.

Mine, I thought again, all mine.

"Truth or dare?" she asked me, reaching up to press my hand harder into her neck.

"Truth."

"Are there?" she asked, her voice breaking on the words.

"What?"

"Are there vampires?"

I squeezed, just enough for her to feel it, and her body shook, sliding against me. "Always," I said. "But they don't sparkle."

She swallowed, her neck writhing beneath my fingers, and then leaned in to kiss me. Soft as promised, quick as a heartbeat, the taste of her lingered long after she pulled back.

"Truth or dare?" I asked, my voice nothing but a breath of air against her ear.

"Truth."

"Do you believe?"

Again, she nodded. "Oh, yes," she said, the words little more than a sigh, almost a moan. Her over-heated skin, beating like a drum, pounded against my fingers where I caressed her heartbeat.

"Truth or dare?" she asked, before kissing me once again, just as quickly. The delicious taste of her, the fragrance of her, left me aching with hunger.

"Dare," I said, my lips brushing against her skin, savoring her, ready to devour. Ready to feed.

Her reply, when it finally came, was the sweetest gift of all.

"Bite me."

Mine, all mine.

When I broke the skin, that soft, burning, fragrant skin, I knew she would finally believe. But now, it was far too late.

Music played around us, people danced, kissed, groped. They were nothing. Less than that, they were…insignificant. Her blood was sweeter than honey, sweeter than anything I'd ever tasted. So fresh, so vibrant, so wonderfully alive.

So very sweet.

Until, it wasn't.

Her hair burned against my skin, her skin burning my lips. I felt her smile as she bent down far enough to whisper. "It's garlic," she said. "In the hair dye. Garlic and holy water. Never could get the color quite right."

I tried to move away but she tightened her hold, keeping me trapped within her embrace.

"It's on my skin, too," she whispered.

I struggled to escape but she pressed my lips harder into her neck.

"Drink up," she said. "It's in my blood as well."

The festive Christmas lights blinked on and off as the music faded to silence.

"My sister sends her regards. You really shouldn't have let her bite you. Cleaning up after her is always such a hassle."

Her blood turned to fire inside of me.

"I win," she said, her voice nothing but a whisper.

29. THE HUNTER
K. Trap Jones

The reaction of people as they near death is a funny thing. Most tend to cry and spit out belligerent, incoherent words, but occasionally I come across a good one and will actually have an intellectual conversation with one of my victims. I find it somewhat soothing. I like to play the game; it is really the only reason why I do what I do. I didn't entrap them or make them turn down my dirt road. I didn't have any false signs that misled them into thinking that it was alright to trespass upon my land. I am an honest person who likes to be left alone, but I am also stubborn as hell and appreciate being isolated. I can't be constantly interrupted by travelers who feel that it is okay to drive on my road and come up to my house to ask for directions. It is all about respecting other people's privacy.

About once a week, I hear the sounds of an engine and can see the headlights from the distance. It makes my skin crawl and irritates me like a flea to a dog, but still I wait. They can certainly turn around and try their luck in finding the highway, but most continue to churn up my dirt road with their city tires once they see my porch light. I guess I could turn it off, but where's the fun in that. The intersection just before my land serves as the crossroads. A left sends them back to the highway; a right sends them to me. Bad luck, I guess.

The back roads that wind through the Smoky Mountains can create quite an illusion sometimes with all the peaceful looking scenery and whatnot. It's rather simple; stay on the paved roads and you'll eventually find your way back to the way you came, but these drunken tourists don't know the difference between tar and dirt. That's what brings them to me. Pigeon Forge, Tennessee boomed in tourism over the years. Some say it is the next big Spring Break destination. I see the whole thing as an invasion of people who don't belong here. Stay upon the lighted roads in order to continue your holiday. Venture into the dark and the outcome is quite different.

Just last night as I watched the sun set behind the rolling trees, I became interrupted by the excessive honking of a car horn. The cherry on my cigar illuminated the shotgun that was sitting on my lap. My hound dog, Gizmo was never startled by visitors. His allergies to pine had destroyed all of his natural born hunting senses. He pretty much just slept and shit all day long. From all of the yelling that was happening, the car sure was having fun as I watched the headlights fishtailing down my road. It takes me at least a day or so to smooth over the damn road with a rake. That was always the first thing that boiled my blood. The headlights grew brighter as they approached. I cocked back the shotgun and saw the golden circles of the two buckshot ends reflecting against my cigar. I petted the metal of the smooth double barrels like it was a long lost cat in my lap. The car drove down my driveway and skidded to a stop, producing a large dust cloud that obscured the car's beams of the light. I found their loud radio to be disrespectful to the mountain animals that were trying to sleep, but nothing scarred my mind more than when they opened their doors and the trash of their partying fell out onto my land. I consider myself a somewhat reasonable person, but I should never be pushed; I should never be tempted to become angry.

"Hey you! Do you know where the highway is?" a young man asked in a slur, wearing some kind of fraternity lettered shirt.

There were three of them; two males and a female. All of them were beyond drunk. I remained silent as they babbled and laughed off their intoxication. I noticed the other man walking away, out of the light of the porch.

"Do you speak English? Where…is…the…highway?" he continued to ask, drooling from his mouth.

"Maybe he speaks mountain man?" the girl asked.

"Wait, what? There's mountain language," he replied as they laughed.

My attention was focused on the other guy. I could see him through a small gap between the two people that were standing on my porch. The walking man came to a stop just off into the shadows. With his back to me, he proceeded to unzip his pants and start to piss on my land. My teeth bit down into my cigar. The cherry ignited brighter as I took another toke. A buckshot shredded the guy's chest in front of me and threw him back off of the porch. The girl became splattered with blood as her eyes widened. I rotated the shotgun and swung it like a baseball bat. The wooden handle cracked her skull and snapped her neck as her body slumped down the steps.

The pissing man was still excreting the many beers he had consumed and didn't even hear the shotgun blast over the loud music that was pumping from the car. Gizmo followed me as my boots treaded within the puddles of blood. Damn if that dog didn't stop and take a few gulps. I always knew it wasn't for their sense of smell as to why they were called *bloodhounds*.

Leaning against the car, I waited for the man to finish marking my land as *War Pigs* by *Black Sabbath* came over the radio. Zipping up his pants, he turned around and saw me. I could see the years of a college education summing up the equation within his mind. The corpses of his friends were a tangled mess near the porch and there I was with a shotgun in my hand with a bloody faced dog at my side.

Again, the reaction of some people towards death is a funny thing. His slurred drunken speech combined with his stuttering fear made him appear like he was speaking in tongues. As the Black Sabbath song ended, I decided to allow the DJ of the radio station to decide the man's fate. If it was a classic rock song, then I would extend his life a little longer; maybe a painless death. Anything else would not be as pretty. An advertisement for air conditioning spilled across the airwaves as the man continued to beg for mercy.

Sometimes bad luck just follows people. Some modern day country song came on and made me twitch with disgust. So much so, that my finger pulled the trigger. The last buckshot ripped through his upper chest, sending his body backwards. Gurgling through the holes in his throat, he slithered on the ground within a mixture of blood and dirt. I turned off the car and walked back to my porch where I sat and waited for the man to bleed out. After finishing my cigar, I turned off my porch light. It had been a long day and I didn't feel like having any more visitors.

30. MAGNUM OPUS
Sydney Leigh

Graham slipped quietly through the side entrance and made his way toward Alan's office. Their cars were parked on opposite sides of the building, but there was little reason for either of them to be there at this hour on a holiday weekend. He knew they were together—he could feel it.

And he was right. There was Lexi—sweet, beautiful Lexi—bent over the smooth mahogany of Alan's desk. Alan stood behind her, hands on her shoulders, pulling her back into him in a sickeningly successive rhythm of thrusts. It was the look on his face that made Graham snap right then and there—the way his lips curled up in a lustful smirk of sheer power and vulgar satisfaction—as though it weren't enough that this was the only woman that Graham had ever loved, and a married man was debasing her on his desk.

Alan was still inside of her when Graham brought the crystal paperweight down in a savage arc and fractured it over Alan's skull. Alan staggered backward in shock while Lexi swirled around and faced Graham, her skirt still bunched up around her waist in a shameful display.

"How could you do this to me?!" Graham screamed, and drove the jagged edge of the paperweight into her throat. Her hands flailed and grabbed at his, and her eyes stayed fastened to Graham's until she sank languidly to the floor.

It made Graham sick to see her reach—crawl, even—toward Alan as the life slipped out of her. It was especially pathetic to see that the last thing she understood in this life was that her lover was already dead.

Graham was pleased with the email he composed from Alan's computer.

Dear friends and family,

With much guilt and regret for your understandably poor opinion of us, we have decided that we can no longer live a lie and are running away to spare you the pain and distress our affair will inevitably cause. Please do not try to find us. We truly believe that this is in fact better for everyone in the end. Do what you wish with our belongings.

Graham made a trip back to the office to clean up the blood after bringing the bodies to his museum. Other than the paperweight, nothing had been destroyed. He kept it with him and removed a few personal items from each of their desks just to be on the safe side. When people returned to work on Monday, they'd see both cars in the lot, their keys on their desks, and the email would explain everything. It was a perfect plan.

Since molding the likenesses out of clay was the most arduous step of the process, it didn't take Graham long to cover their bodies with wax. He worked a bit to alter their faces, carving careful lines and curves to fashion a resemblance to their renowned counterparts. He left the eyes, knowing he would have to replace them at some point. But not until he was finished. By Monday morning, they may very well have become the best figures in the museum. Come October, Graham knew his visitors would be happy with the exhibit.

***

"It's nice," Jade said with a smile. "I'm impressed." She sidled up to the figures of Hester Prynne and Arthur Dimmesdale, lifting the fabric of their clothing and tracing the smooth, hard wax on their faces with a delicate finger. Graham feigned interest.

"Are you familiar with Hawthorne?"

"No, he doesn't look familiar to me at all," she answered. "Who's the girl?"

"No," Graham explained, "that's not Hawthorne. That's a character of his, a Puritan minister. And the adulterous whore he got pregnant."

"Wow, really?" She looked a bit shaken. Graham hoped he hadn't blown it. "Well then, how come they're in here, where you live, and not with the others? They don't seem like the kind of people *I'd* want around."

"No," Graham answered, wishing she would just shut the fuck up so he could get on with it. "You're right. I'm just not finished with them yet." He stepped closer and touched her face. "Would it be alright if I kissed you?" Jade blushed.

121

"Yes, I'd like that very much, Graham." He brought his mouth to hers slowly, being as tender as he could be with a woman for whom he felt nothing. She braced her hands against his chest after they kissed. "You know, I've always liked you, Graham. Since the moment we met at that Halloween party, I could just tell that you were special. And I know we never really got a chance to get to know each other, but I was kind of, well, tied up with other things that aren't a problem for me anymore. I feel like I know you, and, well, I hope you don't mind me being so honest. I'm just really glad that you called me. Surprised, but glad."

"I don't mind at all," Graham lied. "And I'm glad I called, too." He kissed her again, harder this time, and felt her body respond under him. It didn't take much. She was more eager than he expected.

"So," he said, stepping back. "How about a drink?" Jade nodded, eyes still closed in rapture from the kiss. "Good. Have you ever had absinthe?" He smiled and motioned for her to sit down. "I think you're going to love it."

An hour later, he was positioning her perfectly over the arm of the couch so that Lexi and Alan had no choice but to watch. He gripped her shoulders gently at first, but she moaned loud enough to warrant a harder grasp. He worked to recreate the same expression he had seen on Alan's face that night. He would show Lexi what that gluttonous pig had turned her into. He would show her what Alan wanted—the only thing that he wanted, unlike Graham. Graham had loved Lexi, and she snubbed him like it was nothing ... all so she could be the other woman for some lowlife prick. Graham pushed harder and faster with every thrust, drove himself deeper and deeper, never taking his eyes off Lexi's until he came—which was precisely when he recalled the tips of his fingers touching the bare inside flesh of her neck for that one, brief, beautiful moment.

While Graham slept, Jade lit a candle and picked up a book from the coffee table. The pictures and words on the pages seemed to fuse together, and she liked it. She sipped the last of the sweet green spirit swirled with opaline clouds in her glass and listened to the soft rhythm of Graham's breath. She wasn't sure how much time had passed when she placed her head on his shoulder, became one with his skin, with his scent, with his breath, with him—and felt herself fading away, swimming through a sea of euphoric warmth, to find him somewhere in his dreams.

She woke with a sour taste on her tongue and sat up to make sense
of what she was seeing. Long, rippling flames danced on the clothing
of the two life-sized wax figures, stretching all the way from the
leather of their shoes to the collars around their necks. The fire coiled
in serpentine waves and licked at the hair on the heads; and for several
moments, Jade was seduced by the inexorable beauty of it all. She
looked on in awe as the wax began to melt and soften, falling away
from what it covered like liquid silk. She looked on as two faces
gradually appeared from under the rendering flux.

She rose with a start and screamed, but no sound escaped her lips.
Beyond the blazing crackle and hiss, there was only the sharp thud of a
heavy object which slid from the softening wax that sheathed Lexi
Taylor's dead body. Jade leaned down and retrieved a broken crystal
piece of the Scarlet letter which branded the dead woman, the cheating
bitch who had run off with her husband, Alan—but was instead here,
in a death stance beside him in a pyre of sin and guilt, murdered and
enshrined by the one man she had been hoping to seduce all this time.

Jade was prepared to kill Alan to be with Graham—had been
carefully planning it since the night she set eyes on the only man, she
knew in that instant, she'd ever really loved. In the days that followed
the party, Jade had followed Graham. Days turned into weeks, weeks
turned into months, and Jade became more and more certain each time
she watched him from the cloak of darkness that she and Graham were
meant to be together. Alan was the only thing standing in her way. But
he had saved her the trouble of solving that problem by running off
with Lexi. Jade then had Graham all to herself. It was the perfect plan.

She knew now, though, that Graham had betrayed her for that
bitch, and ruined everything—ruined her perfect plan for them to be
together at last.

***

Graham jumped from the couch and lunged toward Jade as she
reeled around and thrust the jagged shard of Alan's paperweight
upwards, burying it deep into the supple flesh of his throat.

"How could you do this to me?!" she screamed. Graham's hands
flailed and grabbed at hers, and his eyes stayed fastened to Jade's until
he sank languidly to the floor.

It made Jade sick to see him reach—crawl, even—toward Lexi's
flame-cloaked body as the life slipped out of him. It was especially
pathetic to see that the last thing he understood in this life was that his
lover was already dead.

123

31. WHY THEY TAKE FIFTEEN BLOOD SAMPLES
C.L. Hesser

Thomas J. Harvey Asylum and Reformatory
A mental hospital, he thought. The loony bin. I guess I'm here at last.

He shuffled along behind his mom as she rolled up to the front desk in her squealing spiked-metal wheelchair; her hair stuck up in points, filthy red. Michael rubbed a knuckle into one eye and shifted his weight from one foot to the other while the sweet little receptionist-nurse eyed him warily.

His mother filled out consent forms, and kept her eyes steadily on the crisp, cream-colored sheets. The nurse wore a white cap strapped firmly to her scalp, with the hospital's insignia printed on the front. Her hair looked like rippling black water, smooth against her neck and shoulders. He had always imagined nurses as ancient crones, silver hair tied back in stiff knots at the tops of their skulls, but this one was slim and young, with voluptuous breasts practically spilling out of her uniform.

The doctors would see him soon. They could go through the check-in process. Some shit like that - he didn't pay much attention to his mother's discussion with the receptionist.

Michael looked about the looming front room, the corridors stretching out in three directions from where he stood, and the click of his mother's wheels as she scratched back and forth on the tile. The nurse began scratching at the base of her scalp, and her fingers came away powdered with white flakes.

A few patients milled around at the end of one of the hallways, while an orderly-type and two nurses crowding them together.

Someone had painted the opposite wall a sickening creamy yellow, like the color of vomit if you had gotten sick after ingesting only milk. Michael watched as the nurse rifled through the papers and filed them away in one of the desk drawers.

He shuffled around and glanced again toward the group of inpatients. One of them looked back at him and winked, a massive woman who appeared to be in her late twenties. Her girth exceeded the height of a ten-year-old child.

He moved back to his mother and gripped her shoulder in a steely vice, causing her to both flinch and cry out. The nurse raised an eyebrow and eyed them curiously.

One of the doctors had arrived just as his mother had begun to leave – her bus waited outside. The doctor looked oddly out of place, dark hair combed back from a high forehead, strong jaw and olive skin. Far too handsome for an institution of the forsaken.

Michael looked at him warily, and the doctor muttered something to the nurse, who took out the forms and handed them over. The doctor leaned in and spoke quietly to his mother and then assisted her to the privacy of an office nearby.

Michael slumped down in the waiting area where the nurse motioned apathetically to the magazines, before sliding the glass window abruptly closed. He picked the first one from the top of the pile and began to flip the pages. Slimy stickers were on the front cover. Painted girls with milky skin, long necks and straight backs. Glossy hair in an abundance of shades, ranging from silky black to alarming crimson.

The doctor returned momentarily and Michael saw his mother rolling immediately for the front door - she hadn't said good-bye to him or wished him well for his stay. He felt the urge to break down but that would only proclaim his weakness and condemn him to further scrutiny.

The swarthy-skinned doctor took his hand and led him into the office.

Was this the usual check-in routine?

The nurse reclined her receptionist's chair until the back tapped against the swatch of chipping yellow paint.

The office was an eclectic mix of neo-Victorian and old-world barbarity. Michael took a seat on a wide sedan type of couch while the doctor sat across from him in a rolling armchair. He propped his elbows up on the mahogany desk and eyed Michael with his piercing dark eyes.

Michael squirmed, and waited in silence until the doctor reached for the forms and unclasped his pen. "So," he said. "There's been some trouble at your home, young man."

No reply.

"A mutilated cat found inside your bedroom."

Michael nodded.

"And you've been experiencing… hallucinations. Auditory hallucinations. Yes?"

"Yes, sir." A weird chill skittered up his spine and made him shiver involuntarily. He shuddered under the doctor's fierce gaze and yanked down his shirtsleeves, so as to cover the crisscross of white scars upon his left wrist and forearm.

The doctor leaned forward just a tad and looked sternly into Michael's eyes. The boy shrank away from him and instinctively turned and began to stand. He then heard a click as the locking mechanism of the door was engaged. Now the only light in the room came in through the slits of closed venetian blinds that hung in the window.

The doctor stood, and his shining fingernails clacked against the desktop. He crossed to the front of the desk, and his spit-polished shoes gleamed black against the deep red of the oriental carpet. The splinters of sunlight glinted off a chain at his neck, and something that hung from it, against his throat beneath his vintage suit.

Michael's eyes flashed wildly as the man leaned over him creepily, holding that expression of wit and malevolence, his countenance perfectly poised.

"You're about seventeen," he said, and his voice was little more than a hoarse whisper that shot through the room like the rumbling of thunder.

"Yes, sir." *Seventeen in April.*

The doctor nodded, and his eyes shone darkly. There was something clasped within one of his fists that Michael hadn't noticed before. "So young," said the man. "You know," he said. "When I picture an angel - a cherubim - I don't picture a round baby with a harp and wings the size of palms." He paused for effect. "I picture something like you."

Something - not someone, something. Michael's uneasiness heightened. The thing in the doctor's hand flashed again in a needle-point of sunlight. Metallic, long, and sharp as a surgical scalpel. The man bent so low and close to Michael that their lips nearly brushed. Suddenly the thing glinted more clearly in the light - a straight razor with pearl handle. Michael caught only the slightest glimpse of it before it slashed deeply in the side of his throat.

He gurgled and clawed at his neck when the man leaned in and licked his tongue against the wound; he clutched the still-struggling boy to his chest and slurped at the gushing blood, wallowing in the stench and the heat. A flow of coppery red washed over his lips and chin, sloshing over the boy's heaving chest. Michael's body fell limply at last, his fingers still trying vainly to push away the doctor's blood-slippery mouth.

His vision went black in great dark waves, as the doctor held the dying body, breathing heavily and still swallowing those final surges of purplish-scarlet blood.

He sat back on the carpet with Michael's chilling corpse still in his arms. Michael's bones jutted against his leg, and that painfully beautiful face had gone ashen and white already. The nurse, minutes later, came in and ordered the resident janitor to begin cleaning the room after removing the body. The handsome doctor clung to it maniacally for a few moments, until the nurse and janitor where able to pull it free.

32. THE LAST STRAW
Vince Liberato

After we set the scarecrow on fire, its mouth twisted into a scream, and a noise unlike any we had heard before filled the air.

It wasn't like the sounds that people or animals make when in pain. It was a sound that made my teeth hurt, almost like the noise wasn't coming from the outside, but from inside of me.

When we approached it, Katrina and I were on guard, keeping the gasoline and matches behind our backs while we crept through the cornfield where it was strung up. I had gone first and soaked it from behind, from the post it was tied to all the way up to the old cowboy hat it wore. I did it quickly for many reasons, but the biggest being because I was too frightened to look it in the face. Then I ran away as fast I could, pouring a long stream of gasoline upon the ground as I fled.

Katrina didn't bother getting any closer than she had to. She just dropped the lit book of matches when the gas trail passed her. The effect was instant.

It didn't know that we'd discovered it had killed Tandi, Seth, Hoss, and all the cattle we'd sent out to graze. We had seen it alive the night before as it prowled. It moved in a jerky and circular amble, like a drunk trying to dance and walk a straight line all at once. One leg would lurch and twitch, striding way too far, and then the other took only a tiny step. It would wobble and then an arm was used to regain balance and close the distance. Each new step would begin as unpredictably as it ended.

That night Katrina and I watched it amble back to the corn fields below us, as we hid up in the barn. When it disappeared from view along the horizon, we had gone to the house and found that both Tandi and Seth had been strangled in their bed. There were bits of straw left behind, wrapped tightly around the swollen arteries of their necks. Katrina and I stayed up that night, armed with a pitchfork and shotgun, just in case it planned to return for us.

This morning, when the sun rose, we were alive and had not been attacked. Everything that had been happening at the ranch came together in our minds. It had started just two days ago with our dead cows out in the open field. It must have taken its time with them, because the entire heart had been ripped from throat to stomach, and all organs pulled out of their chest cavities. When Seth, the ranch's owner saw them, he said it was trespassers or coyotes that were responsible. The rest of us didn't think so. Those damn cows were cut up in a way I had never seen coyotes or even people do to another living creature before. Hoss and Seth argued about it for a bit, Hoss claiming it was the new grass Seth was using, and Seth blaming and then threatening the moonshiners that Hoss visited often and owed a debt to.

When the arguing ceased, the sheriff was notified. With the loss of the cattle, Katrina and I were to tend to the corn, and Hoss was to head out in the pasture, cut the grass, and bale it into hay for the new cows that Seth had to buy.

Then yesterday afternoon, Hoss too was dead. He had been pulled under the tractor and shredded into pieces. Even though it was an old 50's model without the safeties of the newer ones, there was no way Hoss could've found a way to get himself beneath it. Seth, when he was calm enough to, phoned the sheriff again. A deputy picked up and said that he would be by after finishing with the situation at Old Man Kimball's.

The sheriff had gone over to tell Kimball to cut the grass at his property lest he risk a citation, but when he got there, Kimball was dead. He didn't tell Seth exactly what had happened, but he let on that it was messy and that they'd be cleaning Kimball up for a while.

And it was last night when Katrina and I had watched our scarecrow escape as we hid perched out in the loft. Before that, we were helping ourselves to Hoss's moonshine that he kept hidden in the barn. Maybe if we had been in the house, Seth and Tandi would still be alive. Or more likely, the scarecrow would have gotten us too. Either way, we struck first and burned it to ashes. It shrieked and flailed its arms for a few moments, and then surprisingly, that was it. We had killed it before it could get to us.

"Funny thing," Katrina said while we walked back to the house. We expected the sheriff any moment now, especially with the smoke and blaze.

"What? The living scarecrow?"

"Yeah, dummy. That," she said. "You notice the scarecrow ain't had any blood on it? You'd think that it would have, at least something from killing them cows."

"Right," I said. "And how do you think that thing managed to pull Hoss off and throw him under the mower? Hoss'd see that thing coming and run it over - or run like hell himself. Thing wasn't moving that fast last night, so I don't think there was any way Hoss'd get caught unaware. Plus, it was daytime and the field's far away from the cornfield where we had it strung up."

"But it did get Tandi and Seth," Katrina added, "So I imagine the scarecrow at the very least had some strength in it, even if it was slow..." she paused. "Here comes the sheriff. Looks like he's gonna cut through the pasture again." At that moment the police car turned off the dirt road and started driving towards us over the field.

"I guess it was that new blend the county's been using for hay that Hoss hated so much," I told her. "Even so, it seems a little hard to believe a little bit of straw stuffed in a sack could come alive and kill anything, especially when the cows and Hoss weren't even near the scarecrow's spot in the cornfield. I just hope we can convince the sheriff that…"

The sound of crashing metal filled the air, as the grass in the pasture stiffened into tendrils. The sheriff's squad car was stopped instantly and was then pulled apart as the grass tore it, and everyone inside, to pieces.

We could only watch in horror. When it had finished, the grass pasture flattened back out and let out a long, contented sigh.

33. BEAUTY'S END
Shaun Avery

"So why'd you do it?" the detective asks.

His eyes meet mine.

"Why'd you kill all those people?"

We're in an interrogation room, and he's looking at me across a table, on which a bulky-looking folder lies. They caught me at the scene of my last kill and they patted me down before they took me in, but they've not realized that they didn't find something on me that they really should have found.

I stare back at the detective.

And you know, it's funny – I really want to tell him. I want oh so badly to tell someone who, due to circumstance, at least might pretend to believe me. But I can't quite bring myself to say it. Not yet, at least.

So instead I ask, "Why do you think?"

But he's already shaking his head.

"I'm not here to play mind games with you," he tells me, and I find myself strangely pleased with his honesty. "Fact is," he goes on, "we caught you in the act tonight. You match descriptions we've been given from a shit-load of witnesses. And I'm pretty sure your fingerprints are going to match ones we've found at…" – and here the professional mask slips and a sliver of disgust passes across his face – "…the other scenes."

"Interesting," I reply, smiling slightly despite the situation. "Why do you think I allowed fingerprints to be left behind, Detective?"

And I wait for a reply.

But like he's already told me . . .

He's not playing these mind games.

So I sigh.

A little theatrically, but what the hell.

Then I say:

"I wanted to be caught."

I stifle a sob.

Remembering what I saw.

What led me to this moment.

"I needed to be caught."

Our eyes meet once more.

"So that I was no longer part of the problem."

"Problem?" he replies.

Sounding a little bit more interested now.

"Yes," I say. "Problem."

Then a silence descends.

Until I say, "by now, you know what I used to be, don't you?"

He pulls a sheet of paper from the file upon the table and glances at it. A showbiz move, to be sure; he must already know everything there is to know about me. Nevertheless, he speaks as if reciting from the file as he says, "a psychic." He looks back up at me. "So you called yourself, at least."

"Not just what I called myself," I tell him. "What I was."

"There much money in that?" he asks.

I don't answer him, at first.

Instead I'm thinking.

Remembering.

There had been enough money, that I can tell you. It wasn't for financial reasons that I took a mental trip into the future that day, the day all of this began. No, I was chasing the thrill that looking into the future can bring you. The satisfaction of knowing stuff that no one else did.

Only this time, it backfired on me.

When we think of how civilization dies, how beauty ends, we think of nuclear wars, of explosions. But what I saw in that vision, though a bang of sorts, was quite different to that. Rather than seeing a species ending, I saw a species that would not end, that refused to end. I saw a vast orgy of flesh, person upon person, the population of this earth now grown so large that there was no room for anything else. I saw columns of people, one atop the other, reaching up towards the sky, skin skyscrapers. I saw a race whose intellect had long since disappeared, now concerned only with creating further human life, all chance of extinction washed away in a sea of sex. And they were still rutting as the vision faded and I returned to the present.

I came back a different man, though.

One who knew that something needed to be done to prevent this future from taking place.

At first I tried to stop everyone I knew from having sex.

I barged into their rooms when they were trying to get it on.

I got a few punches in the mouth.

But I persevered.

I tried to be celibate.

But I still lusted after women.

So I took care of that.

Then I started killing.

Trying to whittle down the numbers before we were out of time.

As if sensing my thoughts, or maybe just uncomfortable with the silence I have lapsed into, the detective says, "fifty people you killed." He smiles. "It'll be the needle for you."

"I hope so," I say.

And I do.

See, alive, I could still contribute to that dark future I glimpsed. I could adopt. My adopted kids could go on to breed. And all my murderous work would have been for nothing.

That's when the detective stands.

I look up at him.

"Your officers," I say, "missed something when they frisked me."

"Nice try," he replies. "But you're not packing a weapon."

"No," I say. "I'm not."

And I pull down my trousers and show him.

"Did this when I realized I still felt lust," I tell him, as he looks in disgust at the display of scars and stitches that my groin area has become. "Can't pollute the future with offspring if I cut off my equipment, can I?"

And as the guards come in to drag me away for lockup before trial and execution, I decide that you really can't fault logic like that.

Marc Shapiro

Janet gave her pantyhose the final tug that anchored them to her waist. No wrinkles. No sagging. Just right. She snapped the elastic around her firm stomach for good luck.

Turning as double jointed as her 32 year old body would allow, she secured the final snap on 'Old Reliable', a push up, cleavage exploding double D enhancement brazier guaranteed to make a mountain of her admitted molehill.

Janet checked out the apparatus while peering into her floor-to-ceiling mirror and sighed. She really did not want to go out tonight. A typical day at Henderson, Jones and whatever that third name was had given her a yearning for a hot tub and something 50 Shades of trashy. But there were other emotions to contend with.

Fred, the over-aged corporate raider from accounting who had rubbed against her in the elevator, had not seemed quite so insufferable. And she had not minded when Drexel, the only human being she knew whose presence suggested the demeanor of a sea slug, had asked her breasts to take dictation. Janet zipped herself into a red leather skirt so tight and short that it defied her to do anything but breathe. There was no need to ask the question. She already knew the answer.

She was horny. Down in the mud rutting like a pig horny. She wanted something male in her so badly that it took all her will power to keep her fingers from roaming.

"Yeah, Mr. Right," she chuckled as she passed a brush through her hair. "All I want tonight is Mr. Right Now."

The sign flashed 'Meat Market' in tacky yellow and orange bursts. The sign said it all. Walk on by if you're looking for the white picket fence, 2.1 kids and happily ever after. But if pulsating, no strings attached lust is what you crave…, well don't let the door hit you on the way in. Janet stepped inside with confidence, and once inside, discovered that her preconceived notion was right on.

The band was spitting out Foreigner, Bon Jovi and Mötley Crüe as part of their mating dance card. The dance floor, a postage stamp blinking on and off to a flimsy strobe, was packed with the expected suits, skirts and tight jeans doing variations of the bump and grind.

Janet did not see much in the way of competition as she bobbed and weaved through the throng. Secretaries, divorcees, happy hour leftovers, all looking for love or what passed for it. Add to that equation, Janet, a slut among sluts looking for Big Ten Inch.

And then there were the men.

As she dipped to avoid a full tray and an uneasy waitress, Janet found that the pickings were particularly slim.

"Hey baby!" yelled an in-his-cups suit that, odds on, represented the legal profession. "I could be a fool for your stockings!"

Janet was not that desperate. But a little target practice never hurt. "Word on the street is that you sleep with your mother." The scumbag took it the right way and laughed. Janet moved on and into another landmine.

"Hey doll! I've got something you want," roared a creature with a nose so big and so red that Rudolph would ask for best two out of three. Janet bent down so she could lob this grenade face to face.

"And your wife says it's only two inches long."

Janet made the sanctuary of the bar. She sat down and crossed her legs high. The bait was in place. The trap was set.

She stared absently down the bar as the bartender shuffled in her direction. They usually came in two sizes. Stud from Chippendales or Phil from Murphy Brown. Tonight it was Phil. She hoped it wasn't an omen.

"I'll have a…" she started but was confronted by a Scotch Rocks being placed in front of her.

"I didn't order this."

"I know," said Phil. "He did."

She followed his thumb, expecting the worst. What she got was the best.

Janet felt her cheeks flush as she stared into the piercing blue eyes. His hair was fashionably long, curly and black. When he smiled a tight pixy grin, Mel Gibson came to mind. When he brushed back a lock of hair, she saw a trace of a very young Sean Connery.

Janet bit her lip. He was too good for this place. He was too good for her. But there he was, sitting alone, motioning her over.

He said his name was Eddie. Janet didn't care what his name was. He could be Gertrude tonight as long as he delivered the goods.

Things happened fast in a place like the 'Meat Market'. Eddie's eyes instantly broadcast 'between the sheets by midnight' with their hot azure. But, as they danced a raw yet sophisticated counter to the primitive hop going on around them, she had the distinct feeling that she was being courted rather than hustled.

"He's not trying to screw me through my clothes," she mentally calculated as they danced their seductive game of foreplay. "He gets points for that."

"So that's the whole story," demurred Janet as they hit the pits for big drinks and small talk. "My Bob was a very lucky guy…for a while."

"I know the feeling," said Eddie, his eyes locked onto hers. "Mine was a Barbara and she was a slut pure and simple."

They laughed. His hand found hers under the table. Janet immediately went damp in a very private place. Janet blinked and swallowed hard. They both had one thing on their minds and it wasn't how much to leave in the collection plate on Sunday.

"Check please," whispered Eddie.

The next 20 minutes were a blur. The drive back to her place bathed in a full moon just coming into view. Fiddling with the security lock on her building and finally setting the chain lock inside her door as an added, maybe superstitious, addition to the already set deadbolt. Giddy as a school girl, she turned to face Eddie whose stature had seemingly magnified in the half-light of her apartment.

"Those eyes!" her mind and body screamed in unison. "Those damned eyes!"

They embraced and kissed, their tongues shaking hands and exploring those wonderful places where passion dwells. Janet broke away.

"No ground rules," she gasped. "No strings. No promises we can't keep."

Foreplay, with its careful undressing, fondling and caressing, was less stone age than Romeo & Juliet and paved the way for the sexual explosions as his manhood found her inviting and ultimately shook her as the orgasms came and came…

Janet rolled violently with each climax and rush of ecstasy. The nips at her breasts, which had earlier been sweet, had suddenly turned savage. His thrusts more primitive and deep. It was beginning to hurt. But God! It hurt so good!

The bed springs fell silent as animal lust gave way to deep sleep.

A drop of something fell through space and splashed on Janet's cheek. Another drop followed. Janet reached out, slapped at the damp spot and returned to the other side of slumber. Drops, like patterned rain, continued to fall, at last bringing her to full consciousness. She looked at her hand and saw blood. She looked up.

And screamed.

A bloody pentagram on a human palm was dripping into Janet's face. An animal cry widened her view as she lay a terrified witness to the transformation.

Eddie's body was in a whirling, convulsive state. His back buckled, cracked and fractured as bones began to break and realign into something more animal than human. Arms and legs lengthened. Muscles shrank and shaped themselves into monstrous sleekness. Razor sharp talons burst, bathed in blood, from fingers and toes.

The thing's agonized dance cut a destructive swath through the bedroom; knocking over and destroying in a frenzy of primitive pain and anger. The thing howled as its jaw grew swollen and distorted, jutting out in seemingly impossible proportions. Teeth were pushed onto the floor by protruding fangs and, in a final atrocity, black, coarse rivets of fur pushed outward from every pore.

Janet's terror had transformed into a state of resignation. She cowered amidst her nakedness as the creature towered over her. Her hands covered her face in a futile attempt to ward off the demon's sudden charging motion that would most certainly delivery a mortal blow.

But the thing, in mid charge, stopped abruptly. Its growls were still ferocious but less assured. Its eyes, those goddamned eyes, bugged out in a way that reflected confusion rather than rage.

Confusion at the sight of a bleeding pentagram appearing on Janet's palm.

Janet screamed in horror at the spreading red pattern and brought her hands up in a reflexive move that smeared a gore streaked mask across her face. The wrenching staccato of bones cracking and reshaping beat a tattoo upon her eardrums and drew a half human, half animalistic wail from her throat. Her mind screamed as the final remnant of her humanity slipped from the land of the living to permanent residence within the dark side. Her transformation was not the easy methodical thing that Eddie's had been. The elements of unpredictability that composed the female being had instinctively rebelled, and the results were misshapen and malformed limbs. But the malevolent power would not yield, and again the tissues proceeded with another attempt at the intended monstrous anatomy.

The monster that was Eddie backed into a corner, tail tucked between its legs; a nightmarish observer to Janet's stepping over to the other side. It growled mild defiance but was content to watch silently, eyes glistening and tongue lolling to one side.

White fur emerged from Janet's body.

The creature that had been Janet collapsed to the floor, panting and emitting muffled whimpering sounds. It looked foggily around and at the Eddie-thing that had risen up, and now walked cautiously toward her. There was nothing human left in Janet to evaluate the situation. But her new animal instinct told her that there was nothing to fear.

It sniffed her from every possible angle and gazed into her eyes. The growls grew tender as it nuzzled and licked her. The she-beast was unsure but responded in kind.

It mounted her.

The sun came up on a very naked, and once again, very human Janet. She surveyed the damage and contemplated what exactly had transpired the night before. The last vestige of the pentagram faded into her palm.

"What were the odds?" Janet thought. She had always known there were others. In fact it was a bite on a night like this that had turned her all those years ago. She had struggled for years to come to terms with being a creature of the night. How to control it? How to get through the day? And, deep down in her soul, how to address the very human needs that now shared their existence with those of a monster.

Hooking up with a thing like herself? What were the odds?

A rustling amid the wreckage across the room indicated that Eddie was also coming out of the night. He was Gibson and Connery again. Janet looked deep into his eyes and saw something that cut through the confusion and the fear, that all of those who had become demons doomed to walk the earth, shared. Mirrored in those eyes was the memory of the night they made love…

…Like animals do.

35. STILTSKIN
Justin Hunter

Yves picked up the skeletal frailness of his mother and placed her on the freshly laid straw mattress of her bed. He gently lifted her head and placed a down-filled pillow under her head and drew a quilt up to her neckline. He ran his large, gentle hand through his mother's hair until her eyes closed, and she fell into the rhythmic breathing of sleep. He stood slowly and silently gazed upon his wizened, aged mother. Yves was scared to make any sound lest she wake and begin the terrible verbal quavering of the living nightmare that plagued their existence. Her weak uproars had increased of late, which could mean only one thing.

"Impossible," Yves said softly. "We've come so far. We are at the farthest reaches of the kingdom. Nobody knows we're here."

They were living in an impish one-room hunter's cabin deep in the woods, barely within reach of the boundaries of the kingdom. The risk of straying out of the lawfully ruled lands of the king was almost as daring as staying inside of them. Residing there made Yves feel like he was in the grip of the purgatory of indecisiveness. There was no safety. There was nowhere left to run to.

Yves placed a weary and loving hand on his mother's shoulder, taking the chance of waking her. The reassurance he was trying to give by his touch was useless to the lightly slumbering woman. It was his own reassurance he was looking for. Something a mother was supposed to provide, but time steals as much as it gives. His mother had gone beyond the ability for compassion and knew nothing but fear. Her feelings of fear were not for herself, just as they weren't for anyone else. Her fear encompassed her.

Yves took his hand away from his mother's shoulder when her pale hand shot up from the bed and gripped his wrist in a grasp fervent, unexpected and surprising in its strength. Her yellowed eyes opened and looked into Yves' and beyond. Her lower jaw slackened, revealing the perfection of her white teeth.

"He's here," she said. Her thin voice floated up like the dying sparks of a fire.

"There is no way he could find us."

"You have to hide," she said. Yves tried to shake her grip on his wrist. She held fast. Pain ran up his arm from the bite of her fingernails in his flesh.

"We are safe here," Yves said.

Through the open oval window next to the door, the sound of soft laughter drifted along the wind in the darkness.

"Hide." His mother let go of Yves' wrist.

He looked to the window to see the gray, grizzled face of a small man staring back at him. Two gnarled and hairy hands held tightly to the sill as the creature pulled itself up in order to see. Its face looked to have been split in twain, yet mended by hemp rope that was sewn raggedly into the skin and pulled taut. The work was crude and crooked. Its flesh appeared to have healed and re-torn several times. Some lines were pithed scars where others still wept pus and blood. The little man smiled. Broken teeth ran along a misshapen jaw line making the smile almost a look of dumb awe.

He spoke. His words came out wetly and garbled. Saliva dripped from his mouth as his sewn tongue formed words which sent icy fear stabbing up Yves' spine.

The forest is always alive and awake
Nothing can hide forever
By scent and sound and scratch of nail
I, with my whole self severed

I scraped and clawed to find you here
Over miles of woods and vale
Eating rats and snakes and things less nice,
that writhe underneath the shale
A promise was made that saved a life,
and with a life was bought
I will have. I will take. I will make it mine.
Payment for a promise is sought

The little man climbed through the window and dropped nimbly to the floor. Yves' mother sat up in her bed. She shook violently and clutched her blanket close. The dwarf gave her a withering glance as he made a slight bow.

"I saw you die," Yves' mother said. "I saw you plunge into the fiery hell beneath the straw chamber floor. I saw you tear yourself asunder."

The little man grimaced. A long trail of saliva dropped to the floor from his gaping mouth. He spoke.

I am still here and I always will be
No matter how long the sands of time flow
You, my dear queen, of all who dwell in this land
shouldn't be so surprised – I can sew

Yves tried to move, but was spellbound by the little man who limped lightly toward him. Yves measured three times the dwarf's size in height and weight, but found himself helpless under the stare of the little man's red eyes. The imp walked directly up to Yves. He touched Yves on the knee and turned his horrific visage upwards and faced the man. Yves felt like he did when regarded by his father. The look was a mixture of love and compassion, mixed with the yearning the old always feel when faced with youth. The knowledge that time gone can never be replaced. The relentless ticking of seconds making quick way to hours, months and years. The little man spoke.

Mine

He produced a small olive-green sack, no larger than the satchel Yves wore that carried his tackle while fishing. The little man lifted Yves into the air. Yves tried to scream, but found his lungs held no air to make a sound. The unreality of being lifted so easily by one so small was obscured by being stuffed viciously into the small sack. There was no way he could fit into such a small space, but Yves found that he did, with room to spare.

His mother watched Rumpelstiltskin flip the small, now full, bag over his diminutive shoulder. He turned to face her. His efforts had torn a flap of skin from his face away from a strand of hemp. Blood dripped down his chin and onto the dirt floor of the cabin. He spoke.

The debt is now paid. I have what is owed
Now I shall take my leave
A wager won by trick is not true won
I will leave you alone to bereave.

The little man leapt out of the oval window, into the darkness and was gone.

The mother lay back upon the bed. She was alone. She always knew she would be alone one day. She knew they couldn't escape forever. Her fear was now realized. In this terrible moment, she felt something she didn't expect. She felt peace.

36. BABY HANDS
Rebecca Fung

The woman finished playing her song with a flourish. Patrons began to cheer. She nodded. Gone were the days when she would blush. Applause was routine. A pleasant routine, but a routine nonetheless.

Alvin rushed to sit down next to her at the bar.

"You were really good," he said, and then realized how inadequate that was. She was not really good, she had been astounding. He had truly felt transported to another world when her fingers touched the piano keys. It was the kind of playing you expected to pay hundreds of dollars to hear at a piano concert in a prestigious theatre, not from some hotel player.

The woman laid her hands on the bench. Both hands were beautiful, the skin was smooth and the fingers neatly shaped. Tiny hands, compared with the rest of her body. They were more the hands of a little girl than a woman. Her entire hand, outstretched, could fit on the palm of his own, and her fingertips would not even reach the base of his own fingers.

"It's all in the hands," she said.

"You have very petite hands," he said. "You could play anywhere! Why do you play at a little hotel like this?"

"Good piano playing hands," she said. "I play here because it reminds me of a very special night."

*****

The little girl finished playing her song with a flourish. The room erupted with applause. No one had heard such music before. But tonight they were being treated to a concert by a girl who was barely eight years old. She looked up at the crowd, and at her dear father, who sat in the front row. He accompanied her everywhere, and clapped loudest of all.

"Another, my sweetheart!" he cried. She nodded, and set her tiny fingers on the keys of the piano. Her fingers danced across the keys; they knew how to coax the very best from this piano. Audible sighs of pleasure arose from the crowd.

There was one person in the room who didn't applaud. Little Veronica Page scowled and screamed at her Daddy to buy her another creaming soda and a plate of chips.

"Coming right up, sweetheart," said Mr. Page, and pulled out the fat wallet that satisfied all of Veronica's whims and demands. "Daddy loves his princess."

"I want salt and NO PEPPER and LOTS OF TOMATO SAUCE! Daddy!" screamed Veronica. She kicked the table in front of her and ruined the red buckled boots her father had just bought her.

"Veronica, listen to the lovely music. Hasn't Daddy done you a big favor, letting you stay up way past your bedtime? Shouldn't you give Daddy a big smile?"

Veronica scowled. She might be the only child in the room except for the girl who played the piano, but that didn't appease her. *Except for the girl at the piano*. She pouted. She had thought staying up late would be special, and now some other girl was doing exactly the same, and showing off with piano-playing at the same time!

"I want that music to take home!" screamed Veronica. "You get me that music, Daddy!"

Mr. Page plonked the chips and soda in front of Veronica. "How can I? … All right, Veronica. Daddy will make everything better right now. Don't you worry about that!"

Mr. Page walked up to the father of the prodigy at the piano.

"That's your little girl, isn't it?"

"Yes. Gloria. She's good, huh? She's a genius. Watch those little hands, look how fast she is!"

"Excellent. How much are your daughter's CDs? I want to buy one."

The man shook his head. "Sorry, that's not possible."

"I'll give you much more than they're worth. A hundred bucks. Even two hundred. You can't say no to that. I can tell from your shoes you can't afford it. Sell me one."

"I can't. My daughter hasn't made any CDs," explained the man. "We'd love the money if she had recordings. But she just loves playing here. It's a smaller piano. It works well for a little girl." He waved, and his daughter waved back. Amazingly, she did not even seem to miss a note when she waved, she coordinated her playing so well, and her hand flicked up and down so swiftly. "And she gets free ice cream if she plays here. That's all she really cares about, ice cream! Don't you, darling?"

Gloria grinned. "More ice cream the better." Then her hands romped into a sunny march, contrasting with the moody brilliance of the last piece she'd chosen.

"You get me my music, Daddy!" Veronica Page yelled. She hurled her chips into the air to emphasize her point. "I don't want a stupid CD either! I've got a whole roomful of CDs! I want the music! I want the music any time I want it! Daddy!"

"I've got an idea," said Mr. Page. "What if I said you could make a whole lot of money and your little girl could have all the ice cream she wanted?"

"Sounds like a dream come true, but in my experience, dreams don't happen in real life," said the man.

"Sometimes they do," said Mr. Page. "I've got a big house. With five pianos. How about your little girl comes and lives with my little girl and she can eat all the ice cream she wants there, and play any piano she chooses. I can have it brought in by the truckload. I'll pay you three hundred … no, four hundred dollars every day for that."

The man sat up. "Are you serious? What's the catch?"

"No catch. All your daughter would have to do is play the piano occasionally."

"Not just OCCASIONALLY, whenever I SAY!" roared Veronica. "I want my music HOW I LIKE IT!"

"Yes, precious plum princess," said Mr. Page. "So what do you say, my good fellow? Will your daughter come along?"

"Just my daughter?" asked the man.

"Just your daughter," said Mr. Page. "Any ice cream flavor she wants."

"Any flavor? Oh Father, it sounds wonderful!" cried Gloria.

"I don't know. We do need the money, my whole family needs the money," said the man. "We need Gloria too. We'll miss her. You would look after her? See that she lives comfortably, and goes to school, and …"

"Of course," said Mr. Page. "I've got lots of money. She can have her own bedroom, I don't care. I just want that music."

"I – I'm not sure."

"She'll have everything she could ever dream of," said Mr. Page. "That's what you want for her, isn't it?"

"I want what's best for her, of course," said the man. "And for all my family." He looked at Veronica and Mr. Page, and then at the pile of money Mr. Page was already putting on the table.

The deal was done, and Mr. Page and Veronica walked out of the hotel with Gloria. Gloria gave her father a kiss on the cheek.

"I don't WANT just the music," screeched Veronica as they left. "I want to play piano! I want my hands to play music just like her hands!"

"Now honey precious pot, we can't all be prodigies."

"But I want it! You make it happen, Daddy!"

"Of course, darling adorable perfect pumpkin," said Mr. Page. "Daddy will make sure you get whatever you want." He took one of Gloria's special, beautiful hands. "Ready to start your new life? Then come on."

***

"It must have been difficult for you, to leave your father," said Alvin sympathetically. "But I'm sure he had your best interests at heart. People make tough decisions at times."

The woman looked at him, her brow wrinkled for a moment, and then she gave a quick snort. "Oh. No, I think you've got it wrong."

"Veronica, another drink? On the house?" offered the bartender.

"Wait …" said Alvin. "You're Veronica? But you play – you play like a prodigy – you are amazing!"

He looked down again at her hands. So tiny! Only then did Alvin note not only how small her hands were, but how the smooth pale skin of her hands seemed to be at odds with the darker and more wrinkled skin on the rest of her body.

"I wanted to play like her," said Veronica. "Daddy always said he would do anything, pay any price for anything I wanted. The operation wasn't so bad, at the time. But why didn't anyone tell me they wouldn't grow with the rest of me? I feel cramps in my wrists every day. Daddy shouldn't have done it. I'm a freak because of him and I'm stuck with them!"

"No," said Alvin. He recoiled. The hands that had seemed so beautiful just seconds ago now made him want to slink away. Fine morsels of child's flesh sewn to an adult's limbs. "It's not possible. What happened to the other girl, Gloria?"

"It's all right for her, she can eat ice cream through a straw. Her family sold us the hands without much thought, and now she sits around stuffing her fat face all day. But what about me? It's all Daddy's fault. And now I'm like this forever. Daddy! Daddy?"

37. SPHERA
Robert Friedrich

Life and materiality exist but they are only a fraction of what our minds fully perceive. If we explore deeply enough, we would witness the true nature of reality... no matter how dark those truths would be.

Like the woman who sits alone inside of her small apartment. The TV is on but she pays it no attention. Seemingly nothing can disturb her concentration as she stares at a crack in the wall.

The stillness is broken when her left eyeball twitches and then begins to move in all manner of directions. She screams and breaks the entrancement. With both hands she covers her eyeball and falls from the couch to her knees.

Blood begins to drip upon the carpet, filling the tiny spaces between her fingers. Her breathing grows violent as she scurries about on blood covered hands. More blood falls from her eye as it continues to vibrate and pulse violently. Suddenly her eyeball rips itself from her skull, dislodging itself from the nerve connections and hovers in the air before her. The shocked woman stares in disbelief at the disembodied eyeball that now floats and peers back at her.

The organic composition of the floating tissue begins to disintegrate and fall apart, only to reveal a small, black, metallic sphere. As she tries to focus upon it with her right eye, the sphere begins to rotate. While defying gravity and rotating in the air, the orb increases its velocity. The escalating speed of the orb begins generating a low pitched sound. The spinning intensifies till it emits small, fiery sparks. The force which keeps it spinning has created an invisible vortex in the air.

Pieces of paper and hair pins float toward the swirling air, as the lighter objects in the room are pulled forward. The force continues to grow, as blood from the woman's wound is drawn into the vortex. The fiery sparks increase in occurrence and duration. The ever-increasing speed seems to be without end. The low pitched sound has grown to a crescendo that fills the room.

Instantaneously the sparks form into fiery lashes and begin whipping all contents of the room. The TV is sliced in half; the walls display burn marks, and the woman is marred with deep lacerations on her face and body.

Vast amounts of her blood floats toward the orb which lashes everything that surrounds it. The woman staggers to her feet and tries to run but is whipped repeatedly. She falls after only a few steps as her couch is sliced to pieces. Tears from her right eye are pulled toward the sphere and mix with the spinning blood.

The sphere then ceases its spinning in an instant, and hovers menacingly in silence. The absence of sound induces an almost tangible fear. A new, high pitched sound then terminates the silence, shrieking and echoing mightily. Sparks burst outward in all directions, preceding an explosion of immense force. The force obliterates everything inside the apartment, only the walls, windows and doors remain unaffected. The apartment remains intact; but is now empty and hollow.

Even a crack in the wall endures, as complete silence fills the empty room. Right before another scream echoes from the neighboring apartment.

38. FLYTRAP
Jeani Rector

Aaron saw it, and asked the storekeeper, "What's a plant doing in a pet shop?"

The storekeeper looked like someone from a past century, with a handlebar moustache and a stained apron. "That's a Venus Flytrap. Technically a plant, but it sure seems like an animal to me."

Aaron peered at the plant closely. It was in a small, red clay pot and had a rosette of five leaves that arose from a bulb-like stem. The leaves were green, and looked like they had small claws with red interiors on their tips.

The storekeeper spoke again. "Fascinating little thing, isn't it? Did you know that the trapping mechanism is so specialized that it can distinguish between living prey and raindrops? It won't close its claws on raindrops. But an insect…well now…"

Aaron interrupted. "How much?"

The storekeeper smiled. "Last one left. You can have this baby for only twelve ninety-five."

"I'll take it."

***

He brought the plant home and placed it on the mantle in the living room. Then he realized he forgot to ask the storekeeper about how to take care of it. Did it need sunlight like other plants? Was he supposed to catch flies for it, and if so, would it eat dead flies or be so picky that it only wanted those insects when alive?

He stood beside the fireplace, staring at the plant. Impulsively he stuck his finger into one of the red claws. It immediately closed, but the plant's grip was too slight to matter. He removed his finger and figured that flies weren't as strong as he was and therefore couldn't escape so easily.

He decided to find out more about the Venus Flytrap from the internet. He sat at his computer and googled it.

He read:

The Venus Flytrap is found in nitrogen-and phosphorus-poor environments, such as bogs and wet savannahs. It survives in wet sandy and peaty soils. Venus Flytraps are popular as cultivated plants, but have a reputation for being difficult to grow. Place your plant in a sunny window that faces south. As long as the Venus Flytrap receives four or more hours of direct sunlight in the window, it should do well.

So obviously the dark fireplace mantle was an inappropriate spot. Aaron picked up the little plant and moved it to a windowsill. He felt the dirt inside the red clay pot with his finger and decided it needed water.

Next he went to his back porch where he had a flypaper strip hanging from the awning. He felt revulsion at the sight of so many dead insects, but decided that he was now responsible for the plant, so he reached for the sticky yellow strip and plucked a dead fly from it.

Holding the dead insect by its wings, Aaron thought, *How disgusting.*

He entered his house once again and went to the window. With the fly held delicately by his fingertips, he wondered how to serve it to the plant.

He left the dead fly on the windowsill and went to retrieve a toothpick. Impaling the dead insect upon the tip, he nervously aimed it into one of the claws. He was relieved when the claw clamped shut.

Over time, touching flies no longer disgusted him. As the weeks went by, the Venus Flytrap seemed to be happily growing. So much for the internet's claim that they are difficult plants, he thought.

Then came the day when Aaron went to his porch and saw that there were no flies left on the dangling, sticky yellow strip. He felt panicked. How would he feed his plant? By now it had become a pet to him.

What would draw flies? The answer came to him: Animal waste, particularly that of dogs. But he couldn't go to his neighbor's yard with a shovel. Instead, he took a plastic baggie to the park down the street and was rewarded in his quest there.

He placed a paper towel on his back porch and dumped some dog feces upon it. The smell was overpowering. The sunlight glistened on the mess, and Aaron imagined he could see it steam with the heat.

He watched it for a few minutes, trying to breathe through his mouth, then realized that the flies would alight on the dog shit all right, but how would he actually catch them in mid-flight? Unlike a sticky flypaper strip, here the flies could come and go as they pleased.

He went to the store and bought a butterfly net. Bringing it home, he went back to the porch and was surprised to see what looked like dozens of flies buzzing on and off the dog shit. It was a home run! He swung the net around like a crazy person, and felt jubilant that he captured so many flies with his swings.

He brought his prizes inside, and impaled one of the flies with a toothpick. Fascinated by its struggles, Aaron decided that the fly did not have enough intelligence to realize its situation. It floundered and didn't seem to realize that it was now unable to fly.

He found himself staring at the fly. It must be nutritious for his plant to be growing so well. He watched it move on the end of the toothpick. He wondered if his Venus Flytrap could taste its food. What would a fly taste like?

Although he lived alone in his small house, Aaron glanced furtively over his shoulder. He was possessed with a compulsion so strong that it was impossible to resist.

Slowly he brought the toothpick to his mouth, and stuck out his tongue to taste the fly.

He was startled at the fly's movement; he had never put his tongue on anything in motion before. It was an interesting sensation; it seemed to awaken some primal instinct within himself. The fly tasted metallic, but overall, it was not revolting.

Suddenly ashamed at his own weird behavior, he quickly removed the fly from his tongue and took it to his Flytrap plant. He felt happy that the plant accepted the fly. Aaron imagined that the Venus Flytrap was grateful to him for the treat of a living insect.

***

Aaron was unable to go to work. He couldn't motivate himself to leave the house. He was not surprised when his boss left a voicemail stating he was fired.

By now he was used to the stench. It started when he left the back door to the porch open. The warm summer breeze wafted the smell from the dog feces inside. Eventually Aaron realized that flies also liked garbage, so he got into the habit of never emptying the trash can in the kitchen. It was beginning to overflow, the garbage spilling onto the floor.

And now in the kitchen, he swooped upon his prey with the net. He saw with satisfaction that he had captured probably twenty flies. He held the end of the mesh with his hand, blocking any escape.

He loved the green ones. Not only were they beautiful to look at in all their iridescence, but he savored the buzzing activity they created inside his mouth. He liked to allow them to crawl inside his mouth; the sensation was stimulating. And when he bit into them, they had a slight crunch on the outside and were wet on the inside, so he always ate the green ones first.

39. THE HACKER
Doug Robbins

The moon grimaced from the heavens as a maniacal deviant meandered down the street, carrying in his heart rage, and in his hands he carried an ax. He heard Halloween carolers caroling their spooky songs. He's got an axe oozing with blood and he wears a gas mask too. On Halloween Night he'll come looking for you! Beneath his gas mask he smiled knowing fully well that the song was about him. His birth name was Doug Hacker, but now everyone just called him The Hacker. For ten years he had hid, where, no one knows for sure. But on this night he is ready to kill again just as he had a decade ago.

Within his mind he sees his wife's body even now so many years later. She is nude in the image, and still holds a look of post coitus delight upon her painted whore's face. Her hair was still the same mess; frizzy blonde tresses flowing wayward and unkempt. He had driven that axe so deeply into her cranium that the maniac had seen his wife's broken skull protruding through her forehead.

His wife's lover Ramon had then been strangled with piano wire, and after his corpse fell upon the floor Doug had stood over the body and hacked it into infinite bits. He boiled the flesh in a stew and consumed the minced delicacy. His only regret was adding a bit too much spice to the dish.

Tonight he was heading home to the place where it all began, within the quiet town of Harvest Springs. Nearby a party raged into the night. Resident Amy Gelding was hosting a party. She chugged her beer discretely, as the horny young men tried to get laid, and the party churned around her. As fate would have it, there was a break in the noise as a song ended and the party goers heard three loud knocks upon the door.

Amy staggered toward the front door and peered through the peephole. "Oh God," she groaned. "It's that Freshman Clyde Drummond!"

Portly Jeff Rags pulled up his jeans and said, "Well let's not keep the gentleman waiting."

Amy opened the door and greeted Clyde at the door. The young man wore a long, black cape and dark brown khaki pants, with a white t-shirt beneath a black vest. His thin red hair was slicked back upon the gaunt bones of his head.

Amy wrapped her fingers around Clyde's elbow and pulled him inside. "You're just in time to bob for apples," Amy cheered into his ear.

The partygoers chuckled as Amy blindfolded the oblivious freshman. "Alright on the count of three dive right in," she said. "One two three," the kids cheered in unison.

Clyde dove in face first, into the tub filled with water. He clenched something squishy between his teeth and pulled his face upright from the water. He bit through the object with his teeth, spilling the two end-halves into the water, spitting out the remainder that was in his mouth.

Amy pulled the blindfold from his head and that he saw he had just bobbed for a turd. Clyde ran outside and wretched his guts over the front porch while wiping his hand frantically upon his mouth. After finishing, Clyde climbed to his feet and staggered away demoralized. He hopped on his bike and pedaled away as fast as possible, with a heart that was heavy with anger and humiliation and disgust.

"You'll all be sorry," Clyde screamed over his shoulder, and the sound echoed off into the night.

Javier, Amy's boyfriend arrived carrying a six pack of beer and wearing his letterman jacket. He placed the beer on the kitchen table and walked into the living room where he saw his girlfriend. Javier walked over and approached the girls.

"That was really mean to make that poor kid bob for shit," Margo, Amy's friend lectured. Amy rolled her eyes and Javier chuckled.

"Who bobbed for shit?" Javier asked with a smile.

"Rags shit in a tub and that freshman Clyde Drummond bobbed for it," Amy cackled.

"I bet that was hilarious," Javier said excitedly.

"It was a riot," Amy said.

"It was totally sick and obnoxiously mean," Margo said.

"You know what your problem is Margo?" Javier said. "You need to get laid!"

"You know what your problem is Javier, you're a Mexican," Margo shot back.

"Watch it bitch," Javier snapped.

"Just ignore her Javier," Amy said.

Javier took Amy by the hand and led her upstairs. When in bed they were oblivious to the carnage on the main floor. Margo emerged from the bathroom and found herself surrounded by dead bodies. One partygoer had been decapitated, another nearby, the ribcage and heart pierced by the head of the axe. All of the bodies were horribly hacked and mangled. Their dead eyes were wide and their mouths were twisted into grotesque masks of terror.

The Hacker stood in the center of the carnage covered in blood. Speechless with terror, Margo ran up the stairs and banged upon the bedroom door.

"Open the door! There is a fucking maniac out here trying to kill me!" Margo screamed.

The music in the bedroom was too loud and the sex was too intense for either teen lover to hear their friend's desperate pleas for help. The Hacker buried his axe into the back of the terrified teen severing Margo's spine instantly. Her hand, still pressed against the door, left bloody prints as the hands of the corpse slid down the bedroom door.

After sex, Javier dressed quickly and exited the bedroom. Silently the hacker watched from the shadows as Javier walked to the hallway bathroom. The Hacker charged into the bedroom wielding his axe maniacally above his head. Oh how she screamed, as the madman stormed upon her.

Javier raced into the room throwing his shoulder into the back of the killer. He landed on top of the madman and pinned his hands to the floor. Amy, now filled with adrenaline seized the axe from the floor, and swung it down upon the killer's neck. Doug Hacker's head disengaged from his body, and then died with a frozen smile of malevolent joy.

Both Javier and Amy walked away from the room and the carnage completely shaken. He led her down the stairs and past the bodies, shielding her eyes from the scenes of gore.

"It's over now sweat heart," he assured her, whispering quietly into her ear. Javier put her into the passenger seat of his car, then walked around and started the ignition. Instantaneously a brief crackle could be heard, and the car exploded with both Javier and Amy inside.

From behind a tree Clyde emerged, his face displaying a grin of supreme joy. He walked into the house and entered the bedroom where he found the sprawling corpse of the maniac. He removed the gas mask from the disembodied head, and then pulled the mask over his face. From the floor he picked up the bloody axe, and walked confidently outside.

Clyde gripped the axe within his hands as he ambled down the darkened street. His stare was vacant and his mind raced with thoughts of murder and rage. "I am the Hacker now," thought Clyde. "He lives on in me!"

40. CLICKITY-CLACK
J. T. Seate

She was a little girl alone in the big house. It was late and her mother wasn't home from her weekly dance party. She hummed to drown out the occasional creaks and groans, and tried to convince herself the sounds were merely those of ancient wood and brick settling around her.

Then she heard them coming…slowly…closer…coming up the sidewalk toward the front porch. Muffled voices and shoe heels clickity-clacked on the flagstones as they climbed the steps and crossed the porch to her front door.

"Oh God!" she breathed. She glanced at the solid oak door. It stood ajar for her mother, the entrance blocked only by the fragile screen door, secured with a small hook.

She raced to shut and lock the massive door before they broke down the screen. Before they flooded in and descended upon her.

"No!" she screamed as the screen door ripped away, torn from its hinges.

She pushed on the heavy, carved door with all her strength, pushed against the oncoming horde. She slammed her body against it as hard as she could, pushing desperately as gnarled, twisted fingers curled around its edges.

She couldn't stop them. Couldn't escape. Trapped.

A bony hand grasped her shoulder. Another reached in and wrapped around her neck…and squeezed.

Patricia awoke with a start, her head spinning, exhausted from fighting a gruesome enemy in her last terrifying stages of desolation. *This time they'd almost gotten in.* Her heart pounded; the memory of the dream still vivid and terrifying.

How odd, she thought. This childhood dream haunting her so soon after her mother's passing, as if her mind was saying, "She wasn't there to protect you in your dream, and she's not here now…and she won't be, ever again."

Then she heard a quiet murmur. Not a loitering product of the terrible dream, but something tangible. She sat up, taking slow, quiet breaths. Floorboards groan and old pipes rattle, she told herself. She swung her legs off the bed and listened. No further creaks detected. Suddenly, it seemed almost too quiet, but the murmuring sound had unnerved her, filling her with the kind of dread usually reserved for nightmares like the one she'd just endured. She slid unsteadily out of bed, and walked on tiptoes so the sound from sprung floorboards would be less noisy.

She opened the door to her foreboding walk-in closet and reluctantly peered inside. Everything normal. She unlocked her bedroom door as quietly as possible and looked toward her cavernous living room. The aura of her mother still lingered throughout the old house. That aspect of consciousness could be comforting, but it wasn't her mother whose presence that she sensed.

Patricia peered into the room through the dusky haze of dawn filtering through the shutters. The pieces of furniture looked more like sleeping beasts than utilitarian objects. The gloom stretched across the floor like the residue of former inhabitants. She wondered if something could be hiding along the wall just out of sight, something that would grab hold of her ankle when she ventured close enough.

Nothing seemed out of place. But still, she'd heard the sound—the sigh. There were times, and this was one of them, when her old house seemed to be...*organic.* Unlike the essence of her deceased mother, the house felt like something malevolent.

Patricia heard a slight creak between the living room and dining room, and turned to see the door between the adjoining rooms appear to move on its own. She felt a cold spot where her heart was supposed to be. Dark secrets seemed to cling from every rafter. *Stop it. It's an old, creaky house full of warped wood.* She wouldn't be able to relax until she made a thorough sweep of the place.

The dreaded rounds began. She walked quickly through the living room past the oak door from her nightmare, reopened the dining room door, and proceeded to the kitchen. Every door was bolted, every window closed and locked. The most difficult part of her search was her mother's bedroom; too many memories, too much recent sadness. Patricia shuffled safely back to her bedroom, but even then, a nagging unease persisted. Living alone could do these kinds of things to your mind—make you imagine things beyond your dreams. If she was going to manage it alone, she had to get past the loss of her mother, and quickly.

They'd weathered many storms and losing her had been devastating, but Patricia was no longer a child. She could not let these frightening images become like maggots eating away at her thoughts. She would learn to handle difficulties that the world might throw at her, at least in the living, animate world.

The early morning coolness of the house sent both the nightmare and the uneasiness skittering back to a more remote corner of her mind. She walked toward the adjoining bathroom for her morning shower. She reached into the darkness to turn on the light, bracing herself in the event that the nightmare was not completely over. She imagined something cold and slimy from within the darkness, reaching out at her.

Safe again. The dream that held a specter of doom fell away completely in the bright light of the little room taking the creepy, cadaverous thoughts with it. Removing her pajamas, she entered the bathroom. "Silly nightmares," she sighed. "Time to get back to reality."

Looking in the mirror and ruffling her hair, she was further calmed by her opaque, powder-blue shower curtain where passive swans glided languidly across its surface. She crossed the room, reached behind the swans to turn on the water faucets, and stepped into the tub. She hadn't noticed the gnarled, skeletal hand curled around the edge of her curtain that now reached for her throat…and closed, taking Patricia to a place worse than any nightmare, worse than any ominous sounds of the night. She was being pulled into the realm of the Clickity-Clacks through a gateway from which there was no return.

41. HEADS UP
Winifred Burniston

There were 13 people out on Sycamore Street when the head was discovered. It was a typical late-August, Saturday afternoon and people were taking advantage of the last few days of freedom and good weather before the end of summer.

Of course, Mrs. O' Riley was out with her beast of a dog, Schnookums. He was a foul-tempered cur of indiscriminant lineage that outweighed the old lady by about forty pounds. Their daily walks were more like a daily drag up and down the street, with her forever screeching, "Down, Schnookums!" or "Bad, Schnookums!" as he assaulted each neighbor or their lawns while passing.

Next, were the four Johansson boys, or as their neighbors referred to them, Hell on Wheels, playing a game with a soccer ball that defied any definition. Hands, feet, elbows, and knees were being used often and viciously as they scrabbled about on their beaten down front yard.

Across the street, Mr. and Mrs. Lockwood were primping and preening the various flowerbeds decorating their front entrance. Both were keeping an eye on the obnoxious boys across the way, lest their ball bounce over into their property. They would surely pursue it, continuing their shenanigans all over their pristine yard. It would not have been the first time.

Suzie Roth was playing a fabulously imaginative game of tea and Barbies with her three little slumber party girls, waiting for their various rides to show up and pluck them away. Suzie was currently instructing Ann, Holly, and Stephanie on the correct way to hold an imaginary teacup.

And finally, there was Rita Reynolds, standing outside talking to Nick Michaels, of Michael's Deliveries. She was chitchatting about nothing in particular as she signed for the package, the first real one he had ever delivered to her house. All the other deliveries had been part of a thinly disguised affair that they'd carried out over the six months after her divorce. The affair had petered out, but they continued to be pleasant on the rare occasions when they bumped into each other.

What happened on that gloriously serene day can only be described as the perfect storm. Schnookums was slowly edging his owner over to the Johannson yard, as he could hear the troop of boys roughhousing and desperately wanted in on it. As they finally pulled up to the barest edge of the disheveled lawn, the soccer ball came hurtling past them in a beeline for the Lockwood's place, followed by a shrieking horde of boys in hot pursuit. The dog lowered himself down into a prelaunch stance for a fraction of a second before rocketing himself after the soccer ball. His ill-prepared owner was dragged for several feet before falling face first onto the road, breaking her nose for good measure.

Mrs. Lockwood stood up just as her husband turned toward the street with a wide, red rake in hand, both of them setting up their defensive line for the coming onslaught. Neither saw the dog galloping up from behind, and then past the children. Mrs. Lockwood was just bending over to claim the ball while her husband eyeballed the boys menacingly, daring them to try and stop the collection of their offending toy.

It was at this exact moment that Schnookums collided with both the ball and Mrs. Lockwood in an attempt to retrieve the toy for his own amusement. The ball was propelled from the collision of man and beast, and went flying off into the woods between the Lockwood and Roth homes. Mrs. Lockwood flipped ass over teakettle into her own begonias, flattening her husband onto the lawn as she went.

Stifling their laughter the best as they could, the Johannson boys lived up to their mother's protestations that deep down, they were good kids, and stopped to gently help their three neighbors. The dog, possessing no such manners, continued the chase into the woods. Rooting around for a bit, he found a marvelous prize. Half hidden under last year's leaves and lawn debris was what at first glance appeared to be a withered and blackened stump protruding upwards. The mass of flies that had hung over it all summer were long since gone. Now, it was leathered and hardened with a tangle of shredded pieces dangling off the desiccated mass. Schnookums, overjoyed at the delightfully putrid stench wafting off this find, made the executive decision to ditch the soccer ball and retrieve this vastly superior treasure instead.

Darting out of the woods, prize dangling loosely below his shit-eating doggy grin, Schnookums pranced across the street to the little girls gathered on the front lawn. Suzy was so busy being Little-Miss-Bossy-Britches, that she didn't see what the dog had clenched in his teeth behind her. It wasn't until Ann leaned over to throw up, and Holly and Stephanie began shrieking in that brain-piercing way that only little girls can do, that Ann turned around.

It took a moment for her mind to accept what she was seeing. The vile lump that had once been attached to a human body was staring its empty sockets into her pretty green eyes. She inhaled sharply, readying to join her friends in screaming for her mother, when Schnookums did the unthinkable. He began to shake the head, throttling it in a display of doggy superiority. Chunks of gore and ooze spattered all over Suzy's face and hair, the little tea table, and her increasingly frantic friends. Suzy did what any All-American Girl would do…she passed out cold on the front lawn as her friends bolted towards the house, screaming incoherently.

Rita the divorcé, looking up at the first screams, caught part of the action with the girls. Thinking it was a cruel prank being pulled by the boys, she began to approach them to take control of the situation. The dog, spying a less noisy human to impress, started for her in full gallop, his trophy still in tow. He got halfway to her before she saw what he bore with him. The girls were still screaming, and the boys, Mrs. O'Riley, and the now upright Lockwoods were frantic as well, dashing to and fro.

Rita turned towards her ex-lover and managed to scream a single, "Nick!" before the dog slammed into her knees. She toppled over, landing painfully on her ass and whacking her head on the asphalt. Schnookums skidded across the road, dropping the rotten head on the way. It tumbled several times over before coming to a stop at the deliveryman's feet. He looked down at the bashed-in mound of flesh and hair. Dazedly he reached for the cell phone hanging from his belt and dialed 911.

The rest of the neighbors were now gathered around Rita, helping her to sit up, all of them with an eye on the monstrosity perched near Nick's feet. No one moved any closer to him as he quietly relayed the information to the police operator. Everyone stood in silence, waiting to hear the siren coming to the rescue. They all realized that not only summer, but the innocence of life as they'd once known it, had come to an abrupt and disturbing end.

42. THE FIRES OF HELL AND AVONDALE
Julianne Snow

"Oi! John, what do ye make o' this?" Alroy yelled the words down the gangway as he scrubbed his dirty fingers through his sweat-matted red hair. It was against regulations to remove your helmet while in the mine, but many of the men occasionally broke protocol for one reason or another.

"What are ye yelling about Alroy? No' another shiny rock is it?" John Powell was the most imposing member of the dayshift. As the underpaid but highly respected foreman, many of the issues that the miners found were brought to him. Or at least to his attention.

"Can ye no' feel the heat from there John? The closer ye get to the face, the hotter it gets."

Striding over the rough ground of the gangway, John passed by other miners, some of them still working, while others had stopped for a moment to wipe the blackened sweat from their brows. The closer he got to the cut's face, the more he could feel the dry burn of the heat emanating from it.

"Where the heck is that coming from?" John asked the question out loud, not expecting an answer from the men around him. Removing his own helmet, he swept a hand through his sandy brown hair.

In the murky half-light, he examined the metallic lustre of the anthracite's jagged surface. The heat was palpable, radiating outward and upward along the gangway. The monotony of the crisp picks against the vein of coal brought John back to attention.

"Hey boys! Giver a rest for a wee moment." It was all the motivation the men needed to drop their pickaxes and wipe their sweaty brows, leaving lightened streaks across their soot-stained faces.

John dropped to his haunches, his hand extended toward the mineral rich wall of the front cut. While afraid, something within him dared him to touch the surface.

"By the good Lord's graces, that's hot!" John ripped the glove from his left hand, disturbed to see his calloused palm blistering from the brief contact. "Alroy, can ye bring me some water."

The pain in his hand had increased the moment he'd removed the glove to gaze upon the singed skin beneath it. Never before had he injured himself while mining; not even when he'd first started going down with his father at the tender age of thirteen. Hell, he'd even survived being trapped when the shaft of that first mine caved in back in Ireland. But that was before he had come to America in search of better opportunities. The blisters on his hand, red and angry bumps, rang like a warning through his head.

As soon as his mind registered the fact there was a problem, Hell broke loose.

It started with a barely audible hiss that grew in strength, the longer one concentrated on it. Almost as if the mere perception of it gave it life. With each passing moment, the area closest to the cut face got louder and hotter, until the vein of anthracite forcibly vented itself.

Instead of steam erupting from the fissures, there came an unholy utterance of evil that filled the hearts and minds of the miners with dread. The cracks glowed with crimson and teal blue as the flickers of flame resembling taloned fingers licked at the jagged edges.

The smell that quickly filled the crowded end of the shaft was unlike anything they had smelled before. It caused many of the men to retch over and over again, some of them doubling over as the vomit and bile poured from between their lips.

Fear and confusion hung unmistakably in the thick, humid air of the shaft. The men had no idea what was truly happening around them and as a result, they were unprepared and disorganized. Some sought water; their efforts focused on quelling what was sure to start a fire. Others tried to flee, turning on their heels and bolting for the only exit. All of it was for naught.

But the forces behind the wall of anthracite had other plans for the one hundred and eight men below the ground's surface. Golden flames snaked out of the fissures, igniting the wooden beams that supported the three hundred and twenty-seven feet of dense soil above them. Like hungry boys devouring the food put in front of them, the flames gorged on the desiccated planks. As the fire grew and coursed its way up the shaft to the surface, the men knew their time to escape had passed. There was just no way they would be able to climb the steep incline to safety with voracious fires nipping at their flesh.

Their only hope was to stay and fight.

John and Alroy were still at the very face of the cut, mesmerized by the sight before them. While they both sensed the danger, neither of them could break the hypnotic hold those fingers that snaked from the cleft had over them. Voices spoke to them; some aloud and some inside their heads. They spoke of many things, all of them promising wealth and power for just a little help.

It was Alroy that gave them what they wanted. Picking up the closest pickaxe, he swung it up over his heading, bringing it down onto the vein of anthracite that now shimmered like a pane of graphite colored glass. The result was tumultuous.

All of the beings cloistered behind the wall burst forth to dance among the burning timbers and carved walls of the shaft. Like children held for long hours, cooped up in classrooms, they cavorted, their faces lit by the fires around them.

They were all shades of hideous. Demons, each and every one of them, with pointed teeth and black soulless eyes. They celebrated their freedom as the fires of Hell fought to consume the gangway, reaching ever closer to its goal of the surface.

Open air meant more souls, more fire. In fact, Hell on Earth was what it craved. Nay demanded. With ferocity unmatched by human hand, the blaze burned brighter, hotter. John and Alroy were both knocked back; the pickaxe still clutched in Alroy's blistering hand.

It was the impact with the cool floor that brought John to his senses. The voices in his head quieted for a moment, allowing a singular voice to speak to his soul. It told him of the danger. The danger that the demons represented for the world at large. It told him of a choice. The choice he could make to drive them back into Hell. John Powell could save the world.

The choice was not an easy one, even for the pious John. The seductive nature of the demonic dance would have made it easy for him to enjoy the end of the world. Each movement had a narcotic effect upon him and the rest of the miners; once the demons had caught your gaze, you were rendered nearly powerless to tear it away from them.

The voice spoke again, reminding John of his family topside: did he want his wife and son to fall prey to the evil that danced before him?

Gathering his scattered wits, he strove to clear his muddied thoughts. He found that closing his eyes helped to lessen the soporific pull. His mind began to chant Psalm 62:6 - God is my rock, my salvation, my fortress; I will not be shaken – over and over again. Like a shield, the words kept him safe and soon he could hear the scripture tumbling out over the dry surface of his tongue.

The demons danced and taunted him, slinging insults and contempt. Some of them were brave enough to rake their talons over his body, cutting into his flesh.

Carved and bleeding, John struggled to maintain his focus. He needed help. More voices to lend theirs to his, to strengthen his faith with their own.

One by one, he bodily pulled six members of his church into an adjoining chamber. Each of them stood trance-like, captivated by what they had just witnessed. Struggling to close each of their eyes with his soot covered hands, he chanted his new mantra as he circled them. John had no idea if his plan would work, but he needed to try something.

While he was sure that some of the demons had already escaped, he could not allow Hell to swallow the earth. At least not while he still had breath left in his lungs.

A loud crash resounded all around them. Something had caved in, likely blocking the tunnel's exit. With the intensity of the fire surrounding them and the singular entrance, rescue would be slow to reach them. Glancing back out into the gangway, John could see that many of the men had retreated closer to the foot of the incline. Some had even managed to break the stranglehold the demons had placed over them, bratticing themselves into adjoining gangways in the hopes of surviving the backdraft that would build as the oxygen was swallowed by the fire.

John could soon hear the voices of six around him, joining him in repetition. As their voices got stronger, so did the insults and taunts of the demons. One particularly brazen one, a small shriveled little urchin, slunk toward John.

"You'll not defeat the Great One! You? You're small, insignificant, a mere speck of refuse slimed beneath my Master's feet. You shall never win. All the souls will be ours. Oh, how we love to torture and break them. I believe I shall start with wee little Billy! He looks so much like his Father!" It sneered as it cackled, the sound akin to the grinding of glass.

"Oh, little one! I do love how you seek to inflate my ego. It pleases me to hear that my legions trust in my omnipotence. You shall be rewarded greatly for such loyalty."

The vision before John was stunning and completely unsettling. Robed in the finest black leather, Satan leaned almost nonchalantly against the crumbling edge of the barrier between Hell and the gangway. The devil looked very much like a man, but with a few striking differences. Thick muscle crested under the bald skin of its head, leading down into eyes that were blacker than onyx. The nose was flattened across its bridge, and its lips were pulled back in the mockery of a smile to reveal sharp pointed teeth that would likely shred anything they seized. Its skin was a dull ashen color of yellow, pulled tautly over ropes of thick muscle. Satan struck a very imposing figure, but John was too tired to fully comprehend the image. Perhaps it was just stupidity.

Ducking back into the chamber, he grabbed the men and they began bratticing themselves within the room, using their shirts to block the holes they could find. Satan laughed at their efforts, thinking it funny that they thought a few roughly hewn cotton shirts would be strong enough to stop him. Crossing the distance in long strides, he placed one of his massive hands onto the timbers adjacent to the chamber. One deft push and he knocked them into the cavity, destroying the makeshift barrier.

The brilliance of the light that shone forth from the chamber burned into the blackest depths of Satan. Bringing his arm up to shield him from the burning rays, he could barely make out the host of the heavens dressed in their battle gear, swords drawn. The chant of the miners was not meant to defeat Satan, but call forth the one being that could vanquish him back to the depths of Hell. Demons from the gangway squealed as the purity of the light incinerated them where they stood.

"Does my former father think he can send a few of his servants to quell me? Brothers, you know I am stronger, wiser. You cannot defeat me, not this time!"

"I did not send my servants to defeat you Lucifer. I came to send you back myself." A voice so melodious and pure spoke from the centre of the light. "You have no power here, be gone. Go back to the one place that I have allowed you to exist."

It was over in the briefest fraction of a moment.

As the fires still burned, Satan was cast back into the bowels of Hell by the hand of God. Many of his minions were destroyed; those that were not, gratefully cast themselves back before the rift was sealed.

***

The fire raged at the bottom of the Avondale Colliery for two days. Each of the one hundred and eight men on shift that day perished in the fire. The official cause of the blaze has been listed as the accidental ignition of the coal furnace that spread the fire throughout the shaft, by means of the ventilation flue.

Each of the bodies recovered from the shaft showed no evidence of burns, instead many of them were found in the attitude of prayer or hugging the soot covered floor. With eyeballs protruding and blood foaming from their mouths and noses, official consensus was that they died from a lack of oxygen.

Many implored God for answers; asking why these men had to die. The answer they never received was that sometimes, God works in mysterious ways.

43. VISITING HOUR
William Holden

You lay awake in your bed. The air is heavy with the remains of another brutal August day. The small window air conditioner spits and chokes on itself. It expels nothing more than warm, stale air. You pull yourself up and peel off the sweat stained t-shirt. You toss it on the floor next to your bed where your other clothes in similar condition have been discarded. The lack of clothing provides little relief from the heat. You leave your undergarments on, afraid to be...

Naked.

Vulnerable.

Exposed.

You look over at the other side of the bed – his side – the empty side. You remember happier times with your lover lying next to you. A tear pools in your lower eyelid. You reach out and touch the pillow that formerly cradled his head. You blink away the tear. It runs down the side of your face. You let it linger in the crook of your neck. You close your eyes and imagine him lying next to you with his naked body damp with the night's heat. You listen to the stillness that hovers over your bed like a lost soul drifting near the ceiling, looking down at your empty existence. In the silence, you can almost hear his gentle snoring as he sleeps. A small, but welcome smile crosses your face. The painful realization that the sound is only in your head tears the smile from your face. You're left with only the memories of him. You take a deep breath in hopes of chasing the demons away that keep you up at night, with the thoughts of his death, his funeral, and the undying loneliness that has taken his place.

The demons taunt you with their cruel intentions. They visit you in the darkness, bearing gifts of unimaginable suffering now that you are alone. They remind you night after night that you shall never again feel his touch, or hear his voice. Sleep seems as lost to you as your departed lover. You want nothing more than to close your eyes, to sleep, to forget, if only for a few hours that he is no longer with you. With sleep, however, the demons come bringing with them the nightmares. You choose instead to stay awake – again.

The silence of emptiness begins to suffocate you. You roll yourself to the edge of the bed and bring your feet to the floor. You look at the dirty clothes that litter your room. You stand up and dress yourself with the same clothes you've worn for the past few days. You look at the clock. It's nearing midnight. On your way out, you stop by the refrigerator and grab a beer. You leave your apartment, shutting the door on the ghosts, which now haunt your life. You step outside. The steamy night air brings a chill to your skin. You light a cigarette, take a swig of the ice-cold beer, and head out into the night.

You walk aimlessly through the deserted streets, the same streets you used to walk holding hands with your lover. The tips of your fingers begin to tingle from a sudden chill. You rub them together to warm them; the cold creeps up your fingers and grips your hand as the warm, murky air settles in around you.

Without realizing it, you have made your way to the cemetery. You pause at the iron-gate and look out across the landscape of death. You hesitate not wanting to disturb the dead, but the need to be near him draws you over the threshold between the living and the dead.

The air feels different as you walk among the deceased. It chills your overheated body bringing with it gooseflesh that pricks your skin. The old gray tombstones speak to you of the stories of the thousands of bodies that lay beneath your feet. Without conscious effort, you find yourself standing over his grave. You stare at his tombstone and read the epitaph remembering the day you ordered it. There are no tears here in this place. The only thing you feel is a dull, dry grief. You imagine him lying there, six feet below the surface, unchanged from the day you had him dressed in his gray pinstriped suit.

You wonder if he knows you are there, perhaps smiling up at you, wanting to thank you for your visit – and for the fact that you haven't forgotten him yet. You touch the cold headstone as you sit next to him. It's been ten months since you placed him in the ground. You reach out and touch the newly sprouted grass. You dig your fingers into the soil, desperate to feel close to him again. A branch snaps in the distance. You want to brush it off as nothing but nerves, but something inside of you tells a different story. You hear footsteps behind you coming up the gravel path. The steps are slow, uneven. You listen to the thud…drag…thud…drag as it approaches. His scent surrounds you. It's Old Spice, the only cologne he ever wore. You can feel his presence engulfing you – soothing your tired mind and body. You want to turn around, to see him once again, but fear keeps you motionless.

He's standing directly behind you. The smell of him has changed. There's a sickening sweet smell to the air, like rotting fruit floating in the sludge of human waste. You suddenly feel a hand on your shoulder. You turn your head and see the grey putrid skin peeling off of the bones. The ring you gave him hangs loosely from his decomposing finger. You close your eyes hoping it's a dream. The hope is ripped from you as you hear his bones snapping and cracking as he leans into you. The cold dead skin of his lips touches your ear. He whispers, "I'm back."

You wake up in your bed, cold and covered in sweat. You take a deep breath to relax your mind from the same nightmare you've had every night since he died. Tonight, however, your mind doesn't ease. You feel that something is different. You lay still, holding your breath as you expect something to happen. The room is deathly quiet. You turn over on your side ignoring the growing unease. You close your eyes. You feel something behind you shift as you settle in. Your breath gets caught in your throat as the cold, slimy arm of your lover reaches around your body and pulls you into him, beneath the covers, beneath the soil, and into the darkness once again.

44. ACROSS THE STREET
J. T. Seate

The Johnson residence was across the street from us when I was growing up. In his backyard was an old, defunct refrigerator that could be seen from our yard. As it lay rusting upon the ground, it reminded me of King Tut's sarcophagus. Mr. Johnson was as creepy as his yard junk. I'd just seen the movie *Psycho*, so my mind was wired for the strange and unusual. Whenever he looked at me from across the street with that kind of hollow-eyed stare, I felt like someone was walking over my grave.

When not in the mood for a book or movie, I enjoyed sitting on the steps of our small front porch on warm evenings. While my parents watched their favorite TV programs inside, I took pleasure in tuning my trusty transistor radio to a DJ who spun the Top 20 platters for all of us groovy teens out there in radio-land.

My eyes occasionally strayed to the Johnson house and the comatose, rusting behemoth in their yard. For a thirteen-year-old boy, wondering if anything was inside added more spice to a summer night than was possible from a scary book or my radio.

One night, I watched Mr. Johnson walk from his house toward his icebox. I slunk back into the corner of my porch, hoping to become invisible and prevent the night-stalking Johnson from turning his demon gaze upon me.

He then stopped in front of the fridge and began talking to it. The conversation between him and the appliance seemed eerily personal. He placed his hands on top of the door like he was standing over a…coffin.

The lid rose with a crypt-like squawk that cried out for oil. He peered at whatever was inside for a moment, then looked up at the moon.

What could be inside? I pondered. Do I really want to know?

Johnson closed the lid and wandered back inside his house. Inside of *my* house, mom and dad sat in their respective chairs staring at the TV.

"Dad?" I called.

No response. They were lost inside the world of Lawrence Welk and Myron Floran playing *Lady of Spain* on dueling accordions?

"Dad!" I said louder. "Weirdo Mr. Johnson was in his yard talking to the refrigerator."

"That's nice," he answered.

"Don't you think it's awfully weird? I mean, you know, having a conversation with a rusty old appliance?"

"He doesn't bother us, Troy. Don't sweat the small stuff, kid."

That was my Dad's favorite expression, but I thought the man across the street conducting services under a full moon was *big* stuff, at least for our little block. I shrugged my shoulders and went to my room just as The Lennon Sisters fired up into song.

My mind was in overdrive. I had to find out what was in that refrigerator.

My chance came on a night when my parents went out to play cards. Even before they cleared the street corner, I formulated my plan. But what if I somehow end up inside that darned refrigerator with whatever's in there? My parents would come home and…no more Troy.

No guts, no glory.

I bided my time. I waited until the lights in the back part of the Johnson's manse went dark. For better or worse, I started across the street toward no-man's land, traversing the distance in a quick moving crouch, the way Army guys did in the movies. I stopped where a chain-link fence separated the Johnson's yard from their neighbor, pleased that no spotlights had suddenly come on, or that I hadn't set off invisible air raid sirens. I heaved myself over the fence, landing safely on enemy soil.

No turning back now. The dead fridge and the mysteries within were a mere fifteen feet away. I duck-walked toward the white whale, my tennis shoes swishing through overgrown grass. *"Lift, look, and leave,"* I told myself and maneuvered into position. My hand crawled toward the silver handle. My fingers closed around the cool metal.

Another hand joined mine. It was not *my* other hand.

My mouth became an oval. My insides tightened up like a basket full of ribbon snakes. With my heart in my throat, I let go of the handle and turned. Mr. Johnson hovered over me. My eyes turned into saucers. I levitated from shear fright. The hulking man stared while I gaped back. I was shaking in my rubber soles.

"What's going on here?" his voice boomed.

I threw my back against the refrigerator and rolled over the door onto the other side, away from the man, looking for an escape. But Mr. Johnson was trotting toward me in a pincer-like movement.

I screamed like a banshee and ran to the closest section of chain-link. I scrambled up and over just ahead of Johnson's clutches. I ran like the wind to the safety of my side of the street.

I locked the door and made a beeline for the bathroom to see if my hair had turned white.

Dare I tell my parents what I had done? When the time came, I clammed up, but would I ever find out what was inside that you-know-what?

A year later, Mr. Johnson died suddenly. A maintenance company hired by the bank came to haul away the rusty fridge. The monstrosity was turned on its side and dumped. Inside was a foot of soil laden with earthworms. I guess Johnson used them as bait.

But there was more.

Underneath the soil lay the skeletal remains of a woman. It turned out my neighbor had been communing with more than his earthworms.

An old dryer revealed another secret. It held a pair of severed feet and hands below the interior metropolis of worms. The yard was a virtual appliance-center cemetery.

As an adult, I took a course in forensics. I liked the idea that being nosy could have a purpose. I've learned that small stuff can prove to be very big stuff indeed.

45. MYTHIC
Nicholas Paschall

The streets of London are rather beautiful at night, Mary Anne mused as she strolled down the darkened alley. The entire city was awash in the light of a full moon hanging low in a cloudless sky; a dull autumn chill sweeping through the neighborhoods and boroughs, just enough for everyone to begin to dress warmly and drink warm cider in the evening with their mead. Even the lowliest street urchins were in a chipper mood by the change in weather and festive mood that seemed to pervade the city.

Humming softly to herself, Mary Anne drew her shawl tighter about her shoulders and playfully expelled her breath harder than normal, smiling at the visible cloud of air that hovered briefly before her. Her hard soled shoes clicked on the cobblestone road rhythmically as she slowly walked down Roman Road past the old cathedral. A slight smile graced her lips as she viewed the old stone building. Many a wonderful day had been spent as a child playing in the graveyard with the other local children, games of hide and seek amidst the headstones having been so delightful. Now she viewed the old graveyard with reverence, as did any good Christian woman; she said a short Hail Mary as she passed the iron wrought fence surrounding the property, saying the prayer for those interred within their eternal wombs.

Approaching Whitechapel Road, Mary Anne softly sang an old nursery rhyme to herself as she approached the small bridge leading over one of the many inlets from the River Thames. Smiling softly, she gazed up at the moon with admiration as she lazily made her way across the old brick bridge, skipping along like she had as a child.

A sharp scraping noise caused her to stop and whirl around, looking where the sound had echoed behind her. The moonlit streets were narrow and full of thick shadows, so all she could see were ethereal reflections of what she knew to be real by day, and could only imagine at night.

"Hello?" she called out, her voice soft and meek. "Is anyone there?"

A flicker of movement caught her eye, but just as soon as she'd seen it, it would faded back into the cover of darkness.

Backing away slowly, she turned and hastened her pace homeward, pulling her shawl tight over her frame as she hummed louder to herself, trying to drive the fear away from her mind. There was nothing there, nothing but the dark.

And the English didn't have to fear the dark.

Not anymore.

Her brave thoughts were shattered like glass on a street corner as a sinister chuckle echoed through the chilled air, seemingly coming from all around her. She stopped and reached down the side of her dress, unrolling her sash to pull the carving knife she stowed away for nights on which she worked, just in case one of her customers didn't feel like paying.

Pulling the knife out, she twirled it deftly in her hand, holding it by the handle with edge facing out like her late husband had taught her. This brought back a sense of her security, knowing that whoever was playing with her right now would probably be scared off by the glinting steel.

The chuckle grew louder, proving her wrong.

"Wot's all this then? Little Mary has 'erself a little knoife? 'Ow quaint." Came a sibilant baritone from behind her, causing her to whirl around, brandishing her knife at the speaker.

He stood on the side of the bridge, his thin frame accentuated by a threadbare cloak that whipped about him with the cool breeze, a pair of oversized boots and a faint scent of sulfur marking him as somewhat otherworldly to Mary Anne. Despite the darkness, and his wide brimmed top hat, she could see two blazing coals where his eyes should be, as well as a silver set of teeth smiling cruelly in the dark.

Softly, ever so softly, he began to sing as he swayed from side to side, his voice deep as the sea and horribly out of tune.

> "Mary, Mary, quite contrary
> Ever the wavering twat;
> While out one night,
> In the pale moonlight,
> She met a stranger with candy;
> 'To whom do you seek,'
> She asked ever so meek
> His laughter nothing short of a chorus
> 'Why it's you, dear whore,
> So sing no more,
> For come the morn
> You'll be spare pieces.'"

That was all Mary Anne needed to hear as she turned and began sprinting away, running through the streets towards the brothel she called home, a place she knew she could be safe. The rapid clacking of her own footfalls was punctuated by a dull and repetitive thump, the sound of someone dropping something heavy one the ground every few seconds.

She turned to dart down Abney Alley, a road she knew well from her many nights walking the streets; with all its small nooks and crannies she could easily slip past this lunatic without him ever being the wiser.

Her dreams were moot sadly as she felt twin slams peg her just beneath the shoulder blades, throwing her to the ground, knocking her head against the stone wall of the alley as she tumbled.

Head swimming and blood pooling from her mouth, Mary Anne gasped as she realized she'd fallen on her knife, wedging it deep into her side. A cold rush washed over her body as her dark velvet clothes became a deeper shade of red as her blood began to spill out of her. She reached for the blade, but cried in agony as a strong hand grasped the handle, twisting the blade into her side viciously.

Screaming into the night, her vision turned white as she felt an iron grip press around her throat, capturing her shriek midway with a sickening gurgle. Opening her eyes, she peered into the brilliant burning coals just inches from her face.

"You lot 'ave had it easy these past few years," the madman said with a snarl, twisting the knife further into her side, "But now that ole Jackie boy is back on the scene, he'll be makin' sure all you little whores scream!"

Mary Anne tried to scream, she truly did, but the cold grip on her throat only tightened as the blade sank deeper into her flesh, his fingertips pushing at the end of the handle to force the knife into her bloodied flesh, his gloved hands caked with her innards and gore as she bled out around him. Her final moments of consciousness were filled with the sight of those red hot coals, and the scent of sulfur and copper filling the air as the life was snuffed from her frame for good.

46. CONTEMPORARY BY PROXY
Raymond Gates

"I don't want to do it anymore."

"You have to."

"Please, Rose. No more."

Rose sighed and took Lily's hands in her own. She stared at the mirror that was her sister. "You know I can't do it without you."

Lily's huge eyes pleaded with her.

"This is the last time," Rose said. She squeezed Lily's hands. "I promise."

Lily looked at the floor, her eyelids fluttering. Rose cupped her sister's porcelain-like face. Warm droplets splashed against her skin. She lifted Lily's chin.

"I promise."

Tears spilled down Lily's face as her eyes closed. When she opened them, they were glassy. Emotionless.

"I hate doing it," Lily whispered between her teeth.

Rose leaned forward and wrapped her arms around her sister.

"I hate it too." She squeezed her eyes shut, felt her jaw trembling and tightened her embrace. "But after tonight, we'll never do it again."

Lily straightened. Despite the dread radiating from her, a tiny smile found its way to her lips. "I know."

Rose breathed, and kissed her sister's forehead. She'd be okay. God, just get them through tonight, and they'd both be okay.

Lily stood and approached the door. "You'll come find me when it's over, won't you?"

"Of course I will." Rose's brow wrinkled. "I always have, haven't I?"

Lily smiled. "I know. I just ..." She bit her lip and shook her head. "I'm just being silly." She opened the door and made to leave.

"Lily."

Lily peered from around the edge of the door.

"Be careful."

Lily grunted and rolled her eyes, the way she had when they'd been children. It was one of those quirks that made her so lovable.

"You too," she said, and closed the door.

Rose slumped onto the chair in front of the make-up mirror. The clipped headlines stuck to the frame seemed more accusatory than flattering tonight. *The budding Rose of contemporary dance! Rose blooms at festival! 'A Woman's Torment', pick of the bunch!* The reviews she'd received, the accolades, the offers already made were going to ensure a better life for both of them.

But would Lily ever forgive her?

She sighed, reached for a make-up brush, and improved on perfection.

***

The audience hushed as the house lights dimmed. Rose took a deep breath and closed her eyes. She'd mastered the adrenalin rush; learnt to control it, bend it to her will and direct it into her performance.

She crossed her arms over her breasts and curled her head forward. Applause crackled from behind the rising curtain. It crescendoed as a lone, blue light illuminated her solitary figure. The clapping crested and fell away. The air seemed to be sucked out of the theatre as the audience held their breath.

A single note pierced the silence. Rose lifted her head and opened her arms. Her body glided, her bare feet floating across the stage. More notes joined the first, a light, airy melody, and Rose's lithe form swirled around the stage. The music embraced her. Rose surrendered and let it take her. She moved as if through water, or the vacuum of space. Her heart soared and those in the audience soared with her.

She felt the tension building, a suffocating feeling deep in her chest, and knew it was about to happen.

Be strong, she thought. It'll be over soon.

Her head snapped to the right, the force dashing her body to the floor. The spotlight flashed red. She raised an arm in a protective gesture. Pushing with hands and feet, she propelled herself backwards. Her body arched and lifted from the stage. Her breath *woomphed* from her lungs, echoed by the multitude of gasps from the crowd.

Coughing, Rose struggled to her feet. Panic, excitement, anticipation reeked from the audience. She focused through the pain, forcing her form to be light and feminine. She held her hands in a pleading gesture. The music diminished as the circlet of light around her shone pure white.

Rose's body curved sideways and she dropped to the stage. Agony lanced through her chest. Several cries reached the stage as the light turned crimson. Rose gasped for breath. Every inhalation felt like she was breathing needles. She tasted blood in her mouth.

What the hell?

Her mouth curled in on itself. Teeth tore free of their sockets and lacerated soft flesh. The front of her face tingled, a strange mix of severe pins-and-needles and numbness. She rolled over and propped on her hands and knees. A woman in the front row screamed as Rose spat scarlet and ivory upon the hardwood.

It's too much! It's going too far!

Her knees shot in opposite directions. Her hands flew behind her back. Her broken face struck the stage, hard. She felt pressure between her thighs. Her eyes rolled towards the audience. Horrified, intrigued faces met her stare. Her mouth formed words without sounds. Her hips bucked as her loins burned from violation.

Oh God, Lily, stop it! Please stop it!

Her body collapsed. She lay amongst her tears and blood. Her mind begged for it to end. For both their sakes.

Rose's head was drawn back. She could see the wonderment of those closest to the stage. Eyes wide. Mouths agape, some hidden under hands. All attention upon her.

Her head tilted and turned to the side. She felt a winding strain in her neck.

Lily, I'm sorry. So sorry.

The front row heard a sharp click, like a finger-snap. Rose's head spun as if she'd been startled by something behind her, then hit the stage with an audible thud.

The pain disappeared. Her vision swam, losing focus. A sound like rain on a tin roof broke the silence. It rose to a downpour, drowning out the cheers, whistles and cries of, "Encore!"

Her heart fluttered. Her eyes closed.

It's okay Lily. I'm coming.

Rose let the curtain fall.

A million miniature boxers pound a relentless rhythm against every wrinkle in my brain. I wade in fog-mired nightmares of inebriated carousing in shallow ponds of ripe, naked bodies and blurry, blood-streaked faces. I don't dare open my eyes to the glaring reality of dawn. God, this is the worst hangover of my life. Bile-filled guts bob like a corked, half-full bottle on stormy seas. My parched mouth begs for relief. One deep breath and my mustache shadowed lips slam shut to stifle a gag. The stench of layers of sweat dried on black locks of my shoulder length hair, stale perfumed body oils and rancid slime on my disheveled pirate costume brings waves of nausea into waking dreams. Oh yeah, way worse than that first spring break back in '09, when I woke up in jail with bare feet, no pants and a huge hickey next to the fish-shaped birthmark on my neck. Rolling onto my sore, overworked back, a belching groan escapes.

"Froggy come a wakin', he does rise, uh-huh! uh-huh!" echoes a menacing baritone voice in the stone chamber.

Squinting reveals two blurry figures hovering over me, a cowboy and a scarecrow. I must be hallucinating. I manage to sit up on the large granite box, but my brain bangs inside my skull like the clanger in a church bell.

"Oh - oh. Looks like Jimmy-doors here needs some hair of the Halloween dog, eh?" teases the haystack headed guy in coke-bottle bottomed glasses on my left.

"Shhhhh!" I hiss, rocking on the sarcophagus, cradling the top of my head with both trembling hands.

"Volunteer your own damn jug, Scarecrow!" growls that low voice to the right. Each syllable ricochets like bullets in a steel cave, "He got plenty of mine last night."

"Ow! Shit! Shut-up!" I moan, my stomach oozing around my insides like hot wax in a lava lamp.

"Here, Jimmy-doors," soothes that nasally tenor from the shadowy figure to my left. He waves the brown glass bottle six inches in front of my nose, "Just remember, I'm the nice one."

I grab the unlabeled bottle and up-end it. Liquid fire sears my tongue, burns down my throat, and chars my belly into temporary submission.

"Not so much, man!" The blessed brown vial disappears. I watch those thick glasses slide down his nose. Flashing crimson eyes give me a wink while he pricks his middle finger with his razor sharp, pointed thumbnail. Three drops of blood in the bottle, a little swish and it is full again.

"Where the hell am I?" I mumble, "Who are you? And who is Jimmy-doors?"

"Just call me, Boomer," drawls the cowboy, jabbing a burly thumb in his muscle-bound chest. "Your bottle mate over there, is Scarecrow."

"Where am I? Who are you?" whines the skinny, "Wizard of Oz" refugee pretending to rub tears from his eyes like a child with his emaciated fists. "Sheesh, Jimmy-doors, the jokes were better last night!" He back-hands my shoulder and bits of straw fall out of his patched sleeve. He takes a long swig from the brown jug.

My eyes finally focus scanning the dim surroundings. The only light pierces the ornate wrought iron door ahead of me like smoky, ghost fingers in the dingy, cinderblock room. Everything is colorless, like an old black and white monster movie, even the puddle of dried puke just inside the door. I'm sitting on a carved sarcophagus in the center of a small, dark crypt. The only colors to be found are the blood red eyes of my roommates and that brown bottle.

"Don't you remember the party at the marina?" asks the cowboy, "Even with the pirate swagger, bawdy jokes and the mark of Dagon, you weren't having much luck with the ladies. That is, until we came along. We teamed up—"

"Like the three musketeers!" Scarecrow interrupts.

Boomer slaps him on the back of the head. "As I was sayin'," Scarecrow shrugs and takes another couple glugs while the cowboy continues, "We teamed up. A few extra snorts of my brew let our toes float and hips slide, while snappy lines just rolled off our tongues. I have to admit, Scarecrow, you were right. That demon birthmark doesn't lie. Playing Jimmy-doors' bumbling sidekicks was the perfect tactic. We rounded up a nice herd of skirts on the dance floor and drove them right out the backdoor. After a little bronco bustin' and some serious hide the salami on the commodore's yacht, we three decided to try a tour of the town."

"We just followed the yellow brick road, club to club to club," Scarecrow recited wistfully.

Boomer took his hat in hand and began fanning his crotch, "Haven't had that much tail in a hundred years!"

"The Sons of Ba'al and the Daughters of Eve made a few new souls last night!" Scarecrow offers his bottle to Boomer.

The cowboy nodded taking a little sip, then hands the bottle back. "How many did you get, Scarecrow?"

"I lost count after Jimmy-doors stole that brunette from you at that jazz joint."

"That's right!" Boomer looms over me, locking his blazing red eyes on mine. "She was mine, primed and ready!"

Scarecrow waved his bottle in front of Boomer's nose, "He got her fair and square. Besides, you made up for it with that blonde, remember?"

A wistful smile crosses Boomer's face, exposing sharp, pointed teeth. "True enough. I'll let that slide. After all, he did manage to keep pace with us most of the night."

"That is," Scarecrow turns on me, "until you insisted on that one stupid song on the jukebox, again and again! Claiming to be the next Jimmy Morris and Sons, and rambling on about doors! You played that song seven times in a row! AND, you jiggled all over the dance floor like a spastic spider!"

"Don't forget caterwauling like a damned, dying hyena with his balls clamped in a trap!" adds Boomer. "You were yowling, 'Break on through to the other side! Break on through to the other side,' over and over and over again! Shit! We had to haul you out of that dumpster in the alley after you kissed the bouncer and grabbed his ass!"

Scarecrow's mouth sprays a shower of liquor, and he doubles over laughing. "That was priceless!"

"We granted your wish. You earned your nickname," proclaims the grinning cowboy holding his hat over his heart. "Welcome to the Land of the Dead, Jimmy-doors!"

48. NIGHT TERRORS
Marc Sorondo

Danny knew how to make himself invisible to them. He slept with all of the blankets—from the light blue jersey sheet to the thick brown quilt his grandmother had made for his eighth birthday—pulled up to his chin. He kept his arms under the covers, pressed tightly against his sides. The extra pillow, the one cased in a dark cover to match the quilt, rested over his head.

He was entirely covered, except only for a thin sliver where the pillows above and below his head never quite met. Through this crack he tried to watch the strange events that took place in his bedroom.

He wasn't sure why it worked, but it kept him unseen. It had gotten him through years of strange nights; it made the terror bearable.

Often enough, when he'd wake to the sound of odd noises in his room, he'd lie there sweating in his pajamas, his coverings trapping his body heat against him until he felt feverish. He'd peer through the crack in his protection and see nothing. At other times he'd see only reflected light, sickly green and thrown from some unseen source, swirling on the wall. When he tried to imagine what could make such a light, he drew a blank that horrified him worse than any imagined monster.

Sometimes he'd be jolted awake by the sound of furniture moving upon the wooden floor of his room. He occasionally saw his nightstand transported; he would watch it as it squeaked against the floor while it moved away from his bed. He never saw what pushed or pulled those things. Most of the time he was happy he didn't.

He would finally get so hot and light headed—every exhalation adding heat to his closed system, his hair and pajamas saturated with sweat and plastered to his skin—that he would fall asleep. When he woke up in the morning, all was back to normal.

It made him wonder if his mother was right, if they were just bad dreams, nothing to be worried about. Seeing his room lit by morning sunlight, it seemed so ordinary, so very much not the stuff of nightmares.

It wasn't so easy to believe her in the dark. At night, his room wasn't safe. At night, he had to stay hidden, because at night, he wasn't alone.

Sometimes, only rarely, he heard what he thought was them talking, their voices like a blend of whispers and the sound of small, chitinous legs scrabbling over a linoleum floor. That chittering sound went back and forth, calling out from different places in the dark of his room.

Those voices made his skin crawl. The sound of it was like having fleas: itchy and tickling in a dirty way.

When it first happened, Danny thought it was ghosts. He'd heard enough stories about haunted houses at school and thought that it described the activities in his bedroom quite well.

Then something happened that Danny doubted a haunting could explain.

There was a loud crash, as if someone had lifted his dresser completely off the floor and then dropped it. That chittering followed, and Danny thought the hidden terrors in his room were laughing at the ruckus. It erupted from numerous points and then stopped all at once.

Danny waited, wondering why the noises had stopped so abruptly, when a weight eased down onto the bed next to him, painfully trapping his right arm beneath the taught blankets.

He found that he couldn't breathe, no matter how hard he tried. The weight settled and spread until it felt like someone was lying next to him, up against him.

Danny looked through the slit in his armor, facing away from the thing that shared his bed with him. He tried to force his lungs to take in a breath, to suck in some of the hot, moist air trapped in his protective covering. There was pain and pressure behind his eyes, as if they would pop out of his head if he didn't take a breath soon.

He heard the sound of muffled, asthmatic breathing coming through the pillow over his head, as if there was a mouth against it, panting down at him.

A gentle weight fell on his chest and ran back and forth from the bottom of the pillow to just over his belly, as though a hand was petting him.

Danny had begun to doubt the strength of his protection. It was touching his armor, prodding it, and whatever it was, Danny thought it must be able to feel him beneath.

Then he'd exhaled and passed out.

The next morning everything was normal. Scary as it had been, Danny felt oddly comforted by the experience: his defenses had been tested and he'd been protected.

That had been almost two years ago, and nothing even close to that bad had happened since. He'd dealt with the occasional sound and shifted piece of furniture, but he did so with the resolve of a battle-hardened warrior heeding a threat.

Tonight, he heard the voices again, like insects whispering secrets. There were two distinct voices, one of which sounded like it was coming from right in front of him, as if one of those things was whispering directly into the crack between his pillows.

Danny forced himself to breath, to keep it slow and steady. He didn't want to pass out tonight, no matter what.

Then he felt the blankets shift, the tops of them yanked down suddenly from his chin to his chest. Danny stopped breathing. The blankets started moving again, slowly sliding down.

Finally, he lay exposed, shivering in his sweat soaked pajamas. He felt naked.

The pillow over his face shifted, and Danny gasped. He clamped his eyes shut, squeezed up his face to force them as tight as possible.

If he kept his eyes closed, if he didn't see them, he hoped that maybe, just maybe, they wouldn't really be able to see him.

Danny willed himself invisible as he felt the pillow dragged off his head.

He had to keep his eyes closed until morning, he reminded himself as he felt something—not a hand, certainly not a hand—petting him in long, slow strokes down his chest and stomach.

Everything always went back to normal by morning. By the light of dawn his bedroom would be of this world again. If he could just keep his eyes closed until then…

49. THE GRUNT
Ken MacGregor

"You had sex with a werewolf?" Gina said. God, she was such a judgmental bitch. Why did I tell her?

"In human form," I said. "Besides, he was really very sweet. A total gentleman. And he was very, ah, attentive to my needs." I blushed.

"What if he had scratched you, for Christ's sake?" That had worried me too, actually. But Gavin didn't scratch me, or bite me. There was some licking. Rather a lot of licking. I could feel myself blushing again. *What? Am I fifteen?*

"I was perfectly safe, Gina," I said. "He didn't hurt me at all, and we used a condom." I left out the part where the damn thing ripped. We were so caught up in what we were doing that neither of us noticed until it was too late. But, I'm pretty sure you can't catch lycanthropy from semen. Gavin freaked out way more than me about the rubber. I told him it was fine. Werewolves don't get diseases, so I wasn't worried about that. And, I was on the pill, so everything should have been totally cool.

Six weeks later, I discovered that the pill had failed. I was pregnant. I tried to get a hold of Gavin, but he had already moved away. He said he didn't like to stay in one place too long. That he could control his Wolf, but someone always found out about it, and most people are touchy about werewolves. I didn't really care. I mean, if they're not trying to eat you - literally, I mean - what does it matter? I try to judge a person by how they act, and how they treat me. Gavin was a great guy, and he never hunted humans; it was his rule. I felt awful that I couldn't reach him to let him know he's going to be a father.

Yeah, I was going through with it. I didn't really see myself as having any options. I mean, I've always supported a woman's right to choose, but there was no way I was going to have an abortion. I wondered if the baby would have Gavin's eyes. I could remember them vividly, a blue so pale that they were almost grey, tiny flecks of gold at the edges of the irises. I think, looking up into those eyes, I might have fallen a tiny bit in love.

It was hard, the pregnancy: the fatigue; the morning sickness; the constant ache in my lower back; the swollen breasts that weighed twice what they used to. I felt fat and ugly and gross, and I resented people who told me I looked beautiful or that I glowed. I'd smile and offer a sincere-sounding thank you, but inside I was, like, *whatever*.

The first and second ultrasounds appeared normal. My obstetrician assured me everything was on track; my doula friend, who liked to bad-mouth doctors told me I seemed just fine, too. But, in my seventh month, I started to worry.

My boy - I could see that he was male in that second ultrasound - was pushing on my uterus harder than was comfortable. It hurt a little, and I was worried. I know werewolves are stronger than humans, by a lot and this little guy was half lycanthrope. I asked both my experts about it, but neither had any experience with a hybrid and didn't know what to expect. The obstetrician advised me to let her know if I thought there was a chance of internal injury. She said that at this stage, premature birth was an option, and the baby would be small but viable. My doula, Hillary, said that boys especially liked to hit and kick, even before they were born. Hillary had a theory that it was evolutionary: boys were bred to be warriors or something. Seemed kind of far-fetched to me, but so did a lot of what she told me. Hillary was into astrology and numerology and some other -ologies, too I was pretty sure.

The days grew shorter, and my temper did, too. Halloween was only weeks away and I decorated for it every year. In a few years, I would be able to take my son trick-or-treating, but for now, I planned to dress as a pumpkin and hand out candy. I had picked up three pumpkins, hoping to carve them over the weekend. I was on the screened-in front porch hanging a cardboard skeleton right around eight. It was full dark already, but I could see the front yard by the streetlight. Three kids, early teens maybe, were whispering loudly and moving furtively from yard to yard. I saw one of them grab a pumpkin from next door, hoist it over his head and smash it in the street.

I put down the skeleton and hefted a shovel that I hadn't put away yet for the season. The kids snuck into my yard and I could hear their excitement on finding one for each of them. I opened the screen door and stepped out, shovel held like a bat, ready to swing.

"You touch my pumpkins," I said, "and I'll smash your fucking heads."

The kids stood rooted to the spot for a moment, eyes wide in shock and fear. Grown-ups aren't supposed to behave this way, their faces said. Then, all at once they ran.

I lowered the shovel, nodding. That showed 'em. It wasn't until much later that I realized how psychotic my behavior was. I sat, drinking tea before bed and wondered what was wrong with me.

At 35 weeks things got ugly. The Grunt - my nickname for the baby growing inside me: *Gavin's Runt* - was working me over pretty well. He hit me hard enough for the skin to show bruises, and it hurt like hell. I was worried I had internal bleeding or permanent tissue damage. I called Doctor Wells; she could get me in at three. I called Hillary; she said she'd be at my house in twenty minutes.

I lowered my bulk into a chair and worked my way through a ham and Swiss cheese sandwich. I never used to eat ham, but since I got knocked up, I couldn't get enough of it. Bacon, too. Really, any kind of pork product made me salivate. Halfway through the snack, ten minutes after I had called Hillary, the Grunt *changed*. I could feel it happening in my womb: limbs twisting, body shifting; face becoming a snout. I couldn't really feel those things, but that's what I pictured as the baby inside me became something else.

The previous pain had been nothing compared to this. The tiny wolf ripped me open from the inside. I fell off the chair screaming and smacked my head on the floor. Stars burst in my eyes and I thought I'd pass out, but the pain brought me back.

My yellow maternity shirt was soaked with blood. The Grunt pushed his snout through my skin, stretching the shirt in the shape of a baby wolf's face. The shirt gave, and his little head burst through the fabric.

My son forced himself the rest of the way out, wriggling to free his body from mine. I could feel his back feet pushing off my spine; the pain almost made me black out again.

My blood sprayed out, soaking the carpet. *Damn it*, I thought through my state of shock. *That's never going to come out*. The Grunt, fur matted with blood and placental fluid, clumsily crawled onto my chest. The umbilical cord pulled taut against my ribs. He pushed his little Wolf face close to mine. His tiny tongue popped out and licked my chin. I tried to smile, and may have managed. My son opened his eyes; they were a bright blue, not as pale as his father's, but lovely. They looked human, which was so strange in that tiny wolf face.

Hillary walked in the front door, which I'd left unlocked for her. Her scream was the second to last thing I ever heard. The Grunt's low hungry growl followed; at least my baby would eat.

50. LOST
Jeff McFarland

Look, I'm going to be completely blunt here. I don't much give a shit whether you believe me or not. The only reason I'm even writing this down is because I'm not sure I believe it myself. My parents don't believe me, my professors don't believe me, and the police *definitely* do not believe me.

Late in the afternoon last Thursday, three of my buddies and I decided we were going to go hiking. The warm weather was fading fast, and we planned on taking advantage of it. There's a state park about ten miles outside of town, so we figured we would go explore a few of the trails. A couple miles in, our friend Chuck casually mentioned knowing something about an unmarked path leading to a peak. We figured what the hell, we're all adults, right? We still had a few more hours of light; we would be fine.

It was out of the way, hidden behind two tall, thorny bushes. We had been searching for so long that we were ready to call bullshit on the entire thing, but sure enough, behind the bushes was a path where the grass had been beaten down by footsteps. Unlike the trails we had come from, this one was dark. Pine trees towered high above us on both sides, blocking out all but the slightest bit of light. Still, Chuck seemed to know where he was going, so we didn't give it much thought.

After a few twists and turns, the trees had grown thicker, and we had even less light to go by. The walk had suddenly turned into a climb, and we were struggling to keep up with Chuck. Despite having difficulty seeing, the light peering through the bushes ahead told us that we were nearing the end of the trail. As we emerged from the choking foliage, the ground had leveled out, and we were treated to a clear view of the rolling hills below.

As far as the eye could see, the land was a patchwork of different colors. Only the canyon, directly below us, was devoid of any vibrancy. The black, charred corpses of the trees beneath us were a stark contrast to the bustling life sprawling over the horizon. Much of the canyon had been ravaged by wildfire the summer before. We snapped a few pictures of the scene for good measure and unpacked lunch. Just as we were gearing up to leave, James returned from somewhere in the trees, zipping up his pants for effect.

"Hey guys, check this out," he said, holding up something in his hand. It was a small, sleek-looking square of black plastic.

"Is that a phone?" Chuck asked, cocking an eyebrow in surprise.

"Looks that way," James replied.

"Sucks for them," I said. "It's in a pretty good condition for sitting in the woods."

"Is there a name in it somewhere or something?" Tony asked, fidgeting with the bag he had brought his sandwich in.

"A few contacts," James said, playing with the buttons. "But there's no contact card for the owner. Just some unread messages."

After a long pause, Tony timidly asked "You're not going to read them, are you?"

"Hell no, man!" James shot back. "I don't wanna chance looking through this guy's pictures or anything. You can't un-see that shit."

"Yeah dude, one time, we found a busted-up phone at a carnival, and it actually belonged to the guy who ran the gyro stand. He was talking to some chick about sucking her toes, and he had some weird-ass pictures of–"

"NOPE!" I cut Chuck off before he could finish. "We oughta at least see if the messages give us some clue as to who it belongs to."

"Yeah, I guess so," James said, reluctantly flipping through the phone's inbox. "There are only a handful of them. One 'hay wuts up,' one video message I'm not brave enough to look at, and... Hey, look at this," he held the phone up for us to see.

The screen read, *hey, if anyone finds this phone, I must have lost it while hiking with some friends earlier. I'm sending this from a friend's phone, if u could bring it back to [ADDRESS RETRACTED] that would be awesome, thx!*

Chuck forced a laugh.

"Well, I guess that answers that."

"I know that street, it's in a little trailer park like two miles outside of town," I said.

"What's the date and time on the message?" Tony asked.

"2:23 p.m., today," James replied. "It hasn't been here very long."

"We oughta take it back, just to help them out," Chuck said.

"Yeah dude! I mean, what if it's a chick? She'll be super excited and maybe Chuck can take her to dinner," James said with a grin.

"For sure man, I can probably clean her pool while I'm at it." Chuck rolled his eyes. Did I mention that we're all adults?

"Either-or, let's get this done before it gets too dark," I ordered. We took in the scenery one final time before beginning our descent back into the thick bristles of the pines.

***

When we made the five-mile trek back to Tony's SUV, the sun was already starting to hide behind the hills. We all piled in and began the journey back home, eager to get back before nightfall. None of us were feeling brave enough to sift through the phone's pictures, especially not after Chuck's story from earlier, so we sat in a comfortable silence for most of the drive. By the time we reached the turn-off into the trailer park, the lone streetlight's soft, orange glow was nearly brighter than the sunset. We followed a narrow dirt road and were greeted by a large billboard that read "*LAZY MEADOWS TRAILER COURT*" in bold, crimson letters.

Chuck turned around from up front and looked at me.

"Are you sure we're in the right place?"

"Yeah man, when I was a delivery driver I had to come out to this place a couple times. Never been to the house we're going to, though," I said, scoping out the different street signs as they passed by. We pulled up to an off-white trailer with little-to-no lawn and an unattached metal staircase for a porch. James looked down at the phone and back up at the house, comparing the addresses.

"Is this it?" Tony asked.

"I guess so. There's no car parked out front or anything, though..." James answered.

"Yeah, but the lights are on inside. The porch light is on too, so they might be expecting someone," I pointed out.

"Maybe they ordered a pizza," James smirked.

"Yeah, well, they better tip," I retorted, getting out of the car. As we approached the "porch" of the white trailer, Chuck pointed to the trailer next door with sickly-green paint that peeled like a sunburn.

"I wonder what kind of meth lab they've got going in there," he said half-jokingly. A breeze started kicking up gravel from the road, so I flipped my hood up to shield myself while James went to the front door.

Knock knock knock.

"Hello?"

Knock knock knock.

"Hey, we found your phone out at the state park! We thought we'd bring it back to you, cut you a bit of a break."

Knock knock kn-knock knock.

"Hel-looo?"

For a long time, there was nothing. Just the awkward silence of us standing on a stranger's lawn and the moaning of the wind as it began to pick up.

"Should we just leave the phone on the steps or something?" Tony asked, cramming his hands into his pockets.

"There's gotta be someone here, why would they just leave all the lights on?" I replied.

KNOCK KNOCK KN-

"Quit beating down my door, god dammit! Just come in, it's unlocked." We were all surprised by the muffled, high-pitched voice that called out from behind the door.

"Dude, I told you it was a chick!" James said with a grin, prodding Chuck in the ribs.

"Oh yeah, like you actually–"

"Hey, shut it!" I scolded the both of them. I nodded at James and he turned the door's handle. As he did, the breeze turned into a full-blown whirlwind. The pebbles from the road hit my face like a shotgun blast. My eyes stung and the cool air sent chills down my spine, so I was determined to get inside to escape the brewing storm.

As the screen door closed behind us, we were greeted by an overwhelming scent that reminded me of an old book. The place was well-lit by warm, yellow bulbs with no shades or any other kind of covering on them. The walls were all a spotless white, and the floors were covered by a dark, blue-greenish carpet with no stains to speak of. The inside of the house, much like the outside, was neat and tidy. Overall, it was a beautiful home, but there was one detail that we were completely unprepared for.

It was completely empty.

Not a single picture lined the walls. There was not one table, chair, or bed to speak of. Not so much as a dropped penny on the carpet. There weren't even curtains on the windows; the blinds had been drawn so there was no real way of seeing in from outside. We all stood slack-jawed in what was presumably the living room of this trailer home.

"Uhhh… Hello?" James called out, waving the phone in his hand. "We found your phone!" After peering around a few doorways, we all set out to explore the numerous but equally empty rooms of the house.

Tony and I ventured into what we assumed was the kitchen. There wasn't a stove or a fridge, but there were counter-tops and cabinets lining the walls, all spotlessly clean. Searching through the cupboards revealed literally nothing at all. Not even a single dust bunny.

Tony's eyes narrowed as he searched through the cabinets, "Dude, what in the actual fuck? What is this?"

"Maybe we should just leave the phone on the counter or something," I said, finding nothing under the sink. We had all but given up when an airy, high-pitched voice called out from the "living room."

"You guys found my phone? Oh, thank you so much! I'm just in the other room here." I gave Tony a puzzled look before we gravitated back towards the living room. There, James and Chuck were both staring at each other with bewilderment. On the wall opposite from the way we had come in, there was an open door. One that hadn't been there before. The light from the living room poured into it, illuminating only the first few feet of a hallway where before there was nothing but darkness. *"I'm right in here,"* the voice crooned out to us again.

It was coming from the open doorway.

"In here?" James asked, his voice cracking with nervousness. He took a few tentative steps away from the open door. The hair on the back of my neck immediately stood on end.

"We're just going to leave your phone on the floor if that's alright," I said, signaling to the front door with my thumb. Chuck nodded in agreement and turned to lead the way back out. As he did, all of the light bulbs in the house suddenly burst into a shower of glass and sparks.

A horrible shriek, both ear-splitting and thunderous all at once, erupted from the open doorway. The wind outside wailed as rain began to pound against the windows. I clapped my hands over my ears and dropped to my knees, trying to shield myself from the broken glass raining down. The entire room spun wildly as my vision went hazy and my stomach started doing backflips. James only got to take one frantic step towards the front door before his head snapped back with a loud crack and he tumbled back into the darkness. His feet kicked wildly as his muffled screams trailed back into the abyss of the hallway.

I crawled along the floor, frantically searching for an exit. I glanced up long enough to see Chuck cradling his face with both hands, sobbing as blood dripped from between his fingers.

"Jim? Tony?! JESUS CHRIST SOMEBODY HEL–"

I crawled even faster, ignoring the glass shards digging into my palms. Something in the dark sent me sprawling across the floor with a heavy *thud*: Tony's body, twitching sporadically while a yellow froth poured from his lips. I let out a groan and slid back towards the wall, struggling to get to my feet. The house was trembling now. The walls buckled. The floor thrashed like the waves of an angry ocean. Even with my double vision, I could make out a small square of black plastic near the open doorway. I couldn't believe it: James had dropped the phone on his way into the hall. I scooped it up as fast as I could and staggered towards the front door, fighting to keep the contents of my stomach where they were. I crashed through the screen door and down the metal steps, landing face-first in the mud that was now the front lawn. Again I was crawling, trailing blood and dirt and vomit behind me as panic fueled my body away from the house.

I got to my feet, and I ran. I ran into the rain and the mud until I reached the edge of the trailer park, crossed the road, and kept running. I refused to look back. I hoped to Christ that my friends had gotten out as well. I wasn't proud that I had just left them, but what else could I do? I wasn't going to bother with the police, they wouldn't believe me anyway. Going back wasn't an option, not without daylight. If I was ever going to find any answers, I would just have to find my way home, and then try to contact the others. In the morning, I tried giving everyone else a call. None of them answered. I had no other choice but to force myself into my car to return to the trailer. When I pulled up to the front yard, my mind shattered into a thousand pieces. I tried to cry out, but my throat made only a dry croaking sound.

The trailer was gone, and there were no signs of that lot having ever been occupied. No pipes or plumbing in its place, no tire tracks leading to or from the lot, no electrical meter outside. Absolutely nothing. I spoke to the owner of the green trailer that Chuck had pointed out next door. He says that the lot has been empty for years. Only Tony's SUV stood in the otherwise vacant area.

Not knowing what else to do, I finally caved and took the cellphone to the police, hoping to get a trace on who the owner might have been.

They told me it was a dummy model. It had never been functional to begin with.

THE END
To be continued in…

**Demonic Visions
50 Horror Tales
Book 3**

9 780986 111419